A Soldier for Suzie

Love will OUT #3

D.E. Haggerty

Also By D.E. Haggerty

A Hero for Hailey
A Protector for Phoebe
A Fox for Faith
A Christmas for Chrissie
A Valentine for Valerie
A Love for Lexi
My Forever Love
Forever For You
Just For Forever
Stay For Forever
Only Forever
Meet Disaster
Meet Not
Meet Dare
Meet Hate
Bragg's Truth
Bragg's Love
Perfect Bragg
About Face
At Arm's Length

Hands Off
Knee Deep
Molly's Misadventures

Chapter 1

Stop trying to make everyone happy. You're not beer.

"You Cheat, We Eat, Suzie speaking. How can we make your life better today?" I answer the phone with a cheery voice despite feeling nowhere near cheery.

"Um… my husband's cheating on me," whispers the voice on the telephone.

Lucky for her. Cheating husbands is our specialty. "We are here to help, Mrs. …"

"Tyler," she fills in.

"Mrs. Tyler, can you tell me why you think your husband is cheating?"

After some hiccups by clients who were – to put it mildly – bat shit crazy, my partner Hailey insists I get details before scheduling an appointment with a prospective client for our PI business. In my defense, how could I have possibly known there are cat owners in this world who want to approve their cats' lovers? Or people who think a dentist can put a listening device in their crown?

"You see…" she trails off.

This is where my past comes in handy. I know exactly how she's feeling, because – in my unfortunate experience – men are the scum of the earth.

"Take a deep breath, Mrs. Tyler." I hear her inhale. "And let it out slowly. There you go," I coax. "Now, tell me what Mr. Tyler did."

She clears her throat. "It's like this. I was snooping through his things before Christmas because I don't like surprises." She's preaching to the choir. Surprises suck.

"And I found this gorgeous necklace. It was a chunky gold chain with a heart pendant. The pendant even had a ruby in it."

"Sounds nice," I murmur when she goes quiet.

"Yes, it was lovely. I was very excited. My husband never buys me jewelry. I couldn't wait until Christmas day. Imagine my surprise when I got some stupid CDs instead. He must have given the necklace to some other women!" she screeches, and I hold the telephone away from my ear. Ouch. "I bet it was his secretary. She's this pretty young twenty-something while I'm the frumpy mother of his children."

I wait until she runs out of steam to ask, "Mrs. Tyler, you do realize you've told me the plot to *Love, Actually?*"

"And? It could have happened to me, too!"

Could have? Oh great, another nut job. "I'm sorry, Mrs. Tyler, but I don't believe we can be of any assistance to you." I hang up the phone before she has a chance to start screeching again. There's a limit to how much screeching my ears can take, and the limit has been met and exceeded.

The door opens and Hailey walks in with her dogs, Leroy and Lola, trotting behind her.

"Please tell me you walked Leroy first." He's a puppy and has a tendency to pee everywhere, although he prefers to pee on the corner of Phoebe's desk. There is a slight chance I squirted some potty-training spray on her desk.

I couldn't help myself. Phoebe is this super uptight rich girl. Watching her shriek when Leroy pees is the highlight of my week. Of course, Phoebe is no longer uptight. Nope. Since she nabbed herself a man, aka Ryker the smoking hot bounty hunter, she's changed.

Hailey rolls her eyes. "Of course, I walked him."

Hailey and Phoebe are the private investigators at the PI firm *You Cheat, We Eat* that Hailey and I started together. As you can probably tell from the name, we specialize in catching cheating husbands in the act. Although, since Phoebe joined us, we've added a bunch of insurance fraud cases to our docket, too.

I am not a PI. No, I'm the person who holds the whole business together. I do the accounting, invoicing, filing, all the boring administrative stuff. I wouldn't mind going out on a case or two, but Hailey says I'm not inconspicuous. She's just jealous my awesomeness cannot be disguised.

The door opens again and Phoebe strolls in. Lola whines and jumps toward her, but Hailey holds fast to her leash.

"No, Lola. It's not nice to hump our friends," Hailey admonishes her dog.

"I don't know. Some friends are nice to hump."

Hailey's ears perk up at my comment and she settles herself at one of the chairs in front of my desk. I wouldn't be surprised if she starts rubbing her hands in glee. Ugh. Hailey is my best friend from forever. She knows better than to push me on my dating life.

Dating life? What dating life? I don't date. I have fun and move on. I have my reasons. And she was there to witness my reasons come to life.

But since Hailey got engaged to her high school crush, Aiden, she sees love and romance every fricking where. It's annoying as all get out. She's also happy and cheerful constantly. Blech. I shouldn't begrudge my friend her happiness, but sometimes I am the teeniest bit jealous. Because I will never have a man who loves me and wants to marry me. Not a chance. I've learned my lesson. Men and relationships are not for me.

Phoebe takes the chair next to Hailey. Great. Another in love woman who sees hearts and butterflies wherever she looks. Her big, bad bounty hunter proposed to her on Christmas morning. Although I was the one who pushed her to get together with Ryker, I still can't believe she gave him a second chance, let alone said yes to his proposal.

"Speaking of humping friends, are there any particular friends you're humping now, Suzie?" Hailey wiggles her eyebrows.

She's referring to my friend Grayson who, for reasons I cannot begin to fathom, she thinks I'm interested in. But I am not talking to her about my relationship with Grayson, which is one-hundred percent platonic if you must know. I look around for a distraction. I notice Leroy slinking off toward Phoebe's office. Perfect!

"Leroy," I shout and jump up to rush after him. "No peeing!"

I trip over the strap of my bag laying on the floor – of course, I do! – and end up flat on my back. Hailey and Phoebe bend over the desk to check out the train wreck that is Suzie and walking.

"Are you okay?" Phoebe asks.

Yes, I'm okay. I'm a bit of a klutz. I trip on my own two feet more times in one day than I can count. But if I say I'm fine, there's a chance the girls resume their interrogation of my non-existent love life. Not on my watch, they aren't.

"Ow." I scrunch my nose and rub the back of my head. "My head hurts."

Hailey rolls her eyes. "You didn't even hit the back of your head." She stands and walks toward her office. "If you didn't want to talk about Grayson, all you had to do was tell us."

Because she would have listened to me and backed off? Does she think I'm stupid?

"You sure you're okay?" Phoebe asks.

"I'm fine." I wave her away when she holds out a hand to help me stand.

The last thing I need is perfect looking Phoebe helping klutziest girl in the world, Suzie stand up. I know I'm not being fair. It's not Phoebe's fault she's gorgeous. And she is gorgeous. She's tall – five-foot-nine to my measly five-foot-two – and has curves in all the right places. She's blonde with green eyes and plush lips in a heart-shaped face. It's no wonder her husband went nuts trying to get her back and force her to have his babies.

I, on the other hand, am your typical redhead complete with pasty white skin that goes from ghost white to crisp as bacon with no stops in between. My body is curvy, but unlike sexy Phoebe, my curves tend toward pudgy. My face may be considered cute by some, but beautiful? Nah. My eyes can't make up their mind what color they are – the ring around the pupil is blue, but the outer ring is brown – and my lips are way too big for my face. Good thing I'm not looking for a man.

"Where's Ryker?" I ask when I'm on my feet.

"He's chasing a skip."

"He took off the day after Christmas?"

I'm surprised the man let her out of his sight the day after proposing. If you look up alpha male in the dictionary, you'll find a picture of Ryker. Of course, when you see the picture of the six-foot-six bearded man with dark green eyes that can see right through you, you'll also understand why Phoebe threw caution into the wind and took a chance on the man. Ryker is h-a-w-t – Hawt!

At Phoebe's nod, I ask, "Will he be home in time for New Year's Eve?"

New Year's Eve is one of my favorite days of the year. Hailey's dad owns a bar, McGraw's Pub, and he throws the best parties. Of course, the free drinks don't hurt. And then there are the pranks. Hailey's dad has a bunch of former Army buddies he plays poker with who practically live in the pub. They are beyond hilarious when they start playing pranks. I rub my hands together. I can't wait to see what they get up to this year.

"He promised to be home in two days, in plenty of time for the party. I should have gone with him. I don't have any cases right now anyway."

The week between Christmas and New Year's is a dead zone in the PI business. Or at least in our PI business, it is. Most couples are all lovely-dovey during the holidays. But those holiday feelings fade fast. January is our busiest month of the year.

"Why didn't you go with him?"

Her nose scrunches up. "He thinks it's dangerous. As if I can't handle myself."

I bite my tongue to stop my laugh from exploding out of me. Phoebe was a total coward when she first started at, *We Cheat, You Eat.* Handle herself? Ask her about the time she ended up in someone's pool some time. Although she's getting stronger, she literally escaped a kidnapping all by her lonesome, she's still got a ways to go.

"Phoebe!" Hailey shouts. "Can you come in here? I need some help."

"She probably needs me to reach the top shelf for her," Phoebe mutters before sauntering off.

Hailey isn't exactly short at five-foot-eight, but Phoebe never lets the chance pass to needle her about her one-inch height deficiency.

In case you're wondering, Hailey is gorgeous too. I'm literally surrounded by gorgeous women. Although Hailey doesn't realize how beautiful she is. She complains about being too thin constantly. Whatever. I'd take her skinny self with her long, brown wavy hair and dark brown eyes over my chubby ass any day of the week.

I wait until Phoebe shuts the door behind her to roll my chair to the door to eavesdrop. I seriously don't understand why they bother shutting the door. They know I'm going to eavesdrop anyway. When will they learn?

Chapter 2

The answer may not lie at the bottom of the beer bottle, but I'm going to keep checking anyway.

I come to a screeching halt when I walk into McGraw's Pub on New Year's Eve. The place is literally packed with men; none of whom are wearing pants. Thank goodness they're wearing underwear. I can't imagine the amount of cleaning and disinfecting necessary if naked asses had been all over the chairs. Blech.

I walk to the uncles' table because if anyone is behind the place being full of pantless men, it's Hailey's uncles. The four poker buddies of Hailey's dad aren't technically her uncles. Lenny, Barney, Wally, and Sid 'adopted' her after her mom took off when she was twelve. My perfectly normal family can't hold a candle to Hailey's makeshift family. And no, I'm not jealous – much.

Hailey pushes me out of the way and slams her hands down on the uncles' table. Barney opens his mouth – probably to tell a dirty joke, the man can't get enough of his jokes – but Hailey growls and shoots daggers out of her eyes at him. His mouth snaps closed.

"What did you do?"

Wally's eyes widen as he places a hand over his heart in the worst imitation of innocence ever. "Why are you looking at me? It wasn't me."

Hailey rolls her eyes. "Yeah, right. And Suzie didn't fall once today."

"Hey!" I lift up my hands and take a step back. "Why are you bringing me into this?"

"Like you don't get off on these pranks."

I totally love these pranks, but I know better than to open my mouth and say anything of the sort right now. Contrary to popular opinion, I'm not an idiot.

Hailey's attention returns to Wally. "Don't make me ask you a third time."

"Come on, honey." Aiden places an arm over her shoulders and pulls her tight to him. "You knew they'd play some prank."

"But I didn't think I'd have to look at hairy asses in panther print thongs. I get enough of hairy asses at my day job, thank you very much."

"Panther print thong?" I stand on my tiptoes and check out all the asses. What kind of man wears a thong?

"Where?" I cringe when I see the man she points to. Oh my. If you're going to wear a thong, you should wax. It looks like there's a strip of material being hugged by two gorillas.

Hailey grabs my hand when I take a step in his direction. "What? I'm going to give him the number of my waxer. He'll thank me later." She tightens her grip and shakes her head.

"You're no fun," I pout.

"Why does Santa Clause have such a big sack?" Barney asks. This I gotta hear. "He only comes once a year."

He guffaws and sticks out his fist. I bump his fist while rolling my eyes. Barney does love his dirty jokes. And they only get dirtier the more he drinks. Something to look forward to.

"Hey, Barney," Hailey shouts to be heard. "Pretty cool trick Wally pulled off, wasn't it?"

Barney shrugs. "He posted on Twitter. Big deal."

"I knew it," she shouts before rounding on me. "I thought you shut the Twitter account down."

I raise my hands in surrender. "I did! I promise."

Wally snorts. "As if a little thing like a password can stop me."

"International No Pants Day – get a free drink if you show up with no pants," Hailey reads the tweet from the McGraw's Pub Twitter account. "Who is stupid enough to come to a bar on New Year's Eve without pants when it's ten below outside?"

I motion to the room full of men in their underwear. Obviously, a whole bunch of people. The women are much smarter than the men. Naturally. They're all in skirts.

"Hey, Babycakes," Hailey's dad says as he joins us. He kisses her forehead before lifting his chin to Aiden.

"Hi, Pops." Hailey tilts her head toward the crowd. "You're not mad?"

"Nah." He smirks. Oh goodie. If he's not mad, then he's already planning his revenge on his former Army buddies. I can't wait.

"Hey, Shorty," he greets me. "Your Shorty's Holiday Brew is selling like hotcakes."

"You're Shorty of Shorty's Holiday Brew?" Grayson asks as he steps up behind me.

I scowl. I don't like people knowing about my little micro-brewery. Don't get me wrong. I'm not embarrassed. I'm merely not ready for everyone to know is all. I want a chance to figure out what I'm doing with my brewing before I shout about my beer from the rooftops.

"Where's Phoebe?" I ask instead of answering him.

"Right here," Phoebe answers as she pants for breath. One look at her hair is all it takes to know why she's struggling for breath.

"Hey, stud." I wiggle my eyebrows at Ryker. "Did you switch the security cameras off first?"

Phoebe's eyes widen to the size of saucers. "Security cameras," she squeaks.

Ryker pulls her close. "Suzie's yanking your chain."

"Thank you for confirming the location of your make-out session." I clap my hands to get the uncles' attention. "Who had Ryker's truck?"

In addition to being pranksters, the uncles are addicted to betting. They bet about anything and everything. And I do mean everything. They even bet about when Hailey and Aiden would have sexy times for the first time, although the bet ended up being a test. I was not amused. Especially since I won!

"Um, Suzie." Grayson touches my elbow to gain my attention. I quickly snatch my arm back before he can see the goosebumps his touch causes. He raises his hands in surrender. "Sorry. Can we talk?"

Ugh. Do I have to? Grayson and I are just friends. I don't want to have 'the talk' with him. Hell, I don't want to have 'the talk' with any man ever again. But it's my fault he wants to chat. I befriended him before Christmas and then I was a total beyotch when Pops invited him for our family Christmas lunch. It was an accident! I was surprised. I don't do well with surprises.

"Fine," I huff and stomp off to the hallway leading to the restrooms, the only unoccupied floor space in the place.

I lean against the wall and cross my arms over my chest. "What do you want to talk about?" As if I don't know.

"I'm sorry. I don't know what I did to piss you off on Christmas day, but I won't do it again."

I raise an eyebrow. "If you don't know what you did, how are you going to not do it again?"

"Maybe you could tell me what I did wrong, then?"

Ugh. I let my head fall back against the wall. It's me who should be apologizing to him. It's not his fault I have not-friendly feelings for him. And not-friendly as in Little Susan trembles whenever he's near.

I can't blame her, Grayson is one fine specimen of manhood. He's five-foot-ten with the broadest shoulders I've ever seen. I never knew shoulders could be sexy. Let me tell you, they can be. His eyes are the color of whiskey and I do love me some whiskey. And his lips? They look incredibly soft. My lips yearn to touch them and see if they feel as soft as they look. To top it all off, when he smiles, two dimples pop out on his right cheek. Two dimples I want to lick before moving on to lick other naughtier bits of his body.

But I don't get involved with friends. The whole friends with benefits thing is total and complete bullshit. You can't have sex with a friend and stay friends. Nope. You either get involved in a relationship – something I do not do – or you ruin the friendship.

"You didn't do anything wrong," I finally say when the silence stretches on too long. I'm not the most patient of people. Silence and me are not good friends. "I was a bitch. I apologize."

He tilts his head to study me. *Please don't ask why I was a bitch. Please don't ask why I was a bitch.* After a moment, he nods and offers me his hand. "Friends?"

"Friends," I agree, and we shake hands to seal the deal.

Hailey and Phoebe come rushing into the hallway. "What's going on?"

Hailey shushes me with a finger over her lips before she moves to lean against the wall next to me. Phoebe stands on the other side of me.

A few seconds later, Wally comes strolling by. He gives Grayson a chin lift before proceeding to the restrooms.

"What—"

Hailey lifts a hand and cuts Grayson off. "Wait for it."

A loud air horn sounds before Wally can be heard cursing up a storm.

"Classic." Hailey falls into a fit of laughter.

"Cruel," Grayson says with a shake of his head.

"He earned an airhorn on the toilet seat when he tweeted it was no pants day at the pub." Hailey is quick to defend Pops.

Grayson's eyes widen. "I was wondering why there was a bunch of pantless men here. Good thing I don't have Twitter."

Wally barges out of the restroom. His jeans are wet like he had himself an accident. I bite my tongue to stop myself from laughing out loud. He marches toward us.

"Where's your father?" He glares at Hailey. "I'm going to kill him."

"Probably shouldn't mention your plan to commit murder in front of an officer of the law," Aiden suggests as he strolls toward us.

Aiden is a police detective. He'd never tell on the uncles, but he sure likes to threaten to squeal on them whenever he's worried they're getting out of hand.

He gets right up in Wally's face. "And if you glare at my woman again, we're having words."

Hailey pulls Aiden away from Wally. "And if you call me your woman again, you're sleeping with the dogs."

"Good thing Leroy's potty trained." I slap my hands against my cheeks in mock surprise. "Oh wait. He's not."

"No comments from the cheap seats," Aiden says before securing Hailey's hand in his and leading her away. Wally follows them grumbling the entire time. I'm sure he's already planning another prank.

"I guess the fun's over. I better find my man before he starts up a search party." Phoebe waves as she leaves.

She's not joking. Since she was kidnapped, Ryker is super protective of her. I'm surprised he let her walk to the restroom by herself.

"We good?" Grayson asks once we're alone in the hallway again.

I force a smile on my face. "Yep. Perfectly peachy."

I'm a big fat liar. Nothing is peachy. Lusting after your friend is the definition of not peachy. What's the opposite of peachy? Whatever it is, that's what I am.

Chapter 3

Don't worry, be Hoppy

"Uh-huh." I nod my head despite Mom not being able to see me. "Yep." Another nod. "Sure."

I'm standing in my backyard in minus five temps shivering from the cold because I refuse to bring any negativity into my brew shack. Don't get me wrong, I love my parents. Although they retired to Arizona years ago and refuse to visit Wisconsin in the winter – even if it is Christmas – they're good, caring parents.

But my mom is determined to marry me off. She thinks my being single at thirty-one is a personal failure on her part. She also thinks I should 'get over my past' because what Toby did was 'to be expected'. Pardon? I should expect a man to betray me? If so, she can forget all about those grandchildren ever happening.

Who am I kidding? There is no doubt. She can totally forget about grandchildren happening. I am done with men. A picture of Grayson smiling with his two dimples on display pops into my head. Too bad men cannot be trusted.

"At least promise me you'll think about it," Mom insists.

"Sure," I agree although I haven't the first clue what I've agreed to as all my mind can think about is all the places on Grayson's body I'd like to lick. No, Suzie! No! Licking friends is bad!

"Good," Mom squeals and claps. "I think Match.com is the best option. The Tinder app seems a bit raunchy."

Wait! What? Match.com and Tinder? "Um, Mom, I'm not signing up for a dating app."

She huffs. "You agreed to not less than two minutes ago."

Crap. I did, didn't I? I blame Grayson and his lickable body. Damn him.

I backpedal. "I said I'd think about it."

"Fine. I'll send you some links. Love you."

I wait for the click of her hanging up before I sigh. She's getting relentless. I fear she may break her no trips up north during winter rule to come badger me some more. No thanks.

I take a deep breath and clear my mind of all thoughts of partners and grandchildren. No negative thoughts in the brew shack. I unlock the locks. Yes, multiple locks. Do you know how much brewing equipment costs? And then there's all the beer I'm storing. Although, there isn't too much beer stocked now. Pops wasn't kidding when he said the patrons of McGraw's enjoyed my Holiday Brew. I'm plum out.

Today I want to try a new recipe for a Session IPA. A Session IPA is more hoppy and has less body than my regular beers, but I think it'll be a great beer for the spring. We may be deep in a cold-ass Wisconsin winter right now, but spring will come — eventually.

Before I can start brewing, I need to make sure my equipment is clean and sanitized. Hailey thinks I'm an obsessive-compulsive cleaner. I'm not. Seriously, I'm not. But I have experienced an entire batch of ruined beer due to my equipment not being sparkling clean. And ruined beer is putting it nicely. I thought I was going to have rush Hailey to the ER when she started projectile vomiting after drinking one of the contaminated beers. Not an experience I'm anxious to repeat. And I don't think Hailey is either.

I switch on my brewing soundtrack – because all brewers should have a brewing soundtrack – and start cleaning. Thirty minutes later, my stainless-steel equipment is shining and the phone conversation with my mom is completely forgotten.

"Time to steep the grains!" Yes, I'm shouting out loud to myself. What? I really enjoy brewing beer.

I fill up my brew kettle with the exact amount of water. And it does have to be exact. Trust me on this. The first rule in brewing beer is there are tons of rules, and the second rule in brewing beer is to measure, measure, measure!

I set my timer for twenty minutes and open a book on the Kindle app on my phone. It's not one of those sex books Phoebe thinks we don't know she reads. Okay, I read them, too. The girl is on to something with those erotica books. They are addicting! They're also distracting. Rule number three of brewing – no distractions!

Instead of getting all hot and bothered by my next book boyfriend, I'm reading an autobiography about some sister brewers in Amsterdam who are wildly successful now. Not that

I'm trying to make my hobby into a business. Sure, it would be fun to call myself a professional brewer, but I'm realistic. It's not going to happen.

Once the grains are steeped, it's time to bring the kettle to a boil. I put my phone away. Boiling the wort requires my full attention.

When my phone beeps with an incoming message, I'm tempted to ignore it. But when it beeps for a second time, I can't stop myself from looking.

How does a squid go into battle?
Well-armed.

I laugh despite myself. I thought Barney had the market on corny jokes cornered. Looks like Grayson is also a member of the corny joke brigade.

I respond with a gif of a cat eating a piece of corn.

How are you doing, munchkin?

Munchkin? Who you calling munchkin? For good measure, I add a whatchu talkin' bout Willis gif.

Spoiler alert – I'm totally a munchkin. In my defense, I'm surrounded by giants making my slightly short stature of five-feet-two seem shorter than it actually is.

You up for grabbing a beer?

Smart man. He knows better than to respond to my ire about my height.

Can't. I'm brewing.

I cringe when I realize what I wrote. I love brewing, but it's my secret hobby I don't talk about with anyone. Not a secret hobby like learning to speak Wookie or extreme ironing.

Now those are some weird hobbies. Before I have a chance to completely flip out, Grayson responds.

Cool. Any new flavors? The holiday brew was good. And I want to try your stout.

Who told you about the stout? Confession – it could have been me. New Year's Eve got a bit hazy at the end there. There's no guarantee I kept my mouth shut.

He ignores my question. *What are you brewing now?*

Oh, what the hell. I decide to tell him. It's not like it's some super secret like what Wally does for a living. Yes, Wally. Although all of the uncles are retired from the Army, I'm pretty sure Wally is into some black ops super secret shit. He disappears for weeks on end and no one has any idea where he is. All the uncles will say is he's 'off-grid'. And if those words don't spell black ops, I don't know what does.

Session IPA.

What's Session IPA?

While I'm typing up my answer, Grayson calls. "Hey," he says in a rich, buttery voice. Geez. All the guy has to do is say 'hey' and Little Susan wakes up and starts singing Marvin Gaye.

"Hey." My voice comes out husky. Bad voice!

"I thought it might be easier if you explained on the phone instead of typing on the tiny keyboard."

"Are you calling my fingers fat?"

"There's nothing fat about you, Munchkin."

I was joking but now Little Susan is doing the tango while singing Marvin Gaye. And, yes, I realize those two things do not go together. I never said Little Susan had taste.

I hold my hand over the phone to clear my throat. No reason for my *friend* to hear the effect he has on me. "It's like this," I say and then go on to explain what a Session IPA is. I may get a bit over-excited and drone on and on. What? I'm a beer geek. There are worse things in life.

"Oh shit," I say when I open my eyes because I closed my eyes when I started to wax poetic about beer. No judging.

"What's wrong?" Grayson asks. To be honest, I'm surprised he's still paying attention. It's not like I've let him speak for the last twenty minutes.

"Crappity crap."

"You're freaking me out. What's wrong? Where are you? I'm on my way."

"Unless you fancy cleaning up a sticky, goopy mess, there's no need." I switch off the heat and place my phone on the table. "I gotta go," I say and hit the end button before he has a chance to respond.

I study the mess trying to figure out where to begin before realizing there is no good place to begin. Time to roll up my sleeves and dive in. It's no big deal. I can start over. It's Friday night. I've got all night. And, yes, I realize how lame that statement made me sound.

Chapter 4

I only drink beer on days that end with a y.

I GROAN WHEN MY doorbell rings the next evening. I'm laying on my sofa in my flannel pajamas while wrapped in my fuzzy blanket. Obviously, I'm not expecting company. And I'm not going anywhere. I don't care if it is Saturday night. I was up most of last night and this morning brewing. I'm taking the night off from playing happy-go-lucky klutzy Suzie.

There's a knock on the window. I startle and nearly fall off the sofa. "Come on, Suzie. I know you're in there."

Who was the idiot who didn't shut the curtains? Oh yeah, it was me.

I wave at Grayson and shout, "Go away!"

He puts his hands against the window to peer in. "I'm not leaving."

I throw off my blanket and stomp to the door. "What?"

"Someone's grumpy." I grunt. He's not wrong. "I guess someone doesn't want her present." He practically shoves a wrapped package in my face. "Not interested?"

As soon as I reach for it, he yanks his hand away. "Nope. Get dressed. I'm buying you dinner."

My stomach rumbles in response to his proclamation. "I'm not in the mood to go out."

"Your stomach disagrees. Come on. I'll take you to McGraw's for a bite to eat and then let you beat me in a round of pool."

I place my hands on my hips. "Let me beat you?"

He chuckles as he looks me up and down. "Love the pj's."

My face heats. I'm wearing my beer bottle pajamas. They're men's pajamas, meaning they're about a mile too long for me. I have to roll the pant legs up to stop myself from tripping. It's ridiculous. I'm only two inches shorter than average for freak's sake.

Grayson waves the present in my face. "Come on. Get dressed. You know you want to."

I don't. No, really, I don't want to spend the evening with Grayson. And it's a good thing my flannel bottoms are flame retardant because I'm a big fat liar.

"Fine." I twirl on my heel and march toward the stairs. "Make yourself comfortable."

I take the fastest shower a woman can take. I leave my hair wet and throw it into the shortest ponytail known to man. I'm growing my hair out from the short spikes I used to sport, and it's barely long enough to put up. All I need is a pair of jeans and a t-shirt and I'm done.

When I walk into the living room, Grayson chuckles. "Cool t-shirt."

He's not wrong. It's a totally cool shirt with the words *Hoptimist A person who believes everything is better with a good craft beer* on the front.

"You ready?"

At his question, I hold out my hand. "Present first." I wiggle my fingers in a gimme gesture.

He chuckles but hands me the gift. "I wanted to apologize for ruining your word yesterday."

"Wort," I correct absently as I rip into the gift. "A leather-bound brew journal."

I caress the material before flipping it open. There are gravity charts, SRM guides, information on grain and hops, and tips on troubleshooting.

"Thank you. This is awesome."

I stand on my tiptoes and kiss his cheek in thanks. Big mistake. This close to him, I can smell the scent of vanilla wafting from him. Because I'm a glutton for punishment, I take another whiff and notice mint. Mmm… mint and vanilla. Two of my favorite smells in the entire world.

Little Susan wakes up and decides it's time to do the rumba while humming *La cucaracha*. I'm not sure how she learned the rumba. I certainly don't know how to do the rumba.

Grayson clears his throat before grasping my hand. "Come on, let's go. Your stomach sounds like it's trying to eat through your skin to escape."

Yes, let's get out of here before I throw caution to the wind and jump my *friend*. Reminder – Grayson is a friend, not a potential sexual partner. I do not have sex with friends. Little Susan pouts and her shoulders hunch as she slumps off the dance floor.

The bar is hopping when we arrive. Of course, it is. It's Saturday night.

"Honey! I'm home!" I shout when we enter.

"Uh oh, trouble's in the house," Barney says and waves us over.

I debate not joining the uncles at their table for at least five seconds. On the one hand, the uncles will pour cold water on any amorous feelings I'm having for Grayson. But, on the other hand, I do want to spend time alone with the sexy man. That does it! No sexy men for Suzie.

"I'm surprised to see you guys here. After all, you're never here." I wink.

Lenny frowns. "Sarcasm does not look good on you, young lady."

"Sarcasm looks good on everyone, old man."

"Who you calling old?" Sid asks.

"I was referring to Lenny, but if you want in on the action, then ..."

Sid punches my arm. "Ow!"

"Children, calm down," Pops orders as he walks over. He kisses my hair. "Hey, Shorty. I didn't expect to see you in here today."

I thumb my finger at Grayson. "This one held my present hostage unless I agreed to get out of the house."

"Present?" Sid leans close. "What kind of present?"

A bit of background about Sid. The guy is a hopeless romantic. But he apparently sucks at the romance part since he's been married five times. Rumor has it he has wife number six – a nurse from a fire incident – on the hook.

"A brewing journal. It was an apology for ruining my wort."

"Never heard it referred to that before," Lenny remarks.

I slap him. "Wort as in the liquid extracted from the mashing process during brewing. Not my tunnel of love."

Sid tsks. "What a disappointment."

I don't want to talk about my relationship with Grayson. I address Pop, "I'll take a hamburger and fries and a stout."

Pops chuckles. "What a surprise." He takes everyone else's orders and leaves.

Lenny slaps me on the shoulder. "He's a keeper."

"He's a keeper? What are you talking about?" I'm acting dumb, but I have a sneaking suspicion I know exactly what he's going on about.

"Grayson. We approve."

No, no, no. They've got it all wrong. I shake my head.

Grayson chuckles. "We're friends. Nothing more."

Phew. Thank goodness. I don't want Grayson getting the wrong idea about us. Snort. Like that's likely to happen. Grayson would never want me. He's like a fifteen on a scale of ten and I'm a five. Maybe a six if I put on make-up and do something with my hair.

Don't get me wrong. I'm not doing the whole boohoo for me thing. I know my value. I'm loyal, fun, and cute. What I am not is beautiful. No, a short girl with spikey red hair who spills her food and trips on her own two feet is not in the beautiful category. I've made my peace with it.

"Is our Suzie not good enough for you?" Lenny glares at Grayson.

Grayson gulps. "Of course, she is. Too good for me." I start to giggle because he has got to be kidding me, but one look at him and the giggle dies in my throat. He looks serious. What?

"Damn right, she is," Wally mutters.

"Then, why don't you want her?" Sid asks and it takes all my self-restraint to stop myself from reaching across the table and slapping him. Doesn't he know the last thing I need in this world is to hear Grayson explain in detail why he doesn't want me?

"Leave it alone, Sid. We're friends. Nothing more."

Sid waves away my protest. "I know why you have hang-ups about relationships, I want to hear what his hang-ups are."

"Maybe it's none of your business." The uncles think it's their right to not only pry into Hailey's life but also the personal lives of all of her friends. It's not.

"Let the soldier speak for himself," Wally orders.

Alarm! Alarm! When the super-secret spy starts using words like soldier, interrogation mode isn't far off. Not good. I stand.

"Come on, Grayson. Let's eat at the bar."

Grayson doesn't move. To my surprise, he opens his mouth and confesses, "I'm not ready for a relationship." The flash of pain in his eyes is strong enough to make me flinch. The soldier is holding out on me. Now I'm curious and hoping Wally does switch into interrogation mode. And – in case you're wondering – there's nothing wrong with being curious.

Wally's eyes narrow on him. "Why not? Are you married?"

"If I were married, I'd be in a relationship, wouldn't I?"

"If a tag chaser hurt you when she abandoned you while you were overseas, there's no need to worry. Suzie is the most loyal person in the world."

"Oh great. You make me sound like a golden retriever," I whine.

Grayson ignores my comment to respond to Wally. "I didn't hook up with a tag chaser. Do I look stupid?"

"What's a tag chaser?"

No one pays a lick of attention to me.

"Then, what's the problem?" Sid asks. "We know you're attracted to our Suzie."

My eyes widen. They do? Grayson isn't attracted to me. In fact, he hasn't shown a hint of interest in me in a romantic way. No flirting, no accidental brushing of body parts against mine, nada nothing. Despite what Hailey and Phoebe think, I know how to flirt. I simply choose not to.

Grayson glances in my direction. His eyes narrow when he notices my face is the color of a fire engine, which is not a good look for a redhead in case you're wondering. He glowers at the uncles. "Stop. You're embarrassing Suzie."

There's a whole lot of grumbling before Lenny chimes in, "What did the toaster say to the slice of bread?" He wiggles his eyebrows. "I want you inside me!"

A total lame joke but I high-five him as a reward for cutting the tension. Grayson ushers me back into my seat and Pops arrives with our food. He studies the uncles for a moment before setting the plates on the table.

"They're not giving you a hard time are they, Shorty?" he asks with a hand on my shoulder making it clear whose side he's on.

I grin up at him. "I'm fine." I sniff the food. "And this smells delicious."

He winks before glaring at the uncles again for good measure and leaving.

We dive into our food and the conversation switches to the playoffs. I don't pay much attention to football, but I'm happy to concentrate on sports instead of my supposed chemistry with Grayson. As if.

Chapter 5

This beer tastes like I'm not going to work tomorrow.

"You Cheat, We Eat, Suzie speaking. How can we make your life better today?" I throw my jacket down and plop on my chair. I may also swallow a grumpy grumble because it's Monday morning and who doesn't hate Mondays. Sociopaths is who!

"I'd like to speak to Ryker Rossi, please," a woman says.

Since Ryker can't stand to have Phoebe out of his sight, he's renting space at our PI firm. He's also hired us – meaning me – to handle his digital research. I run the names of his skips through a network of tracking data to pin down their location. It's not much different than other digital research I do for the business. I guess I'm also taking calls for him now too.

"Mr. Rossi's not in, may I help you?" Mr. Rossi is hardly ever in. Bounty hunting is outlawed in Wisconsin meaning he mostly works out of state.

"Uh, yes? I think?"

I wait, but she doesn't expand on her answer. "Why don't you start by telling me your name?"

Since the core business of *You Cheat, We Eat* is cheating men, I'm used to fielding calls from wives who are – to put it mildly – apprehensive about calling a PI to catch their husband fooling around on them. I often need to coax the information out of a potential client.

"I'm Nora."

"Hi Nora! My name is Suzie." I infuse my voice with a bunch of cheer. "Now that we're friends, why don't you tell me what the problem is."

"I need Mr. Rossi to find someone for me."

"Okay. Is this someone in trouble for skipping bail?" Why do I have a feeling I'm going to be explaining what a bail recovery agent does in a second here?

"I'm not sure."

Could she be any more vague?

"Why don't you explain who you need found and why." Geez. This is more difficult than getting a teenager to tell you how she did on her math test. And before you start making assumptions, math is my superpower.

"I'm not sure what his name is, but he's harassing me, and it needs to stop."

My ears perk up. Maybe I was too quick to judge Nora. "Harassing how?"

"He won't let me sleep at night."

My heartbeat quickens. "Is he in the house with you right now?" I whisper. "Are you safe?"

"I'm safe. He only appears at night."

"Have you called the police when he shows up?" I love money as much as the next girl, but this does sound like a matter for the police and not a PI, let alone a bounty hunter.

"They laughed at me."

Fuckers. How dare they? I can hear how frightened Nora is. "Why don't you give me some examples of what this guy does."

She clears her throat. "He rattles the windows, he rings the phone at all times of the night, he switches the television on and off, he swings doors open and closed, he—

I'm starting to get a sneaky suspicion I know what's going on. "Nora, is the person who has been harassing you a ghost?" I interrupt to ask.

"Yes!" she shouts. "I knew I'd called the right person."

Technically she called Ryker and I answered, but whatever. "What exactly is it you think Mr. Rossi does?"

"He finds people, and I need a person found."

"I'm afraid Mr. Rossi won't be able to help you. He finds fugitives, people who have skipped bond." And not ghosts, I think but don't say.

"You don't know. Maybe my ghost is a fugitive from justice."

"Seeing as we're in Wisconsin and there's no private bail system in the state, I don't think a bounty hunter can help you."

"What about one of the PIs then?"

I cringe. I deliberately didn't offer her our PI services, thinking she didn't know about them and would hang up. I take a moment to imagine Phoebe and Hailey going to ghostbust a house. They could wear Ghostbusters outfits, and we could convert the SUV into an ectomobile. I snicker. They would kill me if I took Nora on as a client.

"I'm afraid we don't offer ghostbusting services."

"But what am I going to do? No one will help me."

I'm sure there's some firm out there that will offer her ghostbusting services. They'll also most likely rip her off. Not okay.

"I tell you what we can do. I can run a background check and property search to find out if any serious crimes or violent acts have been carried out at your house."

"What good would that do?"

The bell over the door rings and Hailey, Phoebe, and Ryker walk in. I raise my hand for them to be quiet to allow me to finish this bat shit crazy phone call.

"If no serious crimes or violent acts occurred at your house, then you'll know your ghost has come in peace."

Your ghost has come in peace? Hailey mouths at me before biting her lip to stop from laughing.

I narrow my eyes at her. She better not start laughing. Nora may be cuckoo for cocoa puffs, but she's also a woman who is suffering. If we can help her, we should. What we definitely shouldn't do, is laugh at her. I'm sure the police laughed at her enough.

"Oh, I didn't think of it like that. I guess a peaceful ghost is better than a violent one. Okay, I'll do it. What are your prices?"

I quickly explain our prices to her. Once I have her agreement, I tell her I'll have the results for her within a day and hang up.

I point at Hailey who looks like she's about to burst. "No laughing. You refuse to deal with certifiable clients. Guess what? Someone still has to deal with them when they call."

Hailey makes a production of zipping her lips. I ignore her to glare at Ryker.

"You promised I wouldn't get any crazy calls. You owe me, big guy." He grunts and walks off. "And a beer at McGraw's is not sufficient," I shout at his retreating back.

He gives me a two-finger wave before shutting his door. Doesn't he know I have his credit card information? Coffee and cake this afternoon are on Ryker!

Phoebe stares at the closed door. "What in the world? Did he forget he shares an office with me?"

She raises her hand to knock but stops and shakes her head. "What am I doing?" she mutters to herself before opening the door. She marches in and slams the door behind her. I expect to hear her lay into Ryker, but Phoebe hasn't come into her righteous woman yet. She's getting close, though.

My gaze moves to Hailey. "Where are Leroy and Lola?"

The door opens and Aiden enters with the dogs on his heels.

Oh great. "Is it love shack day at the office again?"

Aiden smirks. Not the response I was hoping for. This is what happens when your friends and co-workers get engaged. They get all lovey-dovey all the time. I'd complain I'm disgusted, but I'm actually happy for both of them. They both deserve all the happiness in the world. It sucks I will personally never have a fiancé, but c'est la vie.

I stand and gather my coat and purse. "I'm going for coffee." I point at Hailey. "You better be finished when I get back or I'm taking the day off. A paid day off!"

She raises an eyebrow. "Did you forget you're part owner of the business? You don't need my permission to take a day off."

Here's the thing about owning your own business, it's a shit ton of work. There is no such thing as a paycheck. Nope, it's all about dividends and profit sharing and a whole bunch of other boring accountanty words. I may be a math whiz, but it doesn't mean I like it.

"I'll be back in an hour," I shout.

"Don't forget to bring me a cinnamon twist," Hailey replies.

"And I'll take a Boston cream," Phoebe shouts from behind her closed door.

I place my hand on my heart and heave an exaggerated sigh. "Ah, our little girl is all grown up now."

Phoebe used to be a complete health nut, but she's loosened up since Ryker and her got together. All her secrets have been revealed as well, which was a relief because I was literally dying of curiosity. The woman was all mysterious, and if there's one thing I can't stand, it's not knowing everything about everybody.

I wave at Hailey before taking off. With the way Aiden is looking her up and down like she's a big juicy burger he can't wait to take a bite of, I'm not a second too soon in leaving. I said I was happy for them finding their happily ever afters, but it doesn't mean I need to be an eyewitness. Blech. Happily ever after is for fools. I, for one, am no fool.

Chapter 6

How does a man show he's planning for the future? He buys two cases of beer.

MEET YOU AT MCGRAW'S at 6?

I frown when I see Grayson's text. I'd love to hang out at the pub and throw back a few cold ones. Unfortunately, I haven't got the time. I received a huge order for my Short but Stout brew, and I need to label about a gazillion bottles before I can ship them off. Fun times. Not.

Can't. Have a date.

I don't mention the date is with one hundred bottles and their labels. And yes, I'm being an idiot trying to put distance between Grayson and me when all I want to do is climb him like the monkey bars in my childhood playground. What? Screw trees, the monkey bars rock!

I chew on my thumbnail as I wait for his response. I'm stupid! Why am I testing him? Putting distance between us?

Have a good time.

Great. He's completely fine with me dating another man. Chemistry my ass. It takes me approximately two milliseconds before I break down and tell him the truth.

It's labeling night at the brew shack.

Ugh. I'm beyond lame. I had to tell him I didn't have a date, didn't I? What am I doing? I can't be with Grayson anyway. Stupid. Stupid. Stupid. I slap my forehead for good measure. Maybe I can rattle my brain around in there and fix this 'obsessed with Grayson' glitch.

Need help?

You bet I do. But do I want his help? I don't let any old person in my brew shack. And yes, I realize my shyness about my brewing is becoming weird at this point. Fuck it. It's not like we're going to get it on my brew shack. I'm not exactly sexy when I'm brewing. Pfft. I'm never sexy.

Sure.

I insert an emoji of a shrugging woman and text him my address. I set my phone down and get back to work. Five minutes later it hits me. Shit! I invited the man I'm crushing on to my house. Eek! I send Hailey a text to let her know I'm leaving early, snatch my coat, and skedaddle.

By the time six o'clock arrives, the surfaces in my house are sparkling with cleanliness. Spoiler alert – my house wasn't dirty to begin with. Hailey may be onto something when she calls me an obsessive-compulsive cleaner.

I've also spent the past two hours obsessing about Grayson being in my house. Friends, Suzie, remember? You are friends. And friends visit each other houses. You can handle him being in your home without jumping his bones. Besides, you'll be in the brew shack working most of the time.

The doorbell rings and I nearly shriek in surprise. Geez. Talk about getting caught up in your thoughts. I hurry toward the door in my stocking feet. I slip and slide on my gleaming wooden floors as I move. All of a sudden, my back leg catches on something and gets stuck in place while my front leg continues moving forward. My legs slide in opposite directions until I'm doing the splits. Spoiler alert – I can't do the splits.

"Ow!" I shout.

"Are you okay? I'm coming in!" Grayson rushes in but freezes when he sees me on the floor. "What happened?"

"I tried to do the splits?"

He sets the pizza box he's carrying on the side table before reaching forward and helping me to my feet. A current of electricity zings through my hand and up my arm when he touches me. I yank my hand away before I start to pant after the guy. Not for us, remember!

"You are literally the klutziest person I know." Grayson chuckles.

"I can't help it that you don't know very many people." I gesture to the pizza box. "You brought dinner? You're helping me. I'm supposed to buy dinner."

"It's no biggie."

He's wrong. The pizza is huge. "Are you expecting a family to join us?"

He grins. "I'm a big guy, and I'm hungry."

He had to say he's a big guy, didn't he? Now, my eyes are roving of their own accord over his body. In addition to his broad shoulders, his chest strains against the confines of the sweater he's wearing. The arms of the sweater aren't faring much better.

But he's not like one of those chicken-shaped body lifters. You know the ones I'm talking about – all upper body muscle and freakishly skinny legs. Nope. His thighs fill out his Levi's very nicely. What is wrong with me? I'm finding thighs sexy now?

I walk to the kitchen in search of cooler air devoid of sexy men. "Sorry, but no pizza in my brew shack. Cleanliness is holy in the brew making business."

He chuckles. "I knew you'd be a slave driver."

I'm not going to lie. I'm a total slave driver. "Whatever." I hand him plates and napkins.

We settle at the table and dig into our pizza. Meat lovers, my favorite!

"You're quiet tonight," I say when he hasn't spoken for at least five seconds. What? Silence is the enemy.

"Just thinking."

Thinking is bad. Thinking is the enemy. Thinking is when all your skeletons rattle on your closet door until you open it to let them out.

"About what?"

"Nothing you'd be interested in hearing about."

How wrong he is! I want to learn every nugget of information about this guy I can.

"Come on," I push. "Give me something."

He shakes his head. "Feeling out of sorts today is all."

As if I'll be satisfied with such a lame answer. "What happened?"

"Nothing." Liar. But before I get a chance to call him out, he clears his throat and heads me off at the pass. "Tell me why you need my manual labor to help label your beer. Don't they have automatic labeling machines?"

I study him for a moment before deciding to let my curiosity go – for now. "The bottle label applicator I have my eye on costs nearly a thousand dollars."

He chokes on his pizza. "As in a one followed by three zeros?"

"Brewing is not a cheap hobby."

"Is brewing a hobby for you, though? I thought it was a business since you're selling to bars and all."

I open my mouth to tell him I sell exclusively to McGraw's, but it would be a lie. Since the New Year's Eve party, a few other bars have placed orders too. Including tonight's order for a hundred bottles of my Short but Stout beer.

I don't have an answer for him. My relationship with brewing is complicated. Brewing wasn't always a dream of mine. It was a dream of Toby's – the asshole king of all asshole exes. When things ended, I continued brewing because I actually enjoy it, but do I want to make Shorty's Brewing Sensation a full-time thing? Frankly, I don't know.

"Come on." I stand. "Those bottles won't label themselves."

He follows me outside to where my shack is located. It's not really a shack. It's a double garage I've converted into my 'brewery'. I unlock the door and motion for Grayson to enter before me. His eyes widen as he looks around.

"Wow. This is not a hobby, Munchkin."

Confession. I love it when he calls me munchkin. I know I shouldn't, but who wouldn't love it when a hot man has a pet name all for them? No babe, or baby, or honey for me. Nope. Munchkin is all mine.

I slide a box out from under one of the tables, but before I can lift it, Grayson is there taking it from my hands.

"These are the labels," I say and then point to the bottles of beer lining the shelves above the table. "And those are the beer bottles we need to label."

Grayson opens the box and removes a roll of labels. "Huh."

My brow wrinkles. "Huh? What? Is there a problem with them?" Shit. I need to deliver this order to the bar in two days. I don't have time to re-order labels.

"It's nothing." Grayson shakes his head. "I guess I expected something different is all."

I peer around him at the labels. I admit they're a bit simple. There's a picture of a beer bottle and my brewery name, Shorty's Brewing Sensation, and the name of the beer, Short but Stout. I'll be the first to admit I'm not what you would call 'artistic'.

"What's wrong with them?"

"Nothing." He sets the roll down and reaches for a bottle of beer.

"Nope." I snatch his arm and spin him around. Well, I don't spin him around. I don't have enough strength in my puny arms to move the soldier anywhere he doesn't want to move. "Tell me what's wrong."

He shakes his head. "It's nothing. I'm being a jerk."

"Jerk or not. Tell me."

"I'm doing a course in branding now for my marketing degree."

I stop him right there. "Marketing degree? You didn't tell me you were going back to school."

Pink paints his cheeks as he suddenly finds the floor fascinating. "I started last week. I want to finish my bachelor's degree."

"Cool. I'm sure you'll rock it. Now, tell me what's wrong with my labels." I can take constructive criticism. Really, I can.

"They're a little plain is all. I expected them to represent your personality more."

Huh. I haven't given my labels much attention. After all, I wasn't planning on selling my beer. I know. I know. Why do I have the huge set-up if I'm not selling my beer? I blame the ex. He screwed with my head.

"Do you have a better idea?"

"Not right now, but if you'll let me, I'd love to put some ideas together."

Seeing as his earlier gray mood has nearly dissipated, I can't say no. Besides, maybe he'll come up with a cool idea.

"Okay, but I can't put off labeling these bottles. I have an order to fill."

His smile stretches from ear to ear. I guess he's totally into this marketing thing.

"What are you waiting for? You don't need instructions, do you? The labels are self-adhesive."

He snaps a salute. "Yes, ma'am. Right away, ma'am."

His salute has Little Susan waking up and wanting to give him all kinds of orders, mostly of the sexy variety. Maybe I am one of those tag chasers Wally was referring to the other day.

What's a tag chaser, you ask? I Googled the term. A tag chaser apparently is a woman who is attracted to a man solely because he's in the military.

Personally, I've never been much of a fan of men in uniform. Man was I wrong.

Chapter 7

Beer is not a game. Beer is serious.

"WHAT'S GOING ON?" I ask when I walk into McGraw's Pub on Saturday morning. "Why are we here this early? The pub's not even open yet."

"Early?" Lenny snorts. "You don't know early, Doll."

I'd roll my eyes, but since they're not yet working properly, I don't dare. I settle for mumbling *whatever* instead.

I look around and see there is a row of five chairs set up in the middle of the pub. In front of the row of chairs are two tables.

I notice Grayson standing near the bar and walk over to him. "Do you know what's going on?"

"The uncles want Phoebe to decide who will walk her down the aisle today."

Since Phoebe and Ryker got engaged, the uncles have been pushing her to choose one of them to walk her down the aisle. Her biological father won't be given the honor. Phoebe has completely cut herself off from them after what they did, but that's a long story for another day.

"Today? She hasn't picked her wedding date yet. And how are they going to decide?" I ask as I watch the uncles and Pops push each other around. Geez. You'd think middle-aged men would behave. But no, they act like teenagers.

"We're doing The Newlywed Game. And I'm your host for the morning," Grayson explains.

Hailey and Aiden join us. "Why are you the host? I get why Ryker isn't, but why didn't they pick me?"

Grayson offers Aiden a bunch of cards. "You want to be the host? Have at it."

Aiden holds up his hands. "I didn't say I want to be the host. I want to know why I wasn't asked is all."

Hailey rolls her eyes. "Come on, Mr. Grumpy. Let's grab some seats where we can watch the action."

Phoebe and Ryker enter the bar and the uncles cheer. "'Bout time!"

Phoebe stumbles and nearly falls down the two steps at the entry. Ryker saves her. Of course, he does. Ryker's job in life is to protect Phoebe after all. Barf.

"What's going on?" she asks when she reaches us.

"Apparently, you're choosing your wedding daddy today."

"What?" she squeals. "We haven't even picked a wedding date yet."

"That's what she said," Grayson shouts and I high-five him.

"Come on, come on. Everyone take their places. I need to open in two hours for the lunch crowd." Pop ushers us toward the seats.

"You do realize this here is the definition of bat shit crazy? And I have seen some bat shit crazy stuff in my day."

Wally huffs. "Kid, you ain't seen nothing."

I roll my eyes but don't bother to respond. Despite dealing with a crazed man who thinks aliens stole his sperm and a couple who use Hailey's services as part of their sexy time games – to name but a few examples – I haven't seen anything. Pfff. Yeah, right.

Grayson clears his throat to gain everyone's attention. "Phoebe and Ryker, you sit there." He points to the table in front of the line of chairs, which are now occupied by the uncles and Pops. I take a seat behind the uncles next to Hailey.

"I will read out a question." He shakes the cards. "If one of you knows the answer, raise your hand. No shouting out the answer."

I giggle. If he thinks the uncles are going to play by the rules, he's a fool.

I raise my hand. "How will we know what the correct answer is? Phoebe found out about this *event* like five minutes ago."

Grayson hands Phoebe a pen and paper. "She'll write down the answer after I read the question but before the uncles answer."

I rub my hands together in glee. This is a train wreck waiting to happen. I can't wait to watch it play out.

"Everyone ready?" When the uncles and Pops grunt in response, he reads out the first question. "What is Phoebe's favorite pizza topping?"

Pops chuckles. "Too easy. Phoebe doesn't eat pizza."

"And Phoebe says…." Grayson takes the card from her. "Mushrooms and peppers."

"Exactly what I said," Pops insists.

Lenny scowls. "How is no pizza the same as mushrooms and peppers?"

"Mushrooms and peppers aren't toppings on a pizza. They're vegetables."

Lenny's eyes narrow on Pops but he keeps his mouth shut because Pops isn't wrong. Vegetables on pizza is plain wrong.

"Moving on." Grayson reads the question from the next card. "What is Phoebe's favorite drink?"

"Seriously, when are we getting to the difficult questions? Vodka Martini with Stolichnaya."

"Pops," Hailey scolds. "You're supposed to raise your hand. Not shout your answer out loud."

"Your answer is disqualified. Besides, didn't Ryker take Phoebe on a romantic date to the local distillery and now she drinks the *I Did It My Way* hoity-toity stuff." Sid winks at Phoebe.

"Nah, she hasn't given up on her Stolichnaya. But don't tell Ryker, it annoys him for some strange reason," Pops says with Ryker sitting literally five feet away from him.

"Maybe because Russia is our enemy," Wally points out.

"We ain't at war."

Wally shakes his head. "Sure, we are."

I tap Hailey on the shoulder and mouth *super-secret soldier.* She bobs her head in agreement.

"Um." Phoebe clears her throat to gain everyone's attention. "Maybe we don't tell all of Phoebe's secrets today?"

Ryker throws an arm around her. "Like I didn't know you're still drinking the Russian swill, Princess."

Grayson rasps his knuckles on the bar to gain everyone's attention. "Shall we continue?" He eyeballs the former soldiers until they mumble their assent. "What is Phoebe's maiden name?"

"No fair. Wally is the one who did the background check," Barney grumbles.

A shit-eating grin paints Wally's face as he crosses his arms over his chest. "Which is why I should be the one to walk her down the aisle."

Barney jumps to his feet. "Disagree."

Wally stands and faces Barney. "You want to take this outside?"

Lenny puts himself between the two men and pushes them apart. "Enough. You should both be disqualified for fighting."

"I haven't kicked his ass yet." Barney shakes out his hands like he's getting ready for action.

I lean over and whisper to Hailey, "This is the funnest Saturday morning ever."

"Sure is," she says with her eyes glued on Barney and Wally who are now circling each other like boxers in a ring.

"This? This is the most fun you've had on a Saturday morning?" Aiden leans close and whispers in her ear. Her cheeks flame red and she fans her face.

"I stand corrected," she squeaks.

I get up to move closer to the action. Plus, I don't need to hear about Hailey and Aiden's sexy adventures. Trust me. I've heard them in Hailey's office more times than should be allowed already.

"You want to put those numbskulls out of their misery and tell them who you chose?" Pops asks in a booming voice and everyone settles down.

My eyes widen. "Did you already choose someone? But you didn't tell me! What's all the bs about not having picked a date yet?"

Phoebe giggles. "Like I would have picked someone without letting you know. You're my maid of honor. Well, one of my maids of honor." She looks up at Ryker. "I can have two maids of honor, can't I?"

"You can have whatever you want, Princess," he declares before bending forward to kiss her.

I squeal and push them apart. I also cause two chairs to go crashing to the floor but who cares about some stupid chairs when I've just been named maid of honor?

I squeeze Phoebe's hands as I jump up and down. "I'm your maid of honor!"

Hailey scowls. "What? You picked Suzie over me? You know she's going to trip on her way down the aisle and end up mooning everyone in the church, don't you?"

"I'm not a klutz!" Lie. I'm totally a klutz, although not as much of a klutz as these two think I am. But my actual klutziness level is my little secret.

"You're both my maids of honor," Phoebe explains as Hailey glowers at her.

"Took the wind right of your sails, didn't she?" For good measure, I stick out my tongue at Hailey.

My eyes widen and I clap when I realize, "We get to walk down the aisle together then!"

Hailey bows her head. "Oh great, I'm going to end up rolling down the aisle."

"What?" Pops stops next to her. "Roll down the aisle? Are you pregnant?"

"Hailey's pregnant!" Sid shouts, although there's no need to shout. The word pregnant has everyone in the place freezing with their mouths gaping open.

"I'm going to be a grandpa!" Pops' chest puffs out and a smile covers his face from ear to ear.

"This is news to me," Aiden says as he puts his arm around his fiancé and kisses her forehead. "Something you need to tell me, Hails?"

"Yes." A muscle in Aiden's jaw starts to tick. He wasn't expecting her to say yes. This is awesome.

"I'm going to be an aunt," I shout. I can't wait. I love children. I want a whole bunch of them, but me and children? Not happening. You need a man for the whole procreating part and I'm off men – forever. But an aunt? Awe-some!

"Before you start planning my baby shower, I'm not pregnant."

Aiden exhales in obvious relief, and I deflate.

"This morning was a complete waste. We didn't pick who will walk Phoebe down the aisle and now I'm not going to be an aunt. Barkeep! I need a cold one!"

"Way to make this all about you," Hailey mutters. I ignore her. Of course, her having a baby is all about me. Is she not keeping up?

I settle on a barstool and Grayson takes the seat next to me. Pops plops two drafts in front of us and winks before heading down to the other side of the bar.

"Your family is crazy," Grayson mutters before taking a slug of beer.

"I know. Don't you love them?"

He taps his fingers on the bar as if he's seriously considering my question. "Actually, I kind of do."

My heart starts to pound in my chest at the idea he means me. I tell it to calm the eff down. He means the uncles and Pops. Not fall on her ass and end up doing the splits me. Bummer. Wait. What? Not. A. Bummer. I don't want a man, remember? Oh, yeah. Sometimes I forget.

Chapter 8

Friends bring happiness into your life. Best friends bring beer.

"Huh." I lay my phone down on my desk with a frown on my face.

"What's wrong?" Hailey asks, and I nearly jump out of my skin.

I place my hand over my erratic heart. "What are you doing? Trying to scare me to death?"

She wrinkles her brow. "I'm standing right beside you. It's not my fault you weren't paying attention." She points to my phone. "What's going on?"

"Grayson isn't responding to my messages."

Phoebe comes running out of her office. "What's this? Trouble in paradise?"

"Suzie and Grayson are fighting," Hailey explains except she's got it all wrong.

"Um, no, Suzie and Grayson aren't fighting. Suzie's worried about Grayson is all." And why am I talking in third person?

Phoebe and Hailey take seats across from me like we're going to have some kind of girl gab session. Not happening. I wave them away. "Get back to work. Nothing to see here."

Hailey raises her eyebrow in Phoebe's direction. "Does she think we're going to let her off easy?"

"After what she put me through—"

"Us," Hailey corrects her.

"Right, us. After what she put us through, we are not letting her off the hook."

I can feel my lips pursing. I didn't put them through a darn thing. I merely gave their love stories a little push – a loving tap if you will – but my situation with Grayson is completely different. Love is not part of our vocabulary. We're friends. Nothing more. Nothing less.

Hailey motions with her hand for me to hurry it on up. "Come on. Fill us in."

There's nothing to fill her in about. "I already told you. Grayson isn't answering his messages."

"Sounds like someone needs to go to his house and check up on him. He may need assistance." Phoebe winks in case I'm a total moron who didn't catch her innuendo.

"I don't know where he lives."

Hailey snorts. "And you can't possibly find out." She motions to my computer. My computer which is full of all kinds of tracking data software.

Phoebe stands. "We have a plan, then. You'll find his address and go over there and check on him."

Hailey nods and they both head off to their respective offices. "I didn't agree to any plan!" I shout at their backs. I get no response from the cheap seats.

Despite not agreeing to this stupid plan, I start up the software I need as soon as their doors shut. I look around to make sure no one's watching me. What am I doing? It's not like I'm committing a crime. Geesh. I type in Grayson's name, and all kinds of stuff comes up, but I ignore it all. I'm not invading his privacy. And finding his address is definitely not an invasion of privacy. It's not!

I add his address to his contact information in my phone and then sit there staring at it for a good five minutes. Am I seriously going to his place to check up on him? Do friends check up on friends?

"Just go!" Hailey shouts from her office.

"Yes! If I hear you sigh one more time…" Phoebe shouts from hers.

"I'm the eavesdropper in this company, not you guys!"

"What's good for the goose is good for the gander," Hailey shouts back.

"Go. Before I make you go," Ryker growls.

Wait a minute! Since when is Ryker involved in my private life? "It's none of your business, big guy."

"You made it my business when you started shouting in the office."

"I didn't start it!" Yeah, I know. Real mature.

"No, but I'm going to end it." Ryker may be a softie when it comes to Phoebe, but the menace in his voice is kind of freaking me out now.

"All right. All right. I'm going."

I park in front of Grayson's apartment building ten minutes later. It's a three-story brick building not too far from the college. I study the building while frozen in place until I remember my mantra *just friends*. I'm not here checking up on my boyfriend only to discover— Nope. I am not going there. Those thoughts are most unwelcome in my mind.

I march to the building and straight up to the third floor where Grayson's apartment is. I look around as I knock on his door. Although I'm not a lover of apartment buildings – all those neighbors being nosy – the place looks nice. All the lights are working, and the floor looks clean.

I knock again and end up nearly hitting Grayson with my fist when he opens his door. I yank my hand back when I realize he's shirtless. My eyes rove over his muscles, and my mouth waters. I would love to get my tongue on those. Stop. No, you don't, Suzie. Friends. Just friends.

"Sorry. Were you sleeping? I didn't think soldiers were allowed to be in bed at 11 a.m.," I sass while forcing my eyes to remain above shoulder level.

"What are you doing here?"

"Someone's grumpy," I say and then push my way inside. I shiver when my body rubs up against his. No, not rubs against his. His humongous body was in the way was all. I didn't deliberately rub up against him. Not me.

Little Susan cheers when we're inside his place and starts singing *Finally* while practicing her disco moves. *No, we have not met Mr. Right*, I tell her.

My brow wrinkles when I see his living room. It's a mess. "I thought you military types were clean freaks."

I pick up a pile of clothes to make room for myself on his couch. When I return my attention to Grayson, he's putting on a t-shirt. Little Susan sniffs and the disco moves come to an abrupt halt. *Told you so.*

I wait until he moves the magazines on a chair and takes a seat before I start. "What's going on? You've ignored my messages since Sunday."

"Been busy is all."

I look around the room. "Obviously, cleaning is not included in this busyness."

He grunts but doesn't otherwise speak. Normally, we don't have any problems keeping up a conversation.

"Did I piss you off?" It wouldn't be the first time I inadvertently pissed a person off. Not the second either if I'm being completely honest.

"Nah. Like I said I'm busy."

He won't look me in the eyes, though. I know when a man is being evasive. Trust me, I have a degree in ferreting out evasive men.

"What's really going on?"

"Leave it alone. You're my friend, Suzie, not my girlfriend." I feel like he slapped me. He's not wrong. I'm not his girlfriend, but it doesn't mean I want to hear him growl the words at me.

"Duh. I'm your friend. I'm worried about you. I'm checking up on you. This is what friends do." At least it's how girlfriends act with each other. I don't exactly have any male friends unless you count the uncles who I would never ever check up on. I do not want to know what they get up to when they disappear.

"Really? Like friends tell each other their secrets." I nod. "Then, Suzie Langley, why don't you want anyone to know about your brewing? Why is it a hobby instead of a business?"

Geez. Go straight to the heart, why don't you. "I'll tell you why my brewing is only a hobby if you tell me what's going on with you."

"Deal."

Shit. I didn't think he'd go for it. Son of a bitch. Now, I have to tell him. I reach up to tear at the spikes in my hair before I remember I'm growing my hair out. I drop my hands in my lap where I fidget with the strings from the hole in the thigh of my jeans.

"The brewing thing is a dream I shared with my ex. We were going to take the Midwest by storm with our specialty microbrews. I haven't figured out yet if brewing is a venture I want to take on as a full-time business by myself is all."

And – big time secret – I'm not sure I can brew full-time without memories of Toby the asshole ex ruining it.

"Why did you guys break up?"

I shake my head. "Suzie's revelation hour is up. It's now time for Grayson's revelations."

He rubs the back of his neck with his hand as he focuses on the ground. "Like I said, I'm busy is all. Going back to school takes more time and energy than I expected."

I know he's lying or at least not telling me the whole truth and nothing but the truth. It's kind of obvious seeing how he refuses to look me in the eye.

I don't call him on his obvious lies, though. Because he's right. He's not my boyfriend. I don't have a right to push him. Besides, I have other ways of finding out information. Mwa-ha-ha-ha.

Chapter 9

Beer doesn't ask questions or negotiate. Beer just is.

WALLY SCOWLS WHEN HE opens the door to find me standing on his front porch.

I ignore Grumpy Gus and wave. "Hi, Wally!"

He motions for me to enter without saying a word.

Geez. Would a greeting kill him? It's not like I want to be here either, but my research into Grayson's past came to a dead end. I can tell you all about his credit rating and what schools he attended. Hell, I can even give you his report cards. But can I tell you why the man is depressed? No. Thus, Wally.

I look around Wally's place as I follow him to the living room. His furniture is modern and sleek. The black leather looks pristine. Does he never chill and watch a movie here? What am I thinking? When does he have time to chill? He's either at the bar playing poker with the other uncles and Pops or he's off on some super-secret spy mission.

"What is it with you girls and coming to your Uncle Wally?" he mumbles as he walks to his kitchen and opens the refrigerator to retrieve two bottles of water.

"Who else came to visit you?" I ask when he hands me my water.

"Phoebe."

My eyes widen in surprise. Phoebe never asked me for his address. "How did she find you?"

"Followed me," he mumbles.

"Phoebe followed you without you noticing?" I snicker. "I knew we made the right decision hiring that girl."

Phoebe had no PI experience when she showed up at *You Cheat, We Eat.* Actually, she had no work experience at all. Like zip, zero, nada. She'd never held a job before in her entire life! She was a total spoiled rich girl, although not bitchy spoiled. More like spoiled as in clueless about the world.

"What do you want, kid?"

I roll my eyes. Uncle Wally may have multiple talents – talents I'm pretty sure the government puts to use in black ops – but being charming is not one of them.

"I need a favor."

He takes a long drink of his water before speaking, "Let me guess. You want me to do a background check on one Grayson Neill."

Of course, he knows what I want. The man can probably read minds. I wouldn't be surprised if the government has perfected the art and is keeping the information from the public. I know I sound like a conspiracy theorist. But I'm not.

What I am is an excellent eavesdropper. No one pays much attention to short girls. They probably should. I've heard a bunch of stuff the uncles got up to when they were in the Army. Most of it stuff I wish I hadn't heard.

"What's your price?"

Wally grins and leans back in his chair. "This has possibilities."

I bite my tongue to keep from speaking while he taps his chin and pretends to think of all the possibilities. He knows exactly what he wants, but he likes making me wait because he knows I have the patience of a gnat.

"Fine," I grump when he maintains his silence for more than two minutes. Yes, I counted. "What do you want?"

His eyes sparkle. "I never thought you'd ask."

I hold up my hand. "Nothing illegal."

"As if I would ask you to commit a crime."

Frankly, I wouldn't be surprised if he asked me to do something on the wrong side of the law. The man did teach Hailey how to pick locks and hotwire cars after all.

"I want you to give Grayson a chance."

I raise an eyebrow. "A chance? What do you mean?" I know exactly what he means, and I don't like it one bit.

"Don't play dumb with me, kid. You may have everyone else fooled with your happy go lucky act but not me. I know you're lonely."

I shoot daggers at him. "Don't you dare presume to know what I'm feeling."

He's right. Of course, he's right. I told you the government had perfected mind reading! Because there's no other way he could possibly know about the gut-churning loneliness I'm feeling. I cover it up entirely too well with my jokes and klutzi-ness. Confession – I'm not as klutzy as you might think. But he shouldn't know it!

My daggers have no effect on Wally. I mentally add sharpening my daggers to my to-do list. "Don't you dare presume I'm like all the other schmucks you have fooled."

Oh, goodie. A distraction. "Who are you calling a schmuck? You're not calling your brothers-in-arms schmucks, are you?"

"Don't change the subject. You're not going to divert me from the issue here."

Damn it. He's on to me. "What is the subject?" If I can't distract, I'll delay.

He leans forward in his chair and places his elbows on his thighs. He narrows his eyes on me before answering. "You know darn well what the subject is. But before you act all innocent again, I'll remind you. If you give Grayson a chance – a real chance – I'll do your background check."

"Grayson doesn't want a chance. We're friends. Nothing more."

But we want to give Grayson a chance, my inner voice reminds me. I call her Adult Suzie because she's always pushing me to act like a grown-up, something I have no intention of ever doing. But then Little Susan joins in on the act. *Yeah! We want to make the sweet love to him.* Since when does Little Susan speak with a Spanish accent? I shake my head to try and force all the crazy thoughts out.

Wally only stares at me in response. And stares. And stares. Until I burst out with another lie, "There's no chemistry between us!"

He tilts his head back and laughs. He laughs and laughs until he has to wipe his eyes free of his tears of laughter.

"I don't know what's funny." And I'm back to lying.

"What's funny is you thinking no one can see the chemistry between you and Grayson. A blind person could see the electricity jolting back and forth between you two."

They can? "Doesn't matter. We have agreed to be friends, nothing more. Neither one of us is looking for a relationship."

"How do you know Grayson isn't looking for a relationship?"

"Hello! You were sitting right across the table from him when he said he isn't ready for a relationship." I pause. Have things changed from when we had that particular conversation? "Did Grayson tell you otherwise?"

"No. But your curiosity is a dead give away."

And I fell for it. Ugh. "Doesn't matter," I repeat. "I am not looking for a relationship."

And I'm not. My body may want to tangle in the sheets with him, but my head knows better. I've learned my lesson. Men are extremely dangerous to your health and should be avoided at all costs.

Wally shrugs. "You've heard my terms. What is your response?"

"I do not accept." I stand. "Thank you for listening to me. I'll see myself out."

I stomp through the living room and yank open the front door. I'm annoyed. How dare Wally deny me? He's supposed to support me. Uncles are supposed to help you out when your own father isn't on your side. Hasn't he read the manual?

"Wait!" he calls after me, but I don't stop.

If I do, I'll probably break down and cry. And how embarrassing would that be? No. Happy-go-lucky Suzie does not cry. At least not in public. I practically run to my car. As I'm starting my ignition, I look up and see Wally standing on his porch with his arms crossed over his chest. He does not look happy. He's not the only one.

I'll figure out another way to find out what's bothering Grayson. Trust me. I can badger like no one's business. How do you think Phoebe and Hailey ended up happily in romantic relationships? Without me, they'd both be single and miserable. I got this.

Chapter 10

Why did you get a divorce? My doctor told me I
wasn't allowed to touch anything alcoholic.

I LOOK UP WHEN the bell over the door at *You Cheat, We Eat*
rings. "Good morning," I greet the man who walks inside. He
startles and takes a step back when he hears my voice. What's his
problem? It's not like my voice was overly cheery. Confession:
It totally was.

I study the man as he stands in front of the door. He doesn't
look like our normal client. Although we'll find any cheater –
whether male or female – we usually end up with the wives
as clients. He's also dressed in a suit I would bet a crate of my
Holiday Brew is custom made. Consider my curiosity officially
piqued.

"Welcome to You Cheat, We Eat. How can we make your life
better?"

"I need to hire a PI," he answers.

"Perfect! You Cheat, We Eat is a PI firm."

"And you specialize in adultery cases?"

The name kind of gives it away, doesn't it? "We sure do." I point to a seat in front of my desk. "Why don't you have a seat, Mr...."

"Cafferty."

"I'm Suzie. Why don't you give me a bit of background and then I'll check if one of our PIs is available."

Check if someone's available? As if. I can see from the corner of my eye both Phoebe and Hailey have crept close to their doors to listen in on our conversation. Phoebe is being nosy. She doesn't take the adultery cases. The woman can't be inconspicuous if she tried. And she does try. But she's entirely too beautiful and elegantly dressed to not stick out, although she doesn't wear her Louboutins every day anymore.

Mr. Cafferty takes a seat on the chair I indicated and folds his hands in his lap. I'm not fooled. He's not calm. His knuckles are literally white from him clenching them.

"Go ahead," I coax when his lips remain sealed. "No one will judge you here."

"I think my wife is a prostitute."

"Wh—" I cough to hide my exclamation of surprise. This is a new one. I clear my throat. "Sorry. What makes you think your wife is a prostitute?"

"I'm suspicious of all the extra cash she seems to have at her disposal."

I raise my eyebrows and deliberately let my eyes wander up and down him. In addition to the custom-made suit, he's wearing a pair of lace-up oxfords I'd swear are Berluti. The Italian leather shoes retail for over two-thousand dollars.

So, sue me, I like to look at pretty things online during my lunch break. It's not against the law. And it totally came in handy when Phoebe showed up in her Louboutins with her Prada tote.

Mr. Moneybags' lips purse. "She receives a weekly allowance from me, but the amount of cash she has is significantly more than her allowance."

Don't tell me some gold-digger married Mr. Moneybags and then started turning tricks when her allowance wasn't what she expected. I guess getting a real job takes too much time and effort? Sounds crazy, but we get a lot of crazy here.

"And what makes you think the cash is the result of prostitution?" I have never said the word prostitute this much in my life.

He takes a moment to adjust his tie before answering. "I followed her."

I don't ask him what he saw. Judging by the color of his cheeks, I can figure it out. "If you know she's involved with prostitution, what do you need us for?"

"I need proof she's not only committing adultery but is in fact a prostitute."

I don't bother dancing around the subject. "Prenup requirement?"

"Yes." He nods. "Now, can you help?"

Hailey decides it's time to make her appearance. She walks out of her office. "Of course, we can help." She extends her hand toward him. "I'm Hailey McGraw."

After they shake hands, Hailey takes a seat next to him. "I can take pictures of your wife during her activities."

"No, no, no. I read online someone has to engage in sex with her for it to be admissible in court."

Hailey's mouth drops open before she clears her throat and slams her mouth shut again. "Is your wife bi-sexual?" He inclines his head. "And you're suggesting I have intercourse with her?"

"Either you or better yet." He points to Phoebe who is now standing in the doorway of her office. "Her."

I hear a chair squeak and heavy footfalls before Ryker appears behind Phoebe. He wraps an arm around her waist and draws her close. "This one is not having sex with anyone."

"Not even you?" I can't resist asking.

He ignores me. "And before you ask, I'm not having sex with your wife either."

Mr. Cafferty looks Ryker up and down. "Too bad. You are definitely her type."

Not what I was expecting to hear. Mr. Cafferty looks nothing like Ryker. Ryker is six-and-a-half feet tall whereas Mr. Cafferty is slightly shorter than Hailey who measures in at a measly five-feet-eight. Ryker also sports an out-of-control beard compared to Mr. Cafferty's clean-shaven jaw.

Mr. Cafferty opens his mouth, but Ryker shuts him down. "We're not having a threesome either." Apparently, Ryker can read his mind as Cafferty frowns in obvious disappointment.

Total disclosure. The idea of Ryker in a threesome gives me the shivers. I would never poach my girl's man, but there's nothing wrong with a little material for my naughty dreams.

"Besides, your internet search was wrong. No one needs to have intercourse with your wife to convict her of prostitution. Prostitution in the state of Wisconsin is defined as offering or requesting non-marital sexual intercourse for anything of value. There's no need to commit a sexual act to ensure conviction."

Color me impressed. The bounty hunter knows his sex laws.

"Are you sure?" Mr. Cafferty asks.

"He is correct," Hailey answers. Mr. Cafferty doesn't look like he believes her. "If you want proof, I can call my fiancé. He's a police detective."

"Ah, no. It's fine. I believe you." It only took two people and an offer to call a cop, but sure now he believes us.

Everyone falls silent. Guess it's up to me to make sure we acquire a new client. "Would you like us to take pictures of her activities?"

At his nod, Hailey stands. "Please come into my office and we can discuss this further."

He follows her to her office, and she shuts the door. Like a little thing like a door will stop me. I roll my chair close to the door to listen. Their meeting quickly becomes boring, though. Talk about prices doesn't interest me.

I roll my chair back under my desk and return to what I was doing when he arrived – obsessing over Grayson. His only response to my messages over the past days has been a thumbs-up emoji. Not okay.

Hailey escorts Mr. Cafferty out of her office a few minutes later. As soon as the door shuts behind him, she points at me. "Not a word."

I widen my eyes in feigned innocence. "Whatever do you mean?"

Hailey snorts. "Don't act innocent with me. I know you're dying to make some kind of lame, corny joke."

"I think you have me confused with your pops and uncles."

Phoebe joins us. "What a weird situation. Do you get these types of requests often?"

At the sound of Phoebe's voice, Lola barks and comes barreling out of Hailey's office. She heads for Phoebe, jumps her, and commences humping her leg. Phoebe desperately tries to rid herself of the horny dog to no avail while Hailey giggles herself silly.

Suzie to the rescue! I take hold of Lola's collar and yank her away from Phoebe. Lola is not happy being denied her love interest and strains against my grip. I slip and start to fall.

Confession – I can totally stop myself from falling at this point. It's not difficult. But I don't. I let myself fall on my ass. Phoebe's face lights up at my fall.

"Klutzy Suzie strikes again," she announces and offers me her hand to help me up.

I wave her away. I don't need anyone's help. I can stand by myself as well as I can fall by myself. I've had enough practice by this point.

Don't get me wrong. I am somewhat of a klutz. Okay. Okay. I'm a big 'ol klutz. But I am not nearly as klutzy as everyone thinks. Then, why do I act the fool? Let me explain. After Toby, the asshole did me wrong, I found myself in a depression. And not a little bit of a depression. No, I was walking around with the weight of an eight-gallon brew kettle on my shoulders.

Everyone kept giving me looks to make sure I was doing okay all the freaking time. And they weren't sneaky about it. I was about done with everyone's concern and tired of the uncles thinking up ways to kill my ex.

But then I fell. Honest to goodness fell when I slipped on the ice. Everyone laughed when my skirt flipped up and I mooned the entire city. You know what else they did? They stopped studying my every mood. Super klutzy Suzie was born.

Chapter 11

How do you know if someone likes craft beer?
Don't worry, they'll tell you.

I smile when I open my door and discover Wally on my front porch. "Uncle Wally," I greet and open the door wide. "Come on in."

"Hey, kid. I thought I'd come see what this brew shack I keep hearing about looks like."

Why is it everyone is now bound and determined to see my brew shack? A few months ago, hardly anyone knew about my brewing hobby. I blame Hailey. She had to tell Aiden about my beers. And now look! People are knocking down my door to check out my beer shack.

"Do you want a coffee or something else to drink?" I ask in the lamest attempt at stalling ever.

"I'm all full up," he says and then looks at me expectantly. Told you – lamest stalling tactic ever.

"Fine," I mumble and nab my keys to the brew shack.

We walk out the back door to the garage where I unlock the doors and usher him in. He whistles when he enters and gets a look at the place.

"This is more than a hobby, kid."

I roll my eyes. What is it with everyone telling me I should change my career and become a brewer lately? Don't they know I'm worried making a career of it will continually bring up memories of Toby the asshole? Memories I've worked my ass off to forget.

"Do you want the five-cent tour?"

He grunts and I show him around my brewing set-up. He makes comments at all the right times, but he's obviously not paying much attention.

"All right. What's going on?" I ask after I tell him I'm going to name my next beer The Penis Punisher and his only response is an absent-minded nod.

Wally is usually someone who is one-hundred percent present at all times. His eyes may wander constantly to make sure there are no threats about, but he always knows what's happening in front of him.

"Oh god, it's bad, isn't it? Do you have cancer?" My eyes widen. "Or is it Hailey? Or Pops?" My breaths come faster and faster as I imagine a dozen harrowing situations.

"Calm down before you start hyperventilating."

Too late. Wally places his hand on my neck and forces my head between my knees.

"Deep breaths. That's it. Nice and easy."

I take deep breaths in through my nose and out through my mouth until I can breathe like a normal person again and not like an overexcited pug. No judging. The Animal Planet channel rocks.

I collapse in a chair in the corner. "What's going on?"

Wally stands in front of me with his arms crossed over his chest. "I'm not sure I should tell you."

"You couldn't make up your mind before you came over here and scared me shitless?"

He scratches his head before admitting, "It's about Grayson."

I wrinkle my brow. "What about Grayson?" My eyes widen when I realize what's going on. "You did the background check, didn't you?" I jump to my feet. "Tell me. Tell me. Tell me."

"Are you sure you want to invade his privacy in this way?"

I stop dancing around to gape at Wally. "Invade his privacy? But this is what we do. Anyone new who comes into our lives, you check out. You did a background check on Phoebe, remember?"

"Yes, after she came to me to ask me to help her."

I snort. Does he think I'm stupid? "Tell it to another chump 'cuz I ain't buying. I know damn well and good you ran a background check on Phoebe before she came to you, but you didn't get anywhere because you didn't know her real name."

It's a long story – and super exciting full of kidnappings and drugging and stuff – but it turns out rich girl Phoebe was hiding one whopper of a story. It worked out in the end. The knight in shining armor – aka Ryker – saved the day and they fell in love. Blah. Blah. Blah.

"This is different."

I tilt my head and study him. "Different how?"

"We know Grayson isn't a danger to anyone."

I raise an eyebrow. "And Phoebe was?"

"There were people in Phoebe's life who were dangerous," he points out.

"How do you know there aren't people in Grayson's life who are dangerous?" I rub my hands together as I warm to the idea. "Maybe there's someone who's after him for something he did. Like a warlord or maybe another enemy of some type."

"Whoa!" Wally holds up his hands. "There's nothing of the sort in his background."

"Then you did do the check." I knew it!

"You don't like anyone digging into your past with Toby."

I growl at *his* name. "We don't talk about him."

"Exactly. Grayson obviously doesn't want to talk about his past. Otherwise, he would have told you about it."

"But his past is affecting his present. He's all depressed and living in filth." Filth is a bit of an exaggeration but I'm making a point, darn it! "My history with Toby doesn't affect me now."

Wally crosses his arms and stares me down. "Really?"

I nod and pretend my cheeks aren't burning. For good measure, I cross my fingers behind my back.

We stare at each other for a good thirty seconds. I count the ticking of the seconds from the clock on the wall. Damn it. He knows I have zero patience.

"Fine." I stomp my foot. "If I admit, there's the teeniest tiniest possibility Toby the king of the jerks affects my current situation, will you tell me what you found out?"

Wally makes me wait. They must teach patience techniques in the military. How can he resist my adorable pouting face otherwise?

"You should probably sit down for this."

I bite my tongue before I can start sprouting one of my gazillion questions. I know if I speak now Wally will make me wait even more. And I am done with waiting. I take a seat and look up at him. The picture of decorum. Yeah, I didn't believe those words either.

"When Grayson was in Afghanistan, he got sick with a bad case of diarrhea and couldn't go out on patrol."

Gross, but it happens.

"His buddy offered to take his patrol to allow Grayson to stay in the vicinity of a toilet."

This all sounds pretty tame thus far. What's the big secret? I don't show my impatience, though. Wally is obviously building up to the grand reveal.

"The Humvee his buddy was in hit an IED and everyone in the vehicle was killed."

I gasp. What a total bitch I am. I was practically rubbing my hands in excitement to hear the story. There's nothing exciting about this. No, it's tragic.

"Grayson's buddy was married, and his wife had just given birth to a baby boy."

My eyes well up with tears, but I fast blink to stop them from falling. Once I'm convinced I have control over my tear ducts, I speak. "It's a tragic story, but I'm unsure what this has to do with how Grayson is acting."

"Grayson blames himself. He's the one who should have died not his buddy."

"I call bullshit! He's not god. He doesn't decide who lives or dies. Who knows what would have happened if he went out on patrol? Maybe they would have taken a different route or maybe they would have hit a rock and driven around the IED."

Obviously, I have no idea what I'm talking about.

"You're not wrong, but this is how Grayson feels. It's why he's living in Milwaukee instead of heading back up north to his hometown."

My forehead wrinkles. Grayson told me he moved to Milwaukee because there were more opportunities in the big city. Convenient.

"Okay. What are we going to do about this?"

Wally shakes his head. "You're not going to do a thing. You're going to leave him to figure this out for himself."

Please. As if men know how to handle their feelings. Case in point? Pops still pines after Hailey's mother although she left them nearly two decades ago without so much as a look back in her rearview mirror.

"I'm serious, Suzie Langley," he says using a commanding voice that probably makes terrorists pee their pants. "You will leave the boy alone to sort through his problems."

My full name and the commanding voice? He pulled out the big guns. Time to appease the super-secret soldier. Then, he'll leave, and I can start to brainstorm a plan.

I grin up at him. "Of course, I understand. You're a soldier. You know best how to handle these situations." I pat his chest as I spew my lies.

He narrows his eyes as he studies me. I'm waiting for him to call me a liar, but I don't give him the chance.

"Do you want to try my Session IPA? It's a new recipe I'm trying."

He grunts, which I interpret to mean, *Why yes, Suzie, I would love to try one of your awesome beers.*

"Come on," I drag him to the tasting station.

While Wally oohs and aahs over my beer, my mind whirls around with idea after idea. How am I going to fix Grayson? I don't know, but I'll figure it out. I always do.

Chapter 12

I fear my last words will be, hold my beer and watch this.

STEP ONE IN MY Fix Grayson Plan is not proceeding according to plan. The girls and their men are going bowling tonight, but Grayson is refusing to get off his butt and join us. He must be genuinely depressed. He normally jumps at the chance to compete with Aiden and Ryker.

Come on. For me.

I type and add a GIF of a dog with great big puppy dog eyes for good measure. When I don't get a response, I try again.

It'll be fun. Promise.

I add another GIF of a baby girl with huge eyes begging.

If I say yes, will you stop sending me creepy GIFs?

Probably not. I do love me some creepy GIFs but of course, I lie.

Yep. I'll pick you up in 5.

I'll meet you there.

Fine. Whatever.

I give in because at least I finally convinced Grayson to get out of his house. Gee. I hope he showers. The look of his place when I visited does not evoke confidence in his hygiene habits.

When I arrive at the bowling alley, I look around the parking lot, but I don't see Grayson's truck anywhere. I debate waiting for him at the entrance for all of ten seconds. But I am not his girlfriend. And, more importantly, I am not pathetic. I walk inside and head toward the lane Hailey reserved.

"Hey, Suzie. Where's your boyfriend?" Phoebe calls when I join them.

"He's not my boyfriend."

"He's a boy and he's your friend, thus *boyfriend*."

"That's not the definition of boyfriend and you know it." I show her my back to ask Hailey, "What happened to our shy Phoebe? I don't like the new and improved Phoebe."

Hailey hip checks me. "Sure, you do. You just don't like it when she's sassy with you."

True. I love how Phoebe has come out of her shell. This Phoebe is way more fun than spoiled rich and scared little Phoebe, although spoiled little rich girl Phoebe was okay. She wasn't as much fun is all.

Ryker hooks a hand around Phoebe's neck and drags her close. "Give it a rest, will ya?"

Phoebe pouts. "Why? She pushed and pushed until I gave you a chance and you kidnapped me."

Pain flashes in Ryker's eyes before he blinks, and it's gone again. Someone still feels guilty for what he did despite having his reasons – and they were good reasons.

"I have a feeling pushing Suzie isn't going to get you any-where," Ryker admits.

Damn right, it won't! Suzie is Ms. Single until the end of time. My heart clenches at the thought but my head reminds her of the snake in the grass, aka Toby. Argument settled.

"Hey," Grayson says as he comes up behind me.

Ryker and Grayson do some complicated man hug thing. Aiden gets in on the action by slapping Grayson on the back. Phoebe rolls her eyes at me and mouths *men*. See? Men don't know how to handle their emotions. It's up to me to solve Grayson's problems. It's what friends do.

"How should we divide into teams?" Grayson asks as he looks around at the group.

Aiden's grin is sly. "Men and against women?"

Phoebe shrugs. "Sure."

Hailey laughs and stands on her tiptoes to get in Aiden's face. "We're going to kick your asses."

The men chuckle and shake their heads at us as if we're cute. We'll show them! I nearly rub my hands in glee, but I manage to keep my poker face in place. I happen to be an awesome bowler. Beer and bowling are my jam. Hailey isn't too bad either, since I often drag her to the alley with me.

I plop down to put on my bowling shoes.

"You have your own bowling shoes?" Grayson asks.

"Yep." I don't tell him it's because I bowl all the time. No, I'm having too much fun scamming them. "I'm not putting my feet where other people have. How do I know their socks are clean?" I do an exaggerated shiver.

Of course, he swallows my lie hook, line, and sinker. Being a compulsive cleaner comes in handy sometimes. He looks at his rental shoes for a long moment before shrugging and sitting next to me to change shoes.

I bump his shoulder. "How are you doing?"

"I'm fine." I wait for him to expand, but he doesn't. Whatever. I've got him. I'll fix his problems.

"Suzie," Hailey shouts. "You're up first."

I open my bowling bag and remove my bowling ball.

"You have your own ball?"

I'm prepared for his question. I wiggle my fingers at him. "Tiny hands equal tiny fingers."

He takes a bit longer to swallow this lie, but he does. This is going to be too much fun.

I give my rear an extra wiggle as I walk to the approach area. Once I'm there, I let all the noise fall away and concentrate on my throw. The ball flies down the lane and boom! Strike, baby, strike!

I twirl around and bat my eyelashes at the boys. "Must be beginner's luck."

I watch as Grayson takes his first throw. He's obviously bowled some as he knocks down eight pins. He winks when he notices me watching him. I cross my arms over my chest and wait for his second throw. It should be an easy spare, but he misses both pins on his second chance. I may smirk.

"Phoebe, you're up," Hailey shouts from where she's sitting at the command center.

It's not literally a command center. Everything in bowling is automated nowadays. There's no need to keep score, but she likes to sit in front of the computer and pretend she's in charge. I let her.

Phoebe bites her lip as she stands.

"Do you need help?" I ask, but she waves me away. Alrighty then.

She glances over at Ryker to see how he's putting his fingers in the holes. She follows his lead and adopts a conventional grip. Then she watches as he takes his first chance. When he finishes, she scrunches up her nose and studies our lane.

"You got this, Pheebs." I clap to encourage her.

She swings the ball back and then throws it forward. But instead of the ball flying down the lane, it sails upwards toward the ceiling. "Aaaah!" she screams and covers her head.

The ball curves and drops in front of a young girl, barely missing her. The girl's eyes widen to the size of saucers. She stands frozen staring at the ball that literally dropped from the sky to land at her feet. I hear the sound of water splashing and look down to see the poor girl has literally peed herself.

"Ohmygod!" Phoebe rushes to her, but at her approach, the girl screams and bursts into tears. I can't blame her. The ball scared the stuffing out of me, and I wasn't anywhere near the danger zone.

The girl's dad rushes to her and picks her up and carries her off. Phoebe tries to follow but the man gives her a vicious look stopping her in her tracks.

Ryker tags Phoebe's hand and leads her away. "Come on. There's nothing you can do."

"Clean up on aisle five," I shout.

Ryker snarls. "Not funny, Suze. Not funny."

He sits and places Phoebe in his lap. "I am never bowling again!" she declares.

Probably the best idea she's had all night. I stand and take my bowling towel from my bag. I quickly clean up the puddle of pee and then walk over to the bar to throw the towel away. Yes, I know washing machines exist, but I am not keeping a towel that was once used to mop up pee. Not happening.

As I'm walking past the refrigerator with bottled beer, I pause when something catches my eye. I yank the door open to get a closer look. I can't believe it. What the hell? I grab a bottle of *my* beer and march to the counter.

The bartender startles when I slam the bottle down on the bar. "Where did you get this beer?"

His brow wrinkles as he looks at it. "From the back room?"

"And why was it in the back room? I want to talk to the manager!"

Hailey sidles up to me. "What's going on, crazy girl?"

I point to the bottle. "They have my beer."

"Wahoo!" she cheers. "Awesome." She motions to our group. "Hey, everyone! They have Suzie's beer here."

I bat her hand out of the air. "You don't understand. They shouldn't have my beer."

"Why not?"

"I don't have a contract with them."

She shrugs. "Big deal. They probably bought a couple of cases from your online store and are selling it."

"But—"

Grayson throws his arm around my shoulders. "But Suzie doesn't want anyone to know about how awesome her beers are. Isn't that right? You're scared to let people try them."

I scowl at him and shuffle forward until he has to drop his arm. I may be extremely pissed the bowling alley is selling my beer without signing a distribution contract with me, but my body is more interested in lighting up like a freaking Christmas tree when he touches me. Stupid body.

"Stop trying to bait me."

He smirks. "But it's fun." He lays a five-dollar bill down on the bar before taking the bottle of Short but Stout. "Come on. Let's go."

"But I want to talk to the manager," I grump as they try to shuffle me back to our lane.

"Fine. But if you don't take your turn, you'll have to forfeit." Grayson raises his eyebrow in an obvious challenge.

"Forfeit," I growl. "I am not forfeiting. You want me to forfeit because we are kicking your asses."

Somewhat of an exaggeration since we've only bowled one frame and Phoebe didn't actually take her turn.

"I'll let you bowl for Phoebe," Hailey says.

Darn it. She knows she has me. "Fine," I give in.

We spend the next couple of hours bowling and goofing off. Anytime my eyes stray to the bar, Grayson snaps his fingers in front of my face and shakes his finger at me. What is he? An old lady trapped inside a hot man's body? I force my eyes to remain on his and not go roaming over his body although roaming his body is exactly what my eyes and fingers and tongue want to do.

"That cheered me up!" Grayson declares as he walks me to my truck.

"Ah-ha! You admit you needed cheering up."

He rolls his eyes. "Give it up, girl."

I smile and nod as if I agree. I don't. Sneaky Suzie is coming to your rescue, Grayson. You just wait and see.

Chapter 13

What did the bottle write on the postcard? Wish you were beer!

I HUM AND SING along with the radio as I drive out of Milwaukee. I'm on my way to meet Grayson's buddy's widow. It's taken me a week to put all the puzzle pieces together and figure out who the buddy and widow are. In the end, it was easy. A huge duh moment.

I started my research by going through newspaper accounts of military deaths in Afghanistan. There were way more than I thought. It was heartbreaking. From there, I tried to find a connection to Grayson. But he doesn't talk about his time in the military. I have no idea what unit he was in let alone when exactly he was overseas.

And then I remembered something Wally said. Grayson didn't go back to his hometown after his discharge because of his buddy's death. Maybe his buddy was from his hometown. I know Grayson grew up in Merrill, a small town in northern Wisconsin. Sure enough, I found a story of a soldier from Merrill killed in action when his Humvee drove over an IED.

From there it was a simple Google search to find out where Liz Morris, widow of Bill Morris, lives. And now I'm driving the three hours from Milwaukee to Merrill to meet her. I didn't call in advance. I'm not sure how she feels about Grayson. Maybe he feels guilty because she blames her husband's death on Grayson.

It's all a big fat mess, but I'm going to unravel everything and fix Grayson. He won't see me coming.

After a stop for lunch, I park in front of the Morris residence around two. I would have liked to arrive earlier, but it's Sunday, and I didn't want to have to wait for church to get out. It's way too cold for waiting outside. My mom may be onto something with the whole no coming up north in the winter thing.

There's a car in the driveaway and the lights are on. Looks like Liz and her baby boy are home. No more stalling. My hand shakes as I reach for the door handle. Stop it. I berate myself. There's nothing to be nervous about. I'm sure Liz is a lovely person.

I ring the doorbell and stomp my boots as I wait for her to answer. The door opens and a blonde woman a few inches taller than me wearing her Sunday best answers.

"Can I help you?"

I smile. "Hi. Are you Liz Morris?"

Her eyes narrow. "Who are you?"

"I'm a friend of Grayson's."

A little head peeks around her legs. "I'm Grayson, but I don't know you."

I bend down to look at him face to face. "I'm Suzie. My Grayson is an adult."

"Oh." His eyes widen. "Uncle Grayson?"

I nod before standing and holding my hand out to Liz. "I'm Suzie Langley. Can I come in?"

She shakes my hand. "Any friend of Grayson's is welcome here."

Phew. By the sound of it, she doesn't hate Grayson. Fingers crossed she doesn't blame him for her husband's death. After I take off my boots and jacket, she directs me to the living room.

"Can I get you something to drink? I was making some hot cocoa for us."

"Hot cocoa sounds lovely, but I don't want to put you out."

She waves off my concern. "It's no problem. The pan is still warm."

While she walks to the kitchen, I look around the place. It's small but cozy and organized. Even the corner for Grayson's toys is arranged in a proper fashion. It feels weird referring to a small boy as Grayson. Grayson is a big strong soldier, not a little boy, I think as I survey the rest of the room. The furniture is worn but clean and comfortable. It looks like Liz is doing all right for herself, except for being widowed way too young, of course.

Liz returns and hands me a mug of cocoa. I take a sip to stall. I probably should have rehearsed what I'm going to say, but I like to wing it. It's more authentic.

"You said you're a friend of Grayson. Is he okay?"

I put my mug down on the coffee table. "Not exactly." When she gasps, I quickly continue. "He's fine. Physically at least. Mentally, though, the man is messed up."

Her eyes close and her chin drops to her chest. I feel like a total shit for bringing all this up with her, but I'm letting Grayson wallow in his grief and guilt.

"He blames himself," she says when she lifts her head.

"Yes."

"It's not his fault insurgents planted an IED along the roadside and Bill's patrol drove over it."

She's preaching to the choir. "I agree, but Grayson seems to be spiraling."

"Spiraling how?"

"He hasn't gone on a crime spree or started shooting up drugs, but he's clearly depressed. And his living conditions?" I wrinkle my nose.

"Darn. I told him to stop sending us money. We're doing fine without it."

"Sending you money?"

Wally didn't mention Grayson supporting Liz's family, and as far as I know, Grayson isn't working while he's attending school. He doesn't have money to throw around. I think. I'm starting to realize I don't know much about the man.

"It's not much. Fifty dollars here, one hundred there. But it sounds like he can't miss it. Where is he living? Please tell me he isn't homeless. You hear these horror stories about homeless vets."

I slap my forehead with my palm. "I'm sorry. I didn't mean to exaggerate. He has a perfectly fine apartment, except he's not taking proper care of his place. It's not like him."

Or I assume it's not like him. Frankly, I don't know for sure. But I know I'm not exaggerating about Grayson's depression. He's not acting like himself.

Liz puffs out a breath of air. "At least he has a place."

Her son Grayson comes running into the room full tilt. He doesn't stop until he's at his mother's feet. "Can I watch *Super Why*? Please, please, please."

She ruffles his hair. "Yes, but in my bedroom. We're talking."

He rushes off but returns seconds later. "Thank you!" he shouts before running off again.

"He's adorable."

Her face lights up with my praise of her son. "Yes, and very advanced for his age."

"How old is he?"

"He recently turned four."

For some reason, I assumed he was a baby. The timeline is confusing me, but it's not what is important right now. "You named him Grayson?"

"Bill insisted. Those two – Bill and Grayson – were thick as thieves from kindergarten on. I met them when my family moved here when I was in middle school. I fell in love with Bill at first sight, but it took him longer to get with the program. I went off to college and Bill and Grayson joined the Army. Bill finally noticed me when he was home on leave one summer. We got together and the rest is history."

"I'm sorry you lost him." I can't imagine. I can't get over a man betraying me, and she has to deal with the heartbreak of her husband dying.

"Yes, thank you." She clears her throat. "Anyway, what can I do for you?"

"I was hoping you could talk to Grayson, make him understand it's not his fault Bill died."

She shakes her head. "I've tried and tried. He won't listen. He won't pick up the phone when I call. And when he visits his parents, he avoids me like the plague."

"What if you came to Milwaukee to see him? Like a surprise visit." She starts to shake her head again, but I stop her. "I'll pay for everything. Your gas to drive down, a hotel room if you want to stay overnight. Or you can stay with me. I have plenty of room."

It's true. I bought my house when I thought I was going to marry my shithead ex and have lots of children. I should have sold it when everything went down, but I couldn't. I love my house. And I wasn't going to let *that* man take one more thing from me.

She stands. "I'll think about it."

Looks like it's time for me to leave. I can take a hint. I dig a card out of my purse. "Here's my information. Call me if you decide to come. Or just call me if you want to talk. I'm a good listener." Or at least, I'll try to be for her sake.

She takes my card, but by the way she looks at me, I'm afraid she's going to throw it in the garbage the minute I leave. No problem. I can come up with another plan to help Grayson because I will help Grayson. Come hell or high water, I will not let the man wallow in his depression.

Chapter 14

IPA a lot when I drink beer.

I NEED TO STEP up my efforts to cheer Grayson up since it looks like my plan to fix Grayson is not going to work out anytime soon. UGH! I was sure Liz would be understanding and jump on the bandwagon to fix Grayson. She was understanding, but she wasn't jumping on any bandwagons.

Darts and beer tonight at McGraw's?
No answer. I try again.

Come on. I'll let you win.
Still no answer. I throw my phone in the drawer and slam it shut.

"What's wrong? Trouble in paradise?" Hailey asks as she steps out of her office.

I feign innocence. "What? My drawer is sticking is all."

"Here. Let me try." She leans forward and I slap her hand away.

"You know you're not allowed to dig in my drawers." The woman is a menace. She never puts things back where they belong. After I spent a week looking for my favorite stapler –

and yes, I have a favorite stapler, don't judge – I banned her from going near my workspace.

Phoebe skids to a stop in front of us. "What's going on? Did I hear someone say drawers?" She looks me up and down. "Did you finally let Grayson into your drawers?"

I roll my eyes. "What are we? In Shakespearean England? No one says drawers when they mean panties."

"Actually, Shakespeare didn't—"

I hold up my hand to cut Hailey off. No one wants to hear a lecture about proper Shakespearean dialogue. The woman is a drama geek at heart. Even when Aiden did this elaborate Shakespeare-themed proposal, she kept stopping him to correct him. It was hilarious.

"No one is getting in anyone's drawers or panties."

"Maybe not your panties." Hailey wiggles her eyebrows.

I groan. "Isn't it bad enough I've had to hear you and Aiden going at it in your office?"

Phoebe takes Hailey's side. "It wouldn't bother you as much if you had a man in your panties. Say, Grayson."

"I told you once, I told you twice, I told you a million times. Grayson and are friends. Just friends."

"But you want more, don't you?" Phoebe pushes.

My nose flares. Sure, I want more. But I will never get more. Never ever. Men are not to be trusted. I've had my heart destroyed once. It's not an experience I'm eager to repeat. I don't tell her any of my thoughts, though. She'd jump right in and tell me to give Grayson a chance. No way, Jose.

I open my mouth to lie. Not to brag or anything, but my lying techniques are masterful. To my relief, the phone rings. I knock down my coffee cup in my rush to answer the phone. "We Cheat, You Eat!"

Phoebe frowns, but she walks back to her office. Hailey doesn't move except to cross her arms over her chest and study me while I talk to a saleswoman on the phone. A saleswoman I'm pretending is a potential client. I'm not sure if Hailey is buying my act, but she leaves – eventually. I'll call it a win.

I'm relieved when Phoebe and Hailey leave an hour later. They don't come back to the office and instead send me a message to meet them at McGraw's tonight. By the time I lock up, Grayson still hasn't responded to any of my messages. Does he want another unexpected visit? My nose wrinkles. I need to gather together a bunch of cleaning supplies before I drop by his place again.

I walk into the bar and shout, "Honey, I'm home!"

The uncles grunt but don't respond. Hailey and Phoebe are standing over their table while they play cards, poker by the looks of it.

"What's up?" I ask after I walk over.

"They're holding a poker tournament to decide who will walk me down the aisle," Phoebe explains. She does not look happy.

"A poker tournament?"

Hailey nods. "They're playing for twenty-four hours straight. Whoever has the most chips at the end wins."

"How is that going to work? Don't you need potty breaks?" My eyes widen when an idea hits me. "Tell me you're not wearing adult diapers!"

The ruckus in the bar dies down and heads swivel to gawk at us. The uncles lift their heads from their cards and glower at the crowd. Holy moly! I think I'd need adult diapers if they looked at me like that.

"We are not wearing diapers," Lenny insists.

"We get a five-minute break every ninety minutes," Sid explains.

Pops walks over and slams a round of beers on the table. "This is complete bullshit. If I'm not playing, then this entire circus is null and void."

Barney snickers. "It's not our fault you wouldn't close the bar for Phoebe."

Pops ignores his remark. "Besides, this poker tournament has nothing to do with Phoebe. How does winning a poker tournament mean you care about her and earn you the right to walk you down the aisle?"

Phoebe practically melts into his side at his words. He wraps an arm around her and pulls her close before kissing her hair. "Don't pay any attention to these old cronies, darling. You choose who you want to choose. Even if it isn't one of us."

"Not one of us?" Lenny grumbles. "Who saved her from her ex?"

"I did," Ryker declares as he joins us. He glares at Pops until he unhands Phoebe and urges her toward Ryker who immediately claims her with an arm around her shoulders and a kiss on her temple. For good measure, he scowls at the men in the room. I'm surprised he doesn't growl *mine* at everyone.

Pops chuckles. "I need to get back behind the bar. Walk with me, Shorty."

"What's up, boss man?" I ask as I start walking behind the bar. He grasps my shoulder and guides me toward the kitchen.

"I wanted to check on you."

"Check on me?" I point to myself. "Why?"

He crosses his arms over his chest and leans against the counter. "Don't play innocent with me. I know Hailey and Phoebe being engaged can't be easy for you."

"I am not talking about my ex," I hiss. We were engaged for like a minute. I can handle my friends being engaged, no problem. "Besides, I'm over it," I claim.

Pops snorts. "Sure, you're so over it, you won't give another man a chance."

What is this? National badger Suzie on her dating habits day? I'd prefer flowers and chocolate to be honest, and I don't think much of flowers. Why give someone a gift that is going to die? I don't get it.

I shrug and feign nonchalance. "Maybe the right guy hasn't come along is all."

"Darling, the right man is in front of your face."

Ugh. Not this again. "I'm done here." I stomp off half expecting Pops to come after me, but he lets me go.

I walk over to Phoebe and Hailey who are gathered around a high table near the bar with their men. There's a full stout beer sitting on the table with my name on it. I nab it and chug half of it. Ah, I needed that.

"Hey! You took my beer," Hailey says.

I merely point to the beer she's holding.

"It could have been my beer," she pouts.

I ignore her when I see Grayson walk into the bar. I wave him over.

"You made it!" I shout and raise my hand to high-five him. He stares at my hand for a moment before grunting and slapping it. "Yes!"

"I'm only here because I couldn't stand getting another fifty texts per hour from you."

I roll my eyes. "Please. No one can type fast enough to send fifty texts an hour on those tiny ass keyboards."

"They can if they have tiny fingers."

I cross my arms over my chest. "I have tiny fingers, do I? You know what these tiny fingers can do? They can beat your ass in darts is what."

I march off toward the darts board. When I arrive, I swivel around and notice not only Grayson has followed me but Phoebe and Hailey, too. Of course, where those two go, their men are not far behind.

"What are you guys doing?" My words clearly mean *no one invited you.*

Hailey shrugs. "Like I'm going to miss the chance to see the train wreck that is you trying to play darts."

I yank the darts out of the board. I'll show her. I toe the line and throw my first dart. Bam! I miss the bullseye by a millimeter.

I quickly throw my next two darts. Not as good as the first throw but not bad either.

"Are you seeing this?" Hailey asks.

"I can't believe my eyes. Is this honestly happening?" Phoebe responds.

"It's weird. Suzie hasn't injured anyone, not even herself. And she threw three darts. Three!"

"It's a miracle!"

I clap my hands in front of their faces to get their attention. "You do realize I can hear you?"

Hailey smirks. "Of course, we can. It wouldn't be any fun to tease you if you couldn't hear us."

Phoebe snickers. "And it is fun."

Grayson maneuvers himself so he's blocking my view of them. "Let's make this interesting, shall we?"

I raise an eyebrow. "Bring it on. Whatcha got?"

"This is not going to be good," I hear Hailey grumble from behind me.

"You did promise me a train wreck," Phoebe responds.

Hailey pulls her elbow down in an imitation of a train conductor. "Choo! Choo!"

Chapter 15

One beer, two beer, three beer, four. Then I hit the floor.

"Hold me close, young Tony Danza," I sing as Grayson helps me up the sidewalk to my house. When I'm sober, I think I can't carry a tune. When I've had a few beers, though, I realize I've got it all wrong. I can totally carry a tune.

"Hold me close, young Tony Danza." I may be able to carry a tune when I'm drunk but remember the lyrics to songs? Nah. But I'm nailing the chorus.

"Those are not the words to the song," Grayson grumps.

"Dude! They are! I heard it on Friends." And everyone knows if it was on *Friends*, it's true.

"Why is the song called Tiny Dancer if he's singing about Tony Danza?"

"Your question is irrelevant! Stop being a stick in the mud." I try to slap his chest, but I miss his body completely and stumble forward nearly ending up ass over teakettle on my front lawn.

"Whoa." Grayson grabs hold of my belt and yanks me up before I face plant. "Come on, let's get you to bed."

I shiver. In bed with Grayson? Yes, please! I may be tipsy, but I know better than to say those words out loud. "I don't need your help," I complain instead.

This is all Grayson's fault! Stupid man and his stupid drinking game. Sure, I said. I can slam a beer after every turn. Big mistake. Five – or was it six? – beers later and I suddenly found I couldn't see straight. At which point, Ryker took the darts away from me, Aiden stole my car keys, and Grayson escorted me to his truck.

Phoebe and Hailey, the twin troublemakers, cheered as I was dragged out of the bar by Grayson. I need to up my game. Making Leroy pee on the corner of Phoebe's desk is no longer sufficient. Those girls need to pay!

I search my bag for my keys as Grayson drags me by my belt up the sidewalk to my front door. "Aha!" I shout when I find them. I lift my hand in the air to celebrate and promptly hit Grayson in the chest. "Oops!"

I try to fit the key in the lock, but the lock keeps moving. I stab at it, but it darts left and right avoiding the key. Stupid floating lock.

Grayson holds out his hand. "Give me the key before you punch a hole in the glass."

"Whatever." I hand him the key. He lets go of my belt and I start sliding to the ground. This looks like a good place to sleep. It's not even cold out. "Why isn't it cold out?"

"Because your blood is currently ninety-nine percent alcohol," Grayson mumbles as he sticks the key in the lock and opens the door.

I ignore Mr. Grumpypants. "It's a beautiful night, isn't it?" I point to the stars.

"Those aren't stars. They're the streetlights."

I squint my eyes, but I distinctly see stars. "I don't care. It's beautiful."

"You're drunk," he claims as he lifts me up from where I'm sitting on the porch leaning against my house. Huh. How did I get down there?

"Nah. I'm a little tipsy is all."

He chuckles. "Sure, that's why you declared yourself the queen of darts and demanded I crown you."

I don't remember saying anything of the sort, but it sounds like something I would say. I pat my head but there's no crown up there. "Obviously, you failed."

"I did offer to hit up Burger King and get you a crown, but you wanted Taco Bell."

"Duh. Everyone knows you eat tacos after a night of drinking. I'm starting to think you've led a very sheltered life."

"Which room is your bedroom?"

I look around. We're in my upstairs hallway. "How did we get upstairs?"

"Never mind," he grumbles. "I'll find it."

I bounce as he carries me down the hall. When did he pick me up? "Why are you carrying me? Let me down."

He ignores me and opens the first door. He shakes his head at the empty room before moving on to the next door. It's another empty room.

"It's the last one on the right," I tell him before he has a chance to open the next door to yet another empty room. I haven't had the heart to decorate any of them. Not when they won't be used for what I originally intended them for.

"Why do you have this many bedrooms if you're planning to remain single for the rest of your long, long life?"

I sigh. "I wasn't always planning to die an old cat lady."

Grayson opens the door to the master bedroom and places me on the bed. I love this room. It's obnoxiously large because when I bought this place, I thought I'd have tons of children running around. I planned the bedroom as our escape from the world. In addition to an oversized sleigh bed, walk-in closet, and attached bathroom, there's a sitting area with two oversized armchairs in front of the bay window.

"It's a lot of room for cats," he says as he starts untying my boots. They fall to the ground and he stands. "Do you need any help going to the bathroom or changing?"

"I'm not a child." And there's no way I'm going to try to change my clothes when he's in the room. It won't be the first time I've slept in my clothes, and it definitely won't be the last.

He takes a seat on the armchair in the sitting area and starts taking off his boots. "What are you doing?"

"I'm not leaving until you're settled."

How much more settled does he want me to get? "Dude, I'm going to pass out any second now."

But he doesn't leave like I want him to. *Want?* Adult Suzie snorts. I tell her to mind her own damned business.

"Tell me about this house. Why did you buy such a big one?" Grayson asks.

I blame the liquor for me opening my mouth. I never talk about this stuff. "I planned to fill the rooms with children. Tons and tons of children. Not anymore."

"Why not? What's stopping you?"

I shake my head. Shit. Bad idea. The world starts to spin. I clutch the edge of the bed and wait for the spinning to stop. When it finally does, I answer. "You can hardly have children without a man. Duh."

"You don't need a man to have kids. Women have children by themselves every day."

I've thought about it – adopting or using a sperm donor. But I don't know. It seems cruel to bring a child into this world knowing she will never have a dad. Kids need both parents. Look at Hailey. She's still messed up about her mom leaving when she was twelve. I don't want to screw a kid up before I even start raising her. I'm sure I'll be doing enough screwing up as it is.

I'm not telling Grayson any of this, though. Nope. "Why? You offering to be my baby daddy?" I try to wink but the room starts to spin again.

"Munchkin, I'm not having sex with you when you're ready to pass out."

A vision of Grayson naked and above me thrusting into me pops into my head. My entire body heats as Little Susan cheers and starts blowing tooters in celebration. I'm surprised she doesn't fire off some fireworks. She needs to cool it. I hide my body's response to the sexy man sitting in my bedroom by resorting to sarcasm.

"I meant as a sperm donor. You can spank it and I'll take it."

He doesn't answer for a while. "I'll think about it."

His quiet words wake me from the doze I was failing into. "What? Seriously?"

I must be dreaming this entire conversation. There's no way I asked Grayson to be my sperm donor. Nope. This has to be a dream. A dream I'm going to forget all about when I wake tomorrow.

"You can go," I mumble. "I'm going to sleep now."

I don't know if Grayson leaves or not, because I pass out. When I wake in the morning, I'm alone. The ruffled blanket on the armchair and the glass of water and aspirin on my nightstand are proof I didn't dream he was in my bedroom.

Well, shit. I hope to hell I dreamed the entire conversation when I asked him to be my sperm donor. Knowing my luck, it wasn't a dream. I tug the covers over my head and go back to sleep. I'm not adulting today.

Chapter 16

In the pursuit of hoppiness

"This is going to be epic!" I throw my hands in the air and shout, "Yee-haw!"

"I knew I should have gone with a bridal shower instead of a bachelorette party," Hailey grouches.

Phoebe giggles. "Because Suzie wouldn't have planned anything crazy for a bridal shower?"

"You're right. What was I thinking?"

"I'm going to say you weren't thinking at all when you made Suzie your maid of honor and told her she could plan a bachelorette party."

I place my hands on my hips and glower at the two Debbie Downers. "You do know I can hear you, right?"

"Yes!" they shout in unison before collapsing on the sofa in giggles.

"What are you complaining about? I didn't make the condom crown."

Hailey caught me researching how to make a condom crown while at work and lost her ever-loving mind. She finally calmed down when I promised on my next batch of Session IPA to not make her wear one. I considered making another novelty crown – I found this hilarious penis crown – but I was a good girl and bought a simple bling crown with the word bride on it.

"And I didn't make you wear some stupid outfit." Trust me. I considered it. The matching Baywatch outfits were already in my shopping basket when I discovered the t-shirts we're currently wearing.

I gesture to Hailey's t-shirt with the inscription *Brews before I do's.* It's freaking adorable. I already ordered a second one for Phoebe's party.

Phoebe raises her hand. "I for one am very happy with the t-shirts." She's wearing one saying *Bride's Brew Crew* in pink. I have the same one on except mine's maroon.

"Okay," Hailey gives in. "You have restrained yourself thus far. What are we doing tonight?"

We're currently gathered at my house. Aiden and Ryker are in the kitchen eavesdropping on our conversation. I swivel around to glare at them. They don't bother pretending to not have been listening. I point at them.

"You guys are not coming."

Aiden puts his arms on his hips in an effort to look intimidating. Keep trying, dude. "Why? Are you doing something illegal?"

I snort. "Try your cop voice on someone else. I am not falling for it."

Ryker crosses his arms and tries his luck at intimidation tactics. Seriously? Does he not realize I know he's a great big teddy bear? "You guys will ruin all our fun."

Hailey nudges me with her foot. "Just tell them what we're doing. I'm sure they'll calm down when they realize we're going to the male stripper show."

"You told me you didn't want to go!" I cry. I've spent loads of time setting up tonight's entertainment because she flat out refused to watch male erotic dancers.

Aiden barrels into the room and picks her up from the sofa. "If you go to a stripper show, I'll spank your ass when you get home."

Hailey bats her eyelashes. "Then, as long as we do another activity, other than going to the stripper show, you'll be okay with it?"

The woman is a genius. A genius I tell you!

Aiden grunts. "Yes." She pushes for him to let her down.

Once he's back in the kitchen, I announce, "We're having a bachelorette scavenger hunt."

I hand them each a scorecard with a list of actions and the points each action is worth. It's all fun and somewhat embarrassing stuff like kissing a stranger, getting a guy to give you a condom, asking someone to marry you. Stuff like that.

"Hey big guy, can I touch your muscles?" Phoebe shouts her question in the direction of the kitchen.

"Oh, can we go to McGraw's? I'm going to kick ass at this."

"No! No! No!" I snag the cards out of their hands. "You can't use your boyfriends or fiancés or friends or family to help you win. It's called cheating."

Hailey ignores my order to ask, "What do I get when I win?"

I indicate the box on my side table. It's filled with sweet treats – artisan chocolate, fancy popcorn, peanut butter cookies, shortbread, caramel, etc.

"I'm going to gain ten pounds after I eat all this," Phoebe whines as she examines the items one by one.

"You aren't eating any of it because I'm going to win," Hailey declares and shoves her to the side to study the box for herself.

"You guys are cute. Like you have a chance," I tell them.

"She's right," Phoebe whispers out of the side of her mouth. "Suzie has no shame. She'll be getting a piggyback-ride from a guy and gathering condoms and phone numbers before we can blink."

"This is a hard no," Ryker says as he studies the card.

I snatch it out of his hand but before I get a chance to tell Ryker to mind his own dang business, Phoebe speaks, "You don't get to tell me what to do."

He smirks. "You like it when I tell you what to do."

I clap my hands over my ears. "No. TMI! Too much information!"

"Tell you what, we'll allow this little game," Aiden says as he walks over to Hailey. "But we are coming with to chaperone."

I growl. They are ruining all my fun!

"There are rules," Hailey says as she gives in. "You stay in the corner of whatever bar we are in and interfere if and only if we're in danger. And danger is not a man attempting to flirt with one of us. Actual danger. Like losing a limb danger."

I shake my head. This is not going to work. Ryker sees danger everywhere. I am not joking. I'm the one who ends up doing the background checks on the men who are supposedly stalking Phoebe. Spoiler alert – no one is stalking her. Not anymore at least.

"But who's going to keep Suzie under control? Without a chaperone, she'll have an advantage over us," Phoebe points out.

"I don't need a chaperone."

"Grayson's already on his way." The doorbell rings. "I bet that's him now."

The door opens and my body lights up. Not with excitement. No, I'm all about the embarrassment now. I haven't seen him since the 'be my sperm donor' talk.

"I told you I don't need a chaperone."

"What's the big deal?" Phoebe asks. "You got off easy. Grayson and you are only friends. He won't stop you from kissing the bartender."

"And he can be our designated driver," Hailey adds.

Grayson looks around confused. "Wait. What? I thought we were having drinks at McGraw's."

I snatch the cards off of the table. "Come on. I'll explain on the way."

Once we're in his truck, I direct him toward a row of bars nowhere near McGraw's. With her pops and uncles at McGraw's, Hailey would win before Phoebe and I had the chance to start. Not on my watch.

As soon as he parks, I open the door and rush out. "The scavenger hunt starts now. You've got three hours to get as many points as possible." I run into the bar like my ass is on fire.

By the time Hailey and Phoebe find me, I've got a condom, a guy's phone number, and I'm sipping on a drink the bartender gave me for free. Of course, it's a coke because I told him I'm the designated driver, but nowhere do the rules indicate the drink has to be an alcoholic beverage.

I fan my face with the condom and phone number. "What took you guys so long?"

I ignore their sputtering because I've spotted a guy with a tie. He's also pretty muscular. Score! "Hi, Stud," I greet as I walk up to him.

"Sorry, little lady. I play for the other team." In case I'm stupid, he winks at some hot guy walking past.

"Perfect!" I shout. He startles and takes a step back. "I'm doing this scavenger hunt. Can I have your tie and pet your muscles?"

His mouth drops open and he gapes at me. He didn't say no. I whip out my phone and stand close to him for a selfie while I touch his muscles.

He finds his voice. "I'm not giving you this tie. My boyfriend gave it to me." His boyfriend? Didn't he not two seconds ago wink at some guy? Men, I tell you.

"Is he wearing a tie?" I ask as I look around the room trying to spot his boyfriend. I squeal and clap. "Is he short? Under five-foot-two would be perfect."

He eyes my glass. "How much have you had to drink?"

"A glass of champagne." He tilts his head toward my glass. "This is coke." He looks like he doesn't believe me. I offer him a drink. "Here. Try it."

Grayson snatches my glass before grasping my bicep and dragging me away from my prey. "What? What's wrong?"

"What's wrong?" he seethes. "You offered your drink to a complete stranger."

I roll my eyes. "You're taking this chaperone business too seriously. I'm fine." I pet his chest to console him. Big mistake. I can feel his muscles straining at his t-shirt. I snatch my hand away and shove it in the front pocket of my jeans before I'm tempted to pet other parts of him.

"See?" I use my free hand to point at Hailey and Phoebe who appear to have teamed up. I narrow my eyes on them. This is an individual sport. Not a team sport. "Their men are letting them be."

My eyes widen when I realize what I said. "Not that you're my man." I take a step back and he drops his hand.

As soon as I'm free I take off. "There's a karaoke machine!"

Those twenty points for singing a song in the middle of the dance floor are mine. Mine, I tell you! Nowhere in the rules does it say I can't use a microphone for my song. I push my way through the crowd until I'm at the karaoke machine.

"Why is no one doing karaoke?" I ask the DJ who's setting up the equipment.

"We don't start until ten."

Darn. By then the scavenger hunt will be over and I refuse to lose. "Can I use the microphone? And maybe ask you to play a certain song."

He looks at my t-shirt and sighs. "Bachelorette party?" I give him my best sugar won't melt in my mouth smile. "What song?"

"*We Are the Champions* from Queen." Perfect for rubbing my win into Hailey and Phoebe's faces. I squeal as he hands me the mic and the piano introduction starts.

I push my way into the middle of the dancing crowd and start singing. Unfortunately, I don't know the lyrics, although I know the refrain because a toddler could remember the words.

"I am the champion," I shout-sing at the top of my lungs into the mic.

The dancers start singing with me. Before I know it, everyone is shoving and pushing toward me trying to nab my microphone. I scream and start slapping at the hands. Where is my chaperone when I need him?

The DJ comes to my rescue by stealing the microphone, although I guess it isn't technically stealing. "Enough," he growls and marches off.

Once my microphone is gone the crowd melts away. Oh well, it was fun while it lasted. At least, I got my twenty points.

Hailey accosts me the second my foot steps off the dance floor. "Don't think you're getting points for such a weak performance."

"Yeah, you didn't even finish the song," Phoebe adds.

"It doesn't say you have to sing the entire song."

"Of course, it's the entire song. Otherwise, it would say sing on the dance floor and not sing a song on the dance floor," Hailey argues.

"Fine," I give in. I ignore her and Phoebe as they clap in excitement. I need to get me some more points.

I scan the card. Use the men's restroom. Piece of cake. I make my way through the crowd to the restrooms. As usual, there's a huge line for the ladies and no one is waiting for the men's. Thanks for making this easy stupid sexist architects.

I make my way into the men's room and find an empty stall. I hold my nose as I drop my jeans and squat to relieve myself. At least there's toilet paper in this place.

As I walk to the sink to wash my hands, a guy walks in. He raises an eyebrow at me. "Line at the ladies."

He grunts and lowers his zipper as he walks to the urinal. "Can't you wait until I leave to pee?"

"You're the one who went in the men's room, lady."

My eyes widen when he whips his dick out. "Holy macaroni, you're huge! Are you on steroids?" I clap when I get the best idea ever. "Will you give my girlfriend a lap dance? We're having her bachelorette party tonight and there's this scavenger hunt."

"You're done."

I twirl around to see Grayson standing at the entrance to the restroom.

"I'm winning is what's happening," I tell him.

"You're done," he repeats. I ignore him to continue my conversation with the stranger with the massive schlong. Suddenly, I'm flying. I grunt as the air is knocked out of me when my stomach lands on Grayson's shoulder.

"What the hell? What are you doing?"

"We're leaving." He pushes his way through the crowd of women waiting to use the restroom. Several of them snicker. Whatever. At least I didn't wear a skirt tonight, otherwise, I'd be mooning half of the bar by now. Hold on. Is mooning the bar worth points in the scavenger hunt?

"But we can't leave before someone has been declared a winner." I pound my fists on Grayson's back.

"Like we don't know you made three of those baskets," Hailey says, and I look over. She's also being carried out of the bar.

"What did you do?"

"I asked the bartender if I could kiss him."

I swing my torso in her direction to whisper. "And? Was he a good kisser?"

Aiden growls. "She did not kiss the bartender."

"No frogs for you, young lady," Phoebe giggles. Ryker has her slung over his shoulder like she's a sack of potatoes.

"What? You make no sense."

Ryker scowls. "Because someone couldn't stop at one free shot from the bartender."

"What? It would have been rude not to accept the second shot."

Ryker slaps her ass. "And what's your excuse for taking the third shot then?"

"It was yummy."

Grayson dumps me on the front seat of his truck while Aiden and Ryker get their women settled in the back.

"I declare myself the winner!"

"You're a cheater is what you are," Hailey grumps from the back seat.

"Oh please, like I don't know you two ganged up together to beat me."

"The night is young. Let's hit up McGraw's," is Hailey's response.

Grayson switches on his truck. "McGraw's it is."

It's not the bachelorette party I planned, but the night still rocks since I spend it with my favorite people in the world. Now if only Grayson was mine instead of merely my chaperone, my night would be perfect. Whoa! Where did such a crazy thought come from?

Little Susan raises her hand. *It was me!* We don't need a man, I remind her. *Do too!* She shouts and then does an exaggerated full body shiver in anticipation of Grayson being ours. Behave or I'll put a chastity belt on you, I threaten. *You can try,* she sings.

I hate to admit it, but she's right. No one can control Little Susan. Least of all me.

Chapter 17

Save water, drink beer

"Hey, I wasn't expecting you," I say to Grayson as I open the door.

Don't get me wrong. I'm happy to see him. Little Susan is more than happy to see him. She starts singing *When a Man Loves a Woman* at the top of her voice. I shut that shit down real fast. No one is loving anyone here.

Grayson coughs. "I have some stuff I want to show you."

I motion him inside. "Come in. You want a beer? My first batch of Session IPA is finished. I was getting ready to try the first one."

I may have taste tested while in my brew shack, but the taste can always vary when the beer is bottled and chilled. Yep, I went there. If you didn't think I was a beer geek before, I've confirmed it now.

I grab two bottles from the refrigerator and motion to my dining room table. I'm not stupid. Sitting in my living room together on my sofa is a recipe for disaster. Little Susan mewls in protest. *Yeah, well, learn to live with it*, I tell her.

We clink bottles, but I don't take a sip. I want to watch his reaction to the taste. Bad idea. His throat moves as he swallows and suddenly it's the sexiest thing I've ever seen. My dry spell has obviously been going on too long if I'm finding a man's throat sexy. I need to make some time to hit the club this weekend and find a man to scratch my itch.

Little Susan harrumphs and declares she will not be participating in any cheating on Grayson. I seriously don't have time for her craziness now.

"It's good," Grayson says as he places his bottle on the table. "It's crisp and almost fruity."

I smile. "It should have a fruity hop flavor. I went with grapefruit."

I take a sip of my own, barely enough to coat my mouth. I let it hit my lips, gums, teeth, and all around my tongue. As I swallow, I keep my mouth closed and exhale through my nose. Hmm…not bad.

Grayson clears his throat, and my eyes fly open. His cheeks are flushed. Is he sick? Before I have a chance to ask, he asks a question of his own.

"What makes it a Session IPA anyway?"

"Session IPA is a flavorful beer with a lower alcohol percentage that won't weigh you down."

He takes another sip. "I can taste it's less heavy. Where does the name session come from?"

I raise an eyebrow. "You're awful curious. You sure you want to hear me geek out over beer?"

"It's interesting. Besides, if I'm going to help with your marketing, I need to know more." Help with my marketing? Was he serious about helping out? I thought he was being nice is all. "Now, tell me why it's called a session IPA."

If he wants me to bore him with my beer nerdiness, who am I to deny him? "The name comes from WWI-era England when workers were allowed to drink on the job. Workers were allocated two 'sessions' of drinking. But the beer had to be lighter than usual, thus the lower alcohol percentage."

"Cool. I think it will be a big hit in the springtime."

I beam. "I hope so."

He sets his bottle down on the table and starts to play with the label. "We need to talk."

Those words cause ice to fill my veins. What does he want to talk about? Did he find a girlfriend? Is he getting married? Is he moving away? Leaving Milwaukee? I can think of at least a dozen more disaster scenarios, but I curl my hands into fists and dig my fingernails my palms to stop my mind from whirling out of control.

"About what?" I manage to squeeze out.

"Me being your sperm donor."

"Oh god," I bury my face in my hands as my cheeks heat up. "Can we not talk about it? I can't believe I asked you to be my baby daddy."

He chuckles. "Well, you did ask me, and I've been thinking about it."

My head rears up. "You've been thinking about it? You would seriously donate your sperm to me?" I'm not sure if I'm excited or scared or what.

He clears his throat. "No, I won't be your sperm donor."

"Oh." I deflate. Wait. I'm not disappointed, am I? I shake my head. I'll have to obsess over this some other time. A time when Grayson is not sitting across from me studying my every reaction to his words.

"I want you to have whatever you desire in this world, but I can't give you babies."

My heart squeezes at his words. There's nothing I want more in the world than for him to give me babies, but it's not in the cards for us.

"I understand."

He reaches across the table and grasps my hand. Electricity sparks and runs up my arm. I snatch my hand away. I can't allow my body to get any ideas of where this is going. My head knows better.

"I don't think you do. I'm saying no to donating my sperm, not no to other things. Just no for now."

I squint my eyes and study him. What the hell is he talking about?

"Could you explain for the dummies in the back of the class?"

"You're no dummy," he growls. "But I will explain because I realize it's confusing."

He falls silent. I watch as he peels the label off of his beer. The longer the silence lasts the more I'm convinced I am not going to like what he has to say.

"And? Are you going to explain sometime this year? Or do I need to pencil in an appointment with you for next year?"

"Smartass." He grins. "I can't donate sperm because I don't want my child to grow up without a father."

I'm confused. "I thought you had no problem with single moms?"

Of course, I was drunk the one and only time we discussed this topic, but I'm pretty sure he was the one pushing me to have children without a man.

"I'm not explaining this very well." He isn't, but I don't call him on it. This conversation is awkward enough as it is.

He runs a hand through his hair. "I don't want you, my friend, having children using my sperm without me being involved in the raising of the children."

Ah, I see. "I get it. They would be a part of you."

"Exactly. And I'm around. You're one of my closest friends. I'd see your kids all the time. Be a part of their lives, but not as their father. It would be too weird for me."

I pat his hand but pull away when the temptation to squeeze it becomes too much. "I understand. I wasn't completely serious about you being my baby daddy. I haven't given much thought to having children on my own, to be honest."

"Why not?" He gestures to the house. "You obviously want children."

"But children should have two parents."

"Are we back to you being a man-hater?"

"I'm not a man-hater," I huff.

"The first time I met you, you said, and I quote here, 'Hi, I'm Suzie. I'm a man-hater, but I'll be your friend'."

I drop my head to the table and cover it with my arms. I probably should have a muzzle on me when I drink.

Grayson kicks my foot under the table. "Come on. Men aren't all bad. You have tons of male friends. And your girlfriends have men who you like and trust."

I lift my head and narrow my eyes on him. "Are we back to you being curious about my past? Because it's a waste of your breath. I'm not revealing my deep, dark secrets to you."

"You will eventually. Why not get it over with?"

I am done with this conversation. "You said something about helping me with marketing?"

He stares at me for a long moment before speaking. "I'll let you get away with changing the conversation today."

I roll my eyes. He'll let me? As if I need his permission to change the conversation. "Come on. Tell me what you got."

He removes a folder from his backpack. "Now, these are merely ideas. They need to be worked on further." He opens the folder and pulls out a few sheets of paper, which he slides across the table to me.

My mouth drops open as I look at the different logo designs for Shorty's Brewing Sensation. They are awesome. "Wow. Did you draw these?"

I shift through the different designs. There's one for each type of beer I brew – Shout but Stout, Shorty's Holiday Brew, and Shorty's Session IPA.

We spend the next hour discussing my brewing brand and some marketing techniques. Grayson is really into this marketing stuff. His hands are moving all over the place as he explains his different ideas for each social media platform.

I'm not sure I'm ready for the next step. This marketing stuff is pretty professional. Nothing about it spells hobby. No, if I'm going to take this step then I need to be sure I'm serious about the brewing business.

And then there's *You Cheat, We Eat.* Can I combine working there with running a brewery? And what if the joy of brewing is lost to me when I make it a business?

As I shut the door behind Grayson as he leaves, I realize there's one thing I didn't think about with regard to the business – my shithead ex. Not one thought of my jerk of an ex entered my mind. Huh. Maybe I don't need to worry about how running this business will bring up thoughts of the asshole. Maybe I am ready to move forward with this brewing thing without him.

Chapter 18

Beer never broke my heart

"Are you sure you can handle little 'ole me kicking your ass in pool?" I tease Grayson as we walk to the pool tables at McGraw's.

Since our 'baby daddy' talk, things have gone back to normal between us. Oh sure, I still feel like a live wire smacks into me every time we touch, but I got this. I know how to hide my feelings better than the rest.

Grayson grins. "I think I can handle it."

I do an exaggerated sigh. "That's what they all say until it's ass-kicking time."

"I'll rack."

"Come on, Phoebe." I hear Hailey shout behind me. "Suzie is about to cause chaos."

I narrow my eyes on her. "I don't cause chaos all the time."

She opens her mouth, probably to disagree with me, but I give her my back. I don't want to hear it.

Instead, I find a pool cue, chalk up the tip, and lean over the table to break. I need a good break if I want a chance to win against Grayson, because – despite the fighting words coming out of my big mouth – the guy is an awesome pool player. I use as much force as possible to hit the cue ball. Instead of the cue ball rolling down the table to hit the nine-ball, it goes flying through the air and hits Grayson smackdab in the stomach.

"Oomph," he grunts as he bends over.

"Shit. Shit. Shit." I throw my pool cue down and rush to him. "I'm sorry. Are you okay? Do we need to go to the hospital?"

"I'm fine," he grunts out.

"Suzie strikes again," Hailey announces to the entire freaking world. I glare at her. "What?" She shrugs. "It's true."

She's not wrong. I may exaggerate how much of a klutz I am, but I am still a klutz with a capital K. But usually I reserve klutzy injuries to myself. Other people are normally safe from my klutzy ways.

I rub Grayson's back as he bends over taking deep breaths. "I'm fine," he repeats.

He sure doesn't look fine. At least no one is here to witness this mess as the bar is mostly empty since it's a Monday night. The uncles are playing poker in their corner booth and a couple of barflies are drinking beer at the bar, but otherwise, we have the place to ourselves.

The door opens and the cold wind from outside whips through the bar. I look up and my eyes widen when I see who's standing in the doorway looking unsure of herself. Liz Morris. I didn't think she'd show. In fact, I kind of forgot about inviting her here to talk to Grayson.

I drop my hand and walk toward her with a welcoming smile on my face. "Thanks for coming," I tell her as I pull her into a hug.

"Liz?" Grayson calls. He's looking between the two of us with a frown on his face. "What are you doing here? Is Grayson all right?" He narrows his eyes on me. "And how do you know Suzie?"

"Um." I bite my lip. "I asked her to come."

A vein in Grayson's forehead starts throbbing, but Wally steps in before he has a chance to say a word.

Wally offers Liz his hand. "I'm Wally. And you are?" I have to hold in a snort. He knows exactly who she is.

"Liz," she whispers. Wally uses her hand to guide her toward the corner table where the cards and poker chips have magically disappeared. "Please, have a seat."

When I go to sit next to her, he stops me. "Why don't we let Grayson and Liz chat alone?"

We might as well sit with them. I'm going to eavesdrop no matter what. As if he knows what I'm thinking, he tilts his head toward a table on the other side of the room. Seriously? No way am I sitting on the other side of the room. I take a seat at a booth a table away from where Liz and Grayson are now sitting.

Hailey and Phoebe join me while the uncles move to the bar.

"What's going on?" Phoebe whispers.

I shush her with a slash of my hand. No talking when it's eavesdropping time!

"What are you doing here?" Grayson asks, and I lean back as far as possible without actually lying down to make sure I don't miss a thing.

"I wanted to tell you," Liz pauses, "I don't blame you for Bill's death."

Grayson grunts. "But it is my fault he died."

"No, it isn't," she insists. "It's those rebel forces or whatever they're called who put the IED in the road."

"It should have been me."

"And then you would be dead."

"As I should be." I can't help it. I gasp at his words. I can't imagine a world without Grayson in it.

"No, you shouldn't be." Liz's voice wavers.

"But surely you wish I were dead. Then, you would have Bill back."

"What's to say Bill wouldn't have died in some other way? You don't decide who lives and dies."

Someone seizes my upper arm and yanks me out of the booth before dragging me across the room. I slap at Wally's arm. "Stop it. I was listening."

"You were being nosy is what you were doing. Haven't you been nosy enough?"

I glare at him. "You're the one who gave me the information."

He cringes. "My mistake."

Pops pushes Wally out of the way. He grasps my hands and grins down at me. "Look, darling, I know what you're trying to do, but it won't work."

Phoebe raises her hand. "What is she trying to do?"

"Yeah," Hailey adds. "What the hell is going on here?"

"If I had to guess, I'd say Suzie asked Wally to dig up Grayson's past, and then she went nosing around in it."

I nod at Pops' explanation. He hit it right on the head. Except for the nosing around part. I didn't nose around. I conducted an investigation. Totally different.

"Why?" Phoebe asks. "You know better than to go digging up people's pasts. It leads to trouble."

I raise an eyebrow at her. "Because ignoring your past worked out super awesome for you."

She purses her lips but doesn't say a word, because she knows I'm right.

Pops squeezes my hands to gain my attention. "Darling, I know you care for Grayson, but you can't fix him."

I disagree. "I can too." I tilt my head toward the booth where they're talking. "It's working already."

"Darling, look closer. It's not." He releases my hands and turns me around by the shoulders. "Look at his face."

I study Grayson's face. Shit. He's right. Grayson's jaw is clenched. I look closer. His hands are balled on his lap. Damn. He looks ready to explode. I take a step in his direction, but Pops' hand on my shoulder stops me.

"No. Leave it be."

"But—"

"You can't fix him," he repeats.

I disagree. This has to work. Once Grayson realizes Liz doesn't blame him, he'll lose the guilt he's carrying around. He has to.

Barney takes hold of my chin and forces me to look in his direction. "You can't fix what's ailing him."

Jokester Barney is being serious. Shit. This situation is worse than I thought.

"He needs to find his own way."

"But he wasn't finding his own way," I insist.

"Not your problem to solve."

I disagree. Grayson is my friend. Friends don't let friends drown in their problems alone.

I return my attention to Grayson and Liz sitting at the table. I watch as they stand together. Grayson helps Liz into her coat and then escorts her to the door. As soon as the door closes behind her, he marches in my direction.

He points at me. "You had no right to stick your nose into my past!"

I raise my hands in a gesture of surrender. "I was trying to help."

"By bringing up the past with Liz? Reminding her of the husband she lost?"

I keep my lips closed. He's crazy if he thinks my visit brought up any memories for Liz. That woman thinks about her dead husband every single dang day.

"Who do you think you are? Digging around in my past?"

"I'm your friend." I try to grab his hand, but he steps out of my reach. "I wanted to help. I can tell you're hurting."

"Did I ask for your help?" He doesn't wait for my answer. "No. I did not."

"But you ask about my past all the time."

"Ask. I ask you about your past. I haven't gone digging around. Hell, I can ask Hailey right now and you know she'd tell me everything I want to know. I won't ask her though because I respect your privacy. Like you should have respected mine."

"But—"

He raises his hand to cut me off. "I don't want to hear it. We are done. This friendship is over." And with those damning words, he spins on his heel and marches away. He exits the bar without a glance backward.

A blade pierces my heart and slashes it in two. I look down but there's no blood. There's no blade. No, this is my heart breaking apart. The feeling is achingly familiar. It's also a feeling I promised myself I would never feel again. But I couldn't keep the promise to myself. Not when my heart was confronted with all that is Grayson. Shit. I messed up big time. And I don't think I can fix this.

Chapter 19

I give into beer pressure

"Ta-da!"

At the sound, I shriek and drop the bottle I'm labeling. It crashes to the floor and breaks, spilling beer every-freak-ing-where. But there's no need to use a shard of glass to attack the intruder because I recognize her annoying voice. How dare she break into my brew shack!

My teeth clench as I ask Hailey, "How the hell did you get in here?"

She frowns. "Don't insult me."

"It's harder than it looks," Phoebe comments from behind Hailey. "Hailey tried to show me how to pick the lock, but I couldn't figure it out."

Hailey pats her arm. "Don't worry. You'll get the hang of it with some practice."

"I should have used the deadbolt."

Hailey raises her fist. "A challenge! I like it."

Of course, she thinks circumventing a deadbolt lock is a challenge. And everyone is convinced I'm the crazy one. "What are you two doing here anyway?"

Hailey rolls her eyes. "Duh. We're here to cheer you up."

Phoebe removes a bottle from her bag and lifts it up over her head. "I brought vodka!"

I indicate the bottles and bottles of beer on the wall.

"Those are for you to sell and become a famous female brewer. This," she taps the bottle, "is for drinking." She sets her bag on my labeling station. "I also brought shot glasses and snacks."

"You brought snacks?"

"Of course. This is how you cheer your best girlfriend up, remember? If I recall correctly, we start by plying you with questions about your past until you cry. Then, we sit around and watch movies while drinking and eating too much."

Hailey rubs her hands together in glee. "But instead of asking a ton of questions about your past, we get to pry into your relationship with Grayson."

Oh no, they don't. I snarl, but before I can tell them where they can shove it, Hailey raises her palm and practically shoves it in my face. "Stop. You are not keeping this to yourself. I'd say you've kept enough to yourself as it is."

Phoebe pauses with unloading her bag of snacks on the table. "And the uncles and Pops wouldn't tell us a thing. Who was the woman and why did her arrival make Grayson throw your friendship in your face?"

Ugh. I should have known I wouldn't get away with hiding in my brew shack from the two nosy women. "Pick up your stuff. If we're doing this shit, we're not doing it in my brew shack."

"But I've never been in here before," Hailey pouts. "I want a tour."

I sweep my arm in a circle around the garage. "This is my brew shack. I brew beer here. End of tour."

"I'm not tipping for your tour. It sucked," Hailey whines.

"Shush. Don't be rude." Phoebe is seriously worried about being rude? Did she forget she literally broke into my brew shake five minutes ago?

They follow me into my house where we settle in the living room. Phoebe unloads her bag on the coffee table. Don't tell her I said so, but she did good. Cool Ranch Doritos, Pringles, Cookie Dough Ice Cream. Mmm…

"Vodka?" Hailey wrinkles her nose in disgust. "Where's the tequila?"

"Tequila is for the lower class," Phoebe says, and then her eyes widen, and she slaps her hand over her mouth. "I'm sorry. I don't know where those words came from."

I raise my hand. "I do. Your mother."

Phoebe's mom put the B in bitch. She hasn't bothered to attempt contact with Phoebe once since all the scary shit with Phoebe got started. I think Phoebe's better off without the woman, to be honest.

While Phoebe sputters around blushing and being embarrassed about her faux pas, I walk to my kitchen and find a bottle of tequila and some bowls. I scoop half the ice cream into my bowl and sit back to enjoy it. I know the quiet won't last long. I can see out of the corner of my eye Hailey is bursting to start throwing questions at me.

Best to get this shit over with. I wave my spoon at her. "You may begin."

"Who was the woman at the bar? How is she connected to Grayson? What did he mean when he accused you of digging into his past?"

My stomach sours at her questions. I place my bowl on the coffee table no longer in the mood to eat my way through my depression. What I need to do is ask the uncles to put a security system in at my brew shack to stop Hailey from breaking in and asking her nosy questions again. Oh, who am I kidding? Those same uncles are the ones who taught her how to burglarize.

"It's okay." Phoebe pats my shoulder. "You don't have to tell us if you don't want to."

Hailey gasps. "Are you kidding? Of course, she has to tell us. We're her friends. She has to spill her guts to us. It's in the girlfriend handbook!"

I pat Phoebe's thigh. "Thanks, but you and I both know I'm going to have to reveal my secrets or someone is going to lose her mind."

"The woman in the bar was Liz Morris. Her husband was Grayson's best friend. He was killed in action and Grayson blames himself," I start and then tell them all about Grayson's past. He won't thank me for revealing his secrets, but there's no way I'm going to get out of here alive if I don't tattle.

"Wow." Hailey shakes her head. "Heavy. Poor guy."

"It explains why he's been off lately, though," Phoebe comments.

"Exactly!" I shout. "He's been depressed. I needed to take matters into my own hands."

Phoebe raises a hand for me to stop. "Hold up. Grayson didn't tell you any of this himself?"

"No wonder he made the 'You had no right to dig your nose into my past!' comment," Hailey says in a deep voice in the worst impression of Grayson ever. "What did you do?"

I drop my head to study my jeans. "I had Wally dig into Grayson's background, and then I went and saw Liz."

"Is this the part where I get to say I told you so?" I raise my eyebrow at Phoebe's comment. "I did tell you your nosiness would get you into trouble someday."

"Gee, thanks for the reminder." I pick up one of the shots of vodka and guzzle it. The alcohol burns as it makes its way down to my stomach. I cough and slap my chest.

"What are you going to do? You can't let the man you love slip through your fingers."

Hailey's remark causes my nose to wrinkle in confusion. "I don't love him. The whole baby daddy thing wasn't serious."

"What?" she squeals. "Baby daddy? You've been holding out on us."

Phoebe fills my shot glass. "Some more liquid courage because you know you are spilling your guts to us tonight."

Ugh. She's right. I take the second shot. This one goes down much smoother. My head spins a bit, but I manage to set the shot glass down on the coffee table without dropping it.

"Shit. I dropped a bottle in the brew shack. I need to clean it up." I stand, but Hailey puts a hand on my lower arm and pushes me back into my seat.

"I'll do it. But first I want to hear all about how Grayson is going to be your baby daddy."

"Not. He is not going to be my baby daddy. He said no. He doesn't want to donate his sperm. He wants to be involved with the children."

Phoebe squeals and claps her hands. "I knew it! He wants you." She snaps her fingers at Hailey. "You owe me fifty bucks."

"I do not owe you fifty bucks. I didn't bet with you on whether Grayson wants Suzie. I'm not stupid. Everyone who has eyes knows he wants her."

I groan. "What is it with everyone thinking Grayson and I have chemistry?"

"Because you do!" Hailey and Phoebe shout in chorus and then dissolve into giggles.

"I hope neither one of you is driving tonight."

"We're staying over." Hailey points to their bags by the front door. How did they get there?

"Did you break into my house before coming to the brew shack?"

"I'm not dignifying your question with a response."

"Which means yes, you did." Unlike my brew shack, my house does have a security system. "How did you bypass the security system?" Hailey merely raises her eyebrow in response. "Never mind."

"Her uncles are awesome. They've taught me how to shoot, but I didn't get any lessons on breaking into places. Do you think they'd take me under their wings?"

"We're getting off topic here. We're supposed to fire questions at Suzie until she admits she's in love with Grayson."

My heart speeds up at Hailey's words. They're not true. They can't be true. I can't possibly love Grayson. Adult Suzie, the little voice in my head I love to hate, berates me, *Stop lying to yourself.* I shut her up fast and move on.

"It doesn't matter whether I love Grayson, which FYI I don't, I am done with men, remember?"

"Why?" Phoebe asks. "Is this about the mysterious ex you never name?"

"I'm not talking about it." Time for another shot. Once I've downed it, I continue, "I'll get drunk and listen to you two berate me about my nosiness, but I'm not revealing all my deep, dark secrets."

"But I revealed all my deep, dark secrets," Phoebe pouts.

"It's all about the timing," Hailey responds. "When you need to know, you'll know."

I hope to hell not, but I keep my mouth shut. I'm going to have enough trouble convincing them I'm not in love with Grayson as it is. I don't need to add to my problems, especially since Hailey is letting it go for now.

I pick up the remote and switch on the television. "Since revelation time has ended, I think the schedule calls for us watching movies and stuffing our faces. Let's find a movie and pig out on these lovely snacks Phoebe brought."

Hailey sighs. "When she starts using words like lovely, you know her stonewall is back up."

Phoebe shrugs. "I'm up for watching a movie and eating snacks."

Which is exactly what we end up doing. Every time one of them brings up Grayson, I take another shot to stop myself from answering. They end up having to drag my drunk ass to bed. Serves them right!

Chapter 20

No matter what life throws at you, a cold beer will help.

GRAYSON

I'm half-way to Merrill before my anger starts to abate. I can't believe Suzie betrayed me this way. I thought we were friends. If I'm honest, I'd like to be more than friends, but Suzie has a nine-foot electric fence around her heart. And I'm not in the right frame of mind to start scaling it.

But now? Now I have no interest in seeing her betraying little face again. Especially since she's forced me to drive home – a place I am not ready to visit. I don't care if I've only been back once in nearly four years. I'm not ready. But I can't not visit. Not after the way I treated Liz when she came to see me at McGraw's. I hope she'll forgive me for being a total jackass.

I stop at a gas station when I'm half an hour out from Merrill. I can't show up empty-handed to meet my namesake for the first time. I have no idea what to buy a four-year-old boy, but I settle on a Lincoln Logs building set. I remember I had one as a kid and liked it.

Once I arrive on Liz's street, I park my truck but don't get out. Like the coward I am, I sit there staring at Liz's house until the front window curtains flutter. Shit. If I sit here any longer, the police will come in with lights blazing and sirens blaring to arrest me for being a stalker.

I gather the present and make my way to the front door.

"Grayson!" Liz shouts and envelopes me in a hug when she opens the door.

I feel like a fraud. How can she possibly be happy to see me when I caused the death of her husband?

I awkwardly pat her back and retreat from the hug as soon as possible.

"What are you doing here?"

"I wanted to apologize for how I behaved on Monday." I lift the gift. "I also wanted to meet Grayson."

"I'm Grayson." A boy peeks out from his mother's legs.

I kneel down. "Then this must be for you." I hold out the present. He doesn't take it. He looks to his mother for guidance. At her nod, he snatches the package from my hands and rushes off.

"Grayson Bill Morris," Liz shouts. "You will open the present in front of the person who gave it to you." She nudges me forward. "We better hurry up."

The look of happiness on her face almost has me freezing in her hallway. She can't possibly be happy, can she?

When we enter the living room, Grayson is sitting on the floor holding his present. "Can I open it? Can I?"

Liz shakes her head. "I'd like to introduce you to someone first."

Grayson pouts but he stands and walks to me. "I'm Grayson," he says as he holds out his hand.

I get down on a knee and shake his hand. "I'm Grayson, too."

He pumps my hand up and down. "You must be Uncle Grayson. Look, Mom, it's Uncle Grayson."

Liz ruffles his hair. "I know."

"Is he a hero like my dad?"

My heart squeezes at his words and I lower my gaze to the carpet to buy myself some time to get it together. Once I think I can talk without making a fool of myself, I lift my head and say, "Your dad was a great man."

His back straightens. "I know." He looks up at his mom. "Can I open my present now?" At his mom's nod, he rushes back to the gift and tears into the wrapping.

Liz sits with him on the floor. "It's Lincoln Logs. You can build houses with them. Now, what do you say?"

"Thanks, Uncle Grayson! Can I go play?"

Before his mom can answer, he picks up the box and rushes off. Liz smiles as she watches him leave. "Thank you, Grayson. But you didn't need to buy him a gift."

I shrug. "Actually, I came here to apologize."

She motions to the sofa. "Oh? What for?" she asks once we're seated.

I rub my neck. "I wasn't exactly welcoming on Monday."

She giggles. "I'm the one who showed up unannounced. I have to say I never thought I'd see the day the great Grayson Neill got caught unawares."

"You surprised me all right. I didn't realize Suzie knew my background, let alone that she had visited you. I'm sorry about her by the way."

"No need to say you're sorry. Your girlfriend is sweet. She cares about you and doesn't want you suffering. I can appreciate the sentiment."

"She's not my girlfriend."

Liz smirks. "Okay. Whatever you say."

I open my mouth to correct her assumption, but she speaks before I get the chance. "Did you think about what I said on Monday?"

My hands fist where I've placed them on my jeans. "It is my fault Bill's gone."

She shakes her head. "You're as stubborn as Bill was."

"I miss him." I don't know where the admission comes from. I never talk about Bill.

"I know. I miss him, too. But life goes on. You can't get stuck in the past forever or you'll miss out. And you don't want to miss out on that cute little firecracker of a woman, do you?"

I run a hand over my hair. "I'm too messed up for a relationship."

"I bet Suzie can help you get over your issues."

"You make it sound easy."

"It's not. I know it's not. After I went out on my first date, I came home and cried myself to sleep I was missing Bill so bad."

I whip my head up at her words. "You're dating already?"

"Already? It's been almost four years. It's what Bill would want. We talked a lot about what would happen if he didn't come back before you guys shipped out that last time."

"You did? He never told me."

She winks. "I guess there are some things he didn't tell you after all."

We talk for another half hour before she announces she needs to get ready for work. After I leave, I sit in my truck thinking over everything she said. I'm shocked she's dating again. And she looks happy. I rub a hand over my jaw. Maybe it's time for me to move on too.

I switch on my truck and drive to my parent's house. I visited once when I got my discharge from the Army, but I haven't been back since – not even for Christmas. Mom didn't say a word about it to me, but I'm sure she's disappointed I didn't come home for the holidays.

I don't bother knocking when I arrive at my childhood home. I walk right in and shout, "Is anyone home?"

I hear a squeal before my mother rushes out of the kitchen and tackles me in the hallway. "Grayson! What a lovely surprise?"

"Let the boy go before you squeeze him to death," my father says as he comes up behind her.

Mom releases me and my father gives me a one-armed hug. My dad is my height – five-foot-ten – but my mother is shorter than Suzie. Dad looks like a giant when he gathers Mom, who is now sobbing, into his arms.

"Stop crying, woman. You'll ruin our visit with your tears."

She smacks him in the stomach. "I'll cry if I want to Norman Benedict Neill." She beams a smile my way. "Come in, come in. I've got a pot roast in the crockpot."

Mom walks off but I stand frozen in the hallway. Dad slaps me on the back. "Come on. You better move it to the kitchen before your mother gets in a tizzy."

"Isn't she mad at me for not visiting more often?" I look at him. "Aren't you?"

He shakes his head. "Of course not. We know you had shit in your head to work out. Glad it's finally worked out. Four years is a long time to let your guilt fester."

I spent the majority of those four years deployed without any time to let my 'guilt fester'. But I'm not about to start making excuses with him.

"How do you—"

His chuckle cuts me off. "You think we don't know how you feel about Bill's death?" He frowns. "We may be small town, but we're not stupid."

I help Mom set the table and then we settle down to eat pot roast and mashed potatoes.

"Tell us about the girl." I nearly choke at Mom's words.

"What girl?"

"You think we can't tell you have a woman?" Dad asks. "We know you, son."

"Also, I ran into Liz's mother at the grocery store, and she told me all about this mysterious woman who dropped by Liz's house all riled up to fix you."

"She's not my girl. And I'm mad at her," I growl, although my initial anger has faded. Suzie may have overstepped, but she did it with the best of intentions. I'm half-way to forgiving her already.

"Sounds like she's a firecracker," Dad says. The approval is clear to see in his face.

"You haven't even met her."

"Anyone who would drive all the way up here to talk to a woman she doesn't know to help you gets a gold star from me." Mom was a first-grade teacher. To her, getting a gold star is the highest praise possible.

"You don't know the whole story."

Mom waves a hand to dismiss my complaints. "I know enough."

"I saw Liz," I say to end this conversation about me and Suzie.

"Oh, how's Liz?" Mom goes for nonchalant but she's sending Dad furtive glances.

Shit. I stepped through the flames into the fire with my remark. The last thing I want to talk about is Liz.

When I don't answer, Mom prattles on. "She's dating a lovely man. He recently moved here to coach the football team. Grayson adores him."

I nearly choke. "He's met Grayson?"

"Of course."

The conversation falls away and we finish dinner in silence. My mind is whirling as I eat. I can't believe Liz is moving on from Bill. He's the love of her life. Or, I guess, he *was* the love of her life.

After dinner, Mom hustles us out of the kitchen so she can do the dishes in peace, and Dad asks if I want to go for a walk. It's ten below out, but we always do our best talking while we're moving.

"You going to let your guilt continue to ruin your life or are you going to move on now you see Liz is happy and has moved on herself?"

"Wow. You dove right in."

"No sense beating around the bush."

I shrug. "I don't know."

I'm not avoiding his question. I don't know the answer. Can I get over my guilt? No matter what Liz says, I am the reason her husband – my best friend – is dead.

Dad doesn't respond. He knows he's got me thinking, which was his intention. We walk until the sun sets and it's too cold to continue. I haven't come to a conclusion by the time we return home, although I do think it may be time for me to start living in the present and stop wallowing in the past. Maybe it's time I talk to someone.

Chapter 21

I'm not feeling very Hoptimistic today

"WHAT'S WITH THE HELP wanted sign in the window?" Hailey asks Pops as we join him at the bar at McGraw's on Monday night.

"The cleaner quit," he grumps.

"Maggy quit?" Phoebe asks. "What happened?"

Hailey narrows her eyes at Phoebe. "How do you know Maggy?"

Phoebe rolls her eyes. "I lived with Pops for a while, remember?"

When Phoebe had her troubles, she stayed in Hailey's childhood bedroom to keep safe. The place she had been living was seriously sad. I still can't believe Ms. Perfectly Put Together ever lived in a boarding house full of drug addicts. The woman is full of surprises.

"Why are you grumpy about it?" Hailey asks Pops. "The turnover on cleaners is pretty high. This is not an unusual situation."

"Someone," Pops glowers at the table of uncles who are not hiding their mirth whatsoever, "had a salesman call me at eight this morning. They wanted to sell me a lawnmower and wouldn't take no for an answer despite my explaining I don't have a yard."

"You don't have a yard," I agree. Pops lives in the apartment above the pub. It's a huge apartment as it's the size of the pub, but there's no yard. The 'backyard' is a parking lot, although there is one picnic table where the smokers hang out.

"Someone," he growls, "told him I would deny having a yard, but it was only a negotiation tactic."

I giggle and throw a thumbs-up at the uncles who wink in response. They're a menace but they sure are fun to be around.

"Why didn't you hang up?" Hailey asks.

"I did. He called back. Three times."

"Why didn't you switch off your phone?"

Pops shakes his head at Hailey. "I have a daughter who works as a PI, a son-in-law who's a detective, and a friend who…"

I lean closer. Is he going to finally tell us what Wally does? It has to be Wally he's talking about. To my great disappointment, he mutters, "Never mind."

Argh. I know Wally is some sort of super-secret black ops guy, but I need the details. My curiosity is killing me!

"What are you going to do to get them back?" Hailey asks.

Pops narrows his eyes on his supposed buddies. "You'll see. You'll see."

Goodie! I look forward to whatever revenge he comes up with. Of course, my phone has to beep with an incoming message and ruin my happiness. My mom – tired of waiting for me to sign up for the dating website myself – signed up for one on my behalf and is now trolling the profiles to find a man who is a 'good' fit.

She's been sending me these profiles all dang day. Unfortunately, she seems to think I need an older man who looks boring as all get out. She says he'll tame me. I don't want anyone to tame me. Hell, I don't want a man at all.

How long are you going to lie to yourself? my inner voice – aka that bitch, Adult Suzie – asks. I ignore her and open the message on my phone instead. It's as I thought. Another email from my mom.

Hailey looks over my shoulder. "Yes! More men!"

Phoebe looks over my other shoulder. "Let's see. They can't all be bad."

"What's going on?" Sid asks as he bellies up to the bar.

I don't want to answer him, but Hailey has no problem tattling. "Mrs. Langley sends these daily emails with dating profiles of men she thinks Suzie should date. We're looking at the latest batch."

"What for?" he asks. "I thought you and Grayson were an item."

I groan. "Why does everyone keep saying that?"

"Because you can't deny chemistry." Sid looks around. "Where is Grayson anyway?"

I have no idea. I haven't heard a peep from him since last week when Liz showed up.

He clasps my shoulder. "I'm sure he'll be back. Like I said, you can't deny chemistry." He whistles as he walks away; my eye lasers apparently having no effect on him whatsoever. I need to take them into maintenance for repair.

I return my attention to my mom's email. Looking at potential suitors my mom picked out beats thinking about Grayson and how he ghosted me every day of the week.

Phoebe points to a guy in a suit who looks like he's never drunk a beer in his life. "This one looks good."

"He looks like someone old Phoebe would date, not me."

She scrunches up her face. "Forget I said anything. Why don't you tell your mom to stop sending you suggestions of who to date?"

I snort. "Have you met my mother?"

"Actually, no, I haven't."

Oh yeah, I forgot. Phoebe is such an integrated part of my life, I sometimes don't remember it's been mere months since I met her for the first time.

"You're missing out," Hailey says. "Mrs. Langley is a hoot. You think Suzie's crazy? It's inherited."

"When do I get to meet her?"

Oh great. Another friend who's going to love my mom just like all my other friends. It's easy for them. Them she doesn't try to embarrass. No, to my friends, my mom is sweet as sugar. Growing up, she was the mom who was always making cookies for all the kids on the block. The mom who let us hang around in the basement without too much adult supervision.

Her daughter, on the other hand, she can't help but embarrass her. When I was in high school, she'd remind me to take a condom with me whenever I went out. She couldn't say something discreetly when we were alone. Oh no, my mom had to talk about condoms and safe sex in front of every-freaking-one. And I do mean everyone. Every single boyfriend I ever had got the 'sex' talk from Mom. Needless to say, I learned awful quick to stop bringing boyfriends around. Mom still hasn't forgiven me.

"She doesn't come up to Wisconsin if there's snow on the ground," Hailey explains to Phoebe.

"But Suzie grew up here."

"Yep. And when I finished my first year of college and it looked like I was 'going to stick with it', Mom told Dad they were moving to Arizona."

The door to the bar bangs open and everyone looks over to see who's entering, although everyone isn't too many people as it's Monday and the place is practically empty except for us.

A woman stands in the entryway looking nervous. She's not too tall but definitely taller than me, although almost everyone is. She's wrapped up for the cold making it nearly impossible to see what she looks like, although I do see dark brown hair peeking out of her woolen cap. Her eyes, the only part of her face visible between her hat and scarf, widen when she glances around and realizes everyone is looking at her.

Sid stands and approaches her. "How can we help, sweet thing?"

"Is he hitting on her? I thought he and Mary Ann were engaged," I whisper to Hailey.

Lenny, Barney, and Wally join us at the bar. "Nah, Mary Ann dumped his fat ass."

I tilt my head to study Sid's backside. "I don't think his ass is fat."

"How about I buy you one of those frou-frou drinks?" Sid asks the stranger who looks ready to bolt.

Pops throws his towel on the bar and marches over. "Leave her alone," he orders Sid before giving the woman his attention. "I'm Max. How can I help you?"

"I didn't know his name is Max. I thought everyone called him Pops," Phoebe whispers.

"Not everyone." I wink.

"I-I-I saw the help wanted sign," she manages to say.

Pops grins. "You're in the right place. I'm the owner. How about you come to my office and we'll talk?"

She bites her bottom lip as she glances up at Pops. Pops may be in his fifties, but he is a stone-cold fox. His gray hair doesn't make him look old. No, it qualifies him as a silver fox. Like the rest of his former Army buddies, he's tall and fit thanks to an uber strict workout regime. Trust me. The workout regime is worth it. Especially for all the women who come to the bar to pant after his muscles. And when he looks at you with those bright blue eyes? Stone. Cold. Fox.

The woman's eyes flare as she takes him in. Finally, she nods. Pops places a hand on the small of her back and escorts her to the hallway leading to his office.

As soon as they're out of hearing range, Lenny, Barney, and Wally break into laughter.

"Ka-boom! I never thought I'd see the day the almighty Sid crashed and burned," Lenny remarks as he wipes tears from his eyes.

"Even in the sandbox, the man could pick up women," Wally agrees.

"Who knows if they were women, though? Anyone or thing could have been under those burkas," Barney says and raises his hand toward me for a fist bump.

I oblige because no one is talking about me and Grayson or the numerous dates my mother wants to set me up on. Anything to get the attention off me, I'm down with.

"Fuckers," Sid snarls before leaning over the bar and nabbing a bottle of whiskey.

Hailey's gaze lingers on the hallway where her dad and the lady disappeared. "Do you think Pops likes her? Maybe he'll finally get over my mother."

Wally hangs an arm over her shoulders. "Kid, your pops got over your mom years ago."

"Yeah, right. That's why he's never had a serious relationship since her."

I bump her shoulder. "Maybe he did. Maybe he kept her his little secret."

Hailey's nose wrinkles. "Yuck. My pops doesn't have dirty little secrets."

"You don't know everything about him."

"I'm done with this conversation," she announces. "Who wants to play pool?"

"I'm in." Lenny looks at me. "As long as disaster isn't playing. I think she broke one of Grayson's ribs last time she played."

Damn Grayson. I can't believe the big jerk ghosted me. It's been a week. He should be over his hissy fit by now. The annoying voice in my head – aka Adult Suzie – reminds me I hurt him bad and betrayed him. For once, Adult Suzie is wrong. I would never betray anyone. Not after what Toby did to me.

Chapter 22

Beauty is in the eye of the beer holder.

I TAKE IN HAILEY's outfit when she opens her door for me. "What are you wearing? I thought we were going out." It's Friday night and we're gathering for a girl's night out. And boy do I need a night out, especially since *someone* is still ghosting me.

"This is my going out outfit."

I chuckle. "Yeah, right."

As a kick-ass PI, Hailey lives in her ripped jeans and shitkicker boots. The one concession she makes when we go out is to change the shitkicker boots for a pair of knee-high leather boots. But right now, she's dressed in skinny jeans, a shiny tank top, and a pair of strappy sandals.

I point at her top. "You're going to freeze."

I don't bother remarking upon the shoes. Everyone who lives in Wisconsin and is no longer of college-age knows better than to wear any footwear other than boots when there's a foot of snow on the ground.

"I think she looks gorgeous," Phoebe says.

Phoebe is the one who looks gorgeous. She doesn't have to try much. The woman oozes sex appeal. She could wear a paper bag and men would fall at her feet. She's currently wearing a black halter dress that hugs her curves. I'm going to spend the night beating men off with a stick.

"Where are we going? And why didn't anyone tell me to dress up?"

I'm wearing skinny jeans and a top. Granted the top is kind of sexy. One shoulder and arm are completely bare while the other arm and shoulder are covered in lace. I look okay for a night at the bar, but I have a feeling we're not going to a bar.

"I thought we'd do something different tonight," Hailey answers.

Who does she think I am? Like I can't read her like a book. "Try being evasive with someone who doesn't know you. What are you up to?"

Hailey bites her lip and looks away. She looks at her phone. "I think our Uber is here."

Our Uber? Now, I know she's up to no good. We haven't used a taxi since we were in college and couldn't control our alcohol use. I cross my arms over my chest and wait.

Phoebe can't stand the pressure long. "We're going to a strip club."

I raise an eyebrow. "A strip club? Why are we going to a strip club? And why does she know, and I don't?"

Why in the world does Hailey want to go to a strip club now? She's never shown any interest before. Oh sure, she's gone to one for work, but she is not dressed for work.

Hold on. Friday night. Two weeks after her bachelorette party. I nearly slap myself when I connect the dots.

"Tonight is Aiden's bachelor party, isn't it?" Hailey blushes and looks away. A dead giveaway I am right. "You're letting him go to a strip club?"

I'm surprised. Hailey doesn't put up with shit from anyone and definitely not from her fiancé.

"I told him it was his last night of freedom. As long as his dick stays in his pants, I'm good."

Yeah, right. "Which is why you're now dressed up to go to a strip club?"

"I may have overestimated how okay I was with the scenario of my future husband drooling over big breasted women." She circles her chest. "I can't compete."

"Are you serious? Even if you weren't gorgeous – which FYI you are – Aiden loves you. He would never cheat on you. Not least of all because you'd chop his balls off and then feed them to the dogs."

"You're wasting your time," Phoebe tells me.

"Trust me, I know. I've spent thirty-one years telling her she's gorgeous, and she still doesn't believe me."

"You couldn't speak at birth, you know," Hailey grumbles.

I look around. "Where are Leroy and Lola anyway?"

Hailey snickers. "I crated them up. Lola attacked Phoebe the minute she walked in," she whisper-shouts as if Phoebe doesn't know Lola was dry humping her leg.

A car outside honks its horn. "And now our Uber really is here."

Fifteen minutes later, we're sitting in an Uber looking up at the building housing the strip club. "Are you sure you want to go in there?" It doesn't look as sleazy as I expected. It's a black wooden structure with no windows. And, in case the name doesn't give it away – Larry Flynt's Gentlemen's Club – there's a red lantern.

"We're going in," Hailey says, opens her door, and marches out. I run to catch up with her.

Phoebe grasps my hand. "We need to stick together," she whispers.

What does she think? Men are going to mistake her for the entertainment? I look over at her. It's a definite possibility. Bodyguard Suzie to the rescue.

The bouncer doesn't blink twice at three women walking into a strip club. He's probably seen it all. We pay our cover charge and walk inside. Huh. It's not what I expected. Yes, there's a large stage with several poles on it, but it almost looks classy. The tables have comfy club chairs and the wooden accents everywhere give it – dare I say? – charm.

Hailey scans the half-empty room. "I don't see them anywhere. Can you check to make sure this is the club Ryker was talking about?"

Phoebe digs her phone out. "There's a message from Ryker. Plans changed. New address." She looks up. "I guess they went to a different strip club."

"I'll order an Uber." Hailey marches out of the place without a backward glance. Phoebe sprints after her.

I linger. The woman on the pole is super flexible and her breasts are perky despite her hanging upside down. I look down at my chest. I may be better endowed than Hailey but perky? I shake my head and follow the girls outside.

"Are you sure this is the right address?" I ask when we arrive at our next destination courtesy of Ryker. The place looks like a plain old bar.

Hailey studies the place. "Maybe they have a special stripper night?"

My assumption we're in the wrong place is confirmed as soon as we walk into the bar. There is no stripping going on here unless the college kids get raunchy and start taking their clothes off. Heaven save me from drunk college students.

"Why are we in a college bar?" Phoebe asks.

I look around and spot a table where Aiden, Ryker, and a couple of men I assume are Aiden's colleagues are sitting. "That's why?" I point.

When we arrive at the table, Aiden and Ryker are exchanging money.

"Hi, Princess," Ryker says and hauls Phoebe into his lap. He nuzzles her nape. "Thanks for winning me fifty bucks."

"Fifty bucks?" I ask. "What did you bet about? And why wasn't I in on it?"

Aiden snags Hailey's hand and drags her down to sit next to him. "Ryker said you girls would be here within thirty minutes. I figured you'd want to stay at the strip club and check it out."

I raise my hand. "I wanted to stay."

The two men I don't know chuckle. I hold out my hand. "I'm Suzie."

"Sam," says the man who shakes my hand. "And this is Trey."

Sam stands and finds a chair for me. I sit with them as Hailey and Phoebe are now pre-occupied with their men.

"Some bachelor party this ended up being." I point my thumb toward the couples.

Sam chuckles. "It's fine. My wife wouldn't let me out unless I promised we were having a tame guy's night out."

Trey grunts and I interpret this to mean 'same here'.

"Are you Suzie the brewer?" Sam asks.

I smile. Whoa. What? I'm smiling now when someone asks me about my brewing? It's looking more and more like I'm ready to take the next step and make this beer thing a business. My stomach warms with excitement. Suzie the brewer is going to be epic!

"I am. I recently finished up a batch of Session IPA. It's a …"

My words trail off when I notice Grayson walking in our direction. He's back. My heartbeat quickens and tingles break out across my body. He's back and he's here.

I beam up at him, but he walks past me like I don't exist and takes a seat next to Trey. I try to catch his attention but he angles his seat so his back is to me. Ouch. My eyes itch and I have to blink furiously to stop the tears from falling.

Sam pats my hand. His hand is about twice the size of mine and his patting feels like blunt force trauma but it's sweet. "You okay?"

"I'm fine. I'm fine." I sniff and force thoughts of Grayson into a box in my mind. A box I shut and seal with a lock. For good measure, I wrap a chain around it. "Now, where was I?"

Like the idiot I am, I try several times throughout the night to gain Grayson's attention, but he ignores me like a pro. He laughs and jokes with Phoebe and Hailey, but whenever I try to enter the conversation, he suddenly has to use the restroom. If he really did need the restroom as many times as he's left the table, I'd be worried about his prostate.

I give up and go home around midnight. There's no need to torture myself with Grayson's presence. I know a lost cause when I see one. Time to move on. And no, I'm not crying at the thought of moving on. I have dirt in my eye is all.

Chapter 23

I'm not addicted to beer. We're just in a committed relationship.

I'M DRAGGING ON SATURDAY morning as I clean the brew shack. Unfortunately, I'm not dragging because I have a hangover, since girl's night out last night was a complete and total bust. Not only did we not have a girl's night out since we joined the boys, but Grayson pretended I was invisible.

If I really were invisible it would be beyond cool. I'm not above sneaking into bathrooms and closets to scare the fudge out of people. And just think how cops would freak out if they saw my car driving down the road without a driver. But I'm not invisible. I'm plain old Suzie. A little crazy, a little klutzy, and apparently also forgettable.

Ugh! Why am I thinking about Grayson? If he can easily forget about me, I should give him the same treatment. Step one – delete his information from my phone. Before I can change my mind, I take my phone out of my back pocket and find Grayson's contact information. My thumb hovers over the delete contact button for a second before I force myself to move.

There! I feel better already. I decide to turn on some music. Music will improve my mood. I put on my 80s music playlist and Duran Duran starts singing about a wolf. I hum and tumble over made up words as I wipe down the tables. Don't judge. No one knows the words to *Hungry Like the Wolf*!

When someone starts banging on the door, I ignore it. If Hailey wants in, she can pick the stupid lock. Although this time I did engage the deadbolt. She's the one who said she wants a challenge.

The banging continues. Fine. I'll switch off the music and open the door, but I do not have to pretend to be happy about it. I yank open the door. "Hailey—" Shit. It's not Hailey. "What do you want?"

I don't wait for his answer but retreat into the building and grab a broom. I start sweeping as if I haven't a care in the world. Good thing no one can see how much my hands are shaking. Despite what an ass he was last night, Little Susan sits up and pays attention. There may also be some swooning and talk of how he came for us. Little Susan needs to get a life.

Grayson comes in and shuts the door behind him. "We need to talk."

I snort. "Like you talked to me last night?"

"I deserved that," he says from way too close to me.

He reaches around me for the broom, but I hold on tight. We end up playing tug of war with it. Ugh. Whatever. I let go and Grayson grunts as the broom smacks him in the chest. I don't smile. Too much.

While he leans the broom against the wall, I cross my arms over my chest and prepare to do battle. "What do you want?"

"I came back to tell you I forgive you, but then I saw you sitting all cozy with Sam and I got mad."

I try to not let the shock show on my face. He came to forgive me? And he was jealous? It's upside-down world today, but no one warned me. I take a deep breath and dive in.

"We'll get back to the whole mad thing in a minute. Forgive me?"

His throat moves as he swallows. "Yes, I forgive you for nosing into my life and going to talk to Liz."

My stomach warms and the tension I've been carrying around in my shoulders for weeks releases. "I was only trying to help," I explain.

"I know, but it took me some time to see it. Liz and my mom were pretty adamant you were fantastic for trying to help me."

I wink. "I am pretty fantastic." I allow him to chuckle for a moment before I tackle the second part of what he said. "Why were you mad because I was talking to Sam?"

He growls. "You weren't talking to Sam. You were flirting with him."

"Excuse you? I was not flirting with him. He's a married man. I would never flirt with a married man."

"You sure looked animated."

"He asked about my beer, and I probably bored him to tears with my tales of brewing."

He raises an eyebrow. "You talked openly about your brewing?" I nod. "Does this mean you're ready to take the next step?"

I wag a finger at him. "Don't distract me. Why were you mad when you thought I was flirting?"

Grayson steps closer until I can smell him. Mmm… mint and vanilla never smelled this good before. My entire body wakes up and Little Susan gets out the pompoms and starts cheering. *Here we go!*

He tucks a stray strand of hair behind my ear. Goosebumps erupt where he touches me. "I think you know why," he whispers.

His eyes drop to my lips and my tongue peeks out to wet them. He groans. "Say you want me. Say I'm not alone in this thing."

Maybe I'll regret it in the morning, but I can't stop myself from nodding. I don't think I've ever wanted anything more than to feel his lips at this moment.

His mouth crashes down on mine. I gasp and his tongue immediately seeks entrance. I grab hold of his shoulders to stop myself from melting in a puddle of goo on the ground. He tastes like the coffee he drank for breakfast and something else. Something unique. Something all Grayson.

Grayson shoves a hand into my hair and angles my head until he can dive deep into my mouth. I moan as his tongue explores every inch of my mouth. I can feel myself growing wet and he hasn't touched me yet.

My hands start exploring. If this is to be our only time together, I want to taste and touch every inch of skin and muscle I can. He's wearing a skintight long-sleeve thermal allowing me to feel his muscles beneath my fingers as I run my hands over his shoulders and arms, but I want to feel his skin.

I tug on his shirt until Grayson ends our kiss and leans back. He reaches behind himself and grabs a fistful of shirt, which he whips off. My mouth drops open at the sight in front of me. His skin is brown and smooth with ripples of muscle. I flatten my hands on his chest, but he circles my wrists and removes my hands. I mewl in protest.

"I want to feel your skin, too."

Oh, goodie! I raise my arms to allow him to remove my sweatshirt and t-shirt leaving me in my off-white utility bra. Damn. Had I known this was going to happen today, I would have worn a sexy bra.

Grayson's eyes zero in on my chest. "Even better than I expected."

I reach around to unhook my bra, but he stops me. "Allow me."

My bra falls to the ground on top of my sweatshirt and Grayson's hands immediately cup my breasts. "I need to taste." I squeal when he picks me up and places me on the table. I forget all about the cold table and why I shouldn't be sitting on the sanitized surface when his mouth finds my breast.

His tongue swirls around one nipple while his hand kneads my other breast. My back arches and my head falls back on a moan. I place my elbows on the table to support me before I collapse.

Grayson lifts his head and looks me in the eye. "These are fantastic and wonderfully sensitive."

Words desert me. I couldn't talk if I wanted to. His mouth returns to my breast while his hand sneaks down my chest past my stomach. He snaps open my jeans before shoving his hand down my pants. He doesn't mess around and immediately zeroes in on my pulsing clit.

He moans. "You're already wet for me."

Of course, I am. He's touching me in all the right places. All the places I've dreamed of him touching me since the first time I looked into his whiskey-colored eyes.

"I want to taste you." I am down with this plan. "But I'm too impatient. I can't wait to be inside you." An even better plan.

He removes his hand from my pants, and I whimper. He smirks. "I need to get you naked before I can get inside you."

Good idea. I use my feet to push my slippers off my feet while he yanks my jeans down my legs. The table is cold when my naked ass hits it, but I could care less about a little discomfort right now. I unsnap Grayson's jeans and lower his zipper.

"Careful," he cautions.

I release his cock and wrap my hand around it. I need two hands to fist him. Shit. He's more than big. He's huge. Lucky me.

He kisses my shoulder and trails his tongue to my ear where he bites the lobe. I shiver.

I pump his length a few times before he moans and grasps my wrist to stop me. I lean back on my elbows and watch as he lines himself up.

"Condom." I remember right before he enters me.

"Shit. I nearly forgot." He places his forehead against mine. "Need a second before I explode the moment I enter you."

I do a full body shiver at his words. No one has ever said anything as sexy as his words to me. He takes a deep breath before reaching down to remove his wallet from his jeans, which are now sagging around his knees. He finds a condom and sheathes himself.

"You ready?" he asks as he lines his cock up with my opening.

I bite my lip and bob my head. I am more than ready. He enters me slowly, inch by delicious inch. "You're so tight. I'm not going to last long."

I run my nails down his back and squeeze his ass in an effort to get him to move faster. "Me either," I whisper.

He finally bottoms out and pauses. I grunt. "Move. I need you to move."

"If you want this to last more than five pumps, you'll wait."

His words cause excitement to build and leak out of me.

"I can feel how wet you are," he says as he retreats at a snail's pace. I can feel every single ridge of his cock rubbing against me. It's amazing.

When only the tip of him remains inside me, he pauses before slamming into me. The entire table moves with the force of his thrust and bumps against the wall. I lay back on it. The smooth cool surface is a direct contrast to the heat emitting from Grayson's body. He pulls out and strokes in again. My back arches of its own accord as I moan his name.

"That's it," he grunts. His hands are now grasping my hips tight enough I can feel his fingernails digging into my skin. "Take all of me, Precious."

My belly heats as the excitement builds and my walls begin to tighten.

"I can feel how close you are. Come for me, Suzie. Come all over my cock."

My body is totally on board with the idea. I moan and my head drops to the table as my entire body convulses with my orgasm.

When I come down, Grayson starts pounding into me. "Nothing better than seeing you take me." His strokes become erratic. "Gonna come. Fuck," he moans as he plants himself deep and stays there.

Drips of sweat roll down his chest and I lick my lips. "Don't look at me like that."

"Like what?" I bat my eyelashes like I don't know what he's thinking.

"I need a moment before round two." He looks around my brew shack. "And I need a bed."

I giggle. "Sounds like a plan to me."

Chapter 24

It's all fun and games until the beer runs out.

"Wow," is all I can say. I'm lying naked on my bed covered in sweat and gasping for air. My entire body is tingling from the most recent orgasm Grayson gave me.

The man of the hour is laying next to me trying to catch his breath. I swivel my head to look at him as every other muscle in my body is too exhausted to move at the moment. He looks magnificent. I was not wrong to be enamored with his shoulder muscles, but the rest of his muscles aren't anything to sneeze at either.

His hand raises to cup my face. "We need to talk."

I know he's right. We just leaped into a mess of sexy complications but talking is the last thing on my mind. "Dude, don't crush my buzz."

He chuckles before rolling off the bed. "Come on. Get up. Get dressed. I'll make you something to eat and we can talk."

I raise an eyebrow. "You're going to cook?"

He shrugs and my eyes can't help devouring his muscles as they bunch with the movement. He must have been first in line when they were handing out muscles and didn't bother leaving any for the other poor shmucks.

A smack on my belly wakes me from my Grayson muscle trance. "What?"

"Stop objectifying my body and get your smoking hot ass up."

I force myself off the bed. "If my body is smoking, I blame you and your love stick."

"My love stick?" He chuckles.

"I thought you were going to make me food," I comment when he stands there watching me walk around searching for the clothes we threw on the floor as we made our way to the bed.

I should be self-conscious. After all, I'm completely naked with my boobs hanging out there, but this man has literally licked every inch of me. There's nothing he hasn't seen.

Heat flares in his eyes before he blinks and – poof! – it's gone. "Pizza okay?"

I snicker. "By making me food you meant ordering take-out, didn't you?"

He steps into his jeans and I can feel my bottom lip forming a pout as all those delicious muscles disappear. He bops me on the nose. "Food now. Sexy times later."

I'm down with that plan. "Meat lovers for me." He nods as he takes his phone out and leaves the bedroom.

When I enter the living room, he's sitting on the couch playing with his phone. As soon as he sees me, he sets it down and pats the place next to him. I snort. Does he think I'm an obedient dog? He should know better by now. To be contrary, I sit on the armchair next to the couch.

Grayson shakes his head but doesn't comment. "Before the pizza gets here, I want to clear the air." I grunt. I hate 'talks'. "I want to apologize."

Hey now. This is a talk I can get into. "Apologize for what?"

"I may have overreacted when Liz showed up at McGraw's."

I raise an eyebrow. "May have?"

"I was shocked, and I took it out on you." He swallows. "Will you forgive me?"

"Considering everything we've done today; I think it's pretty obvious I forgive you." I wink.

"Thank you."

"But I won't put up with you ghosting me again. I get you were mad, but I was completely freaking out. I didn't know if you were okay. Hell, I didn't know where you were." I'm not proud of it, but I may have kind of sort of stalked his apartment when I didn't hear from him. A whole lotta good it did me. He was nowhere to be found.

"I drove up to Merrill."

I stand and move to the couch to sit next to him. "Did you talk to Liz?"

"Yes." He pauses, and I bite my tongue to stop the barrage of questions banging around in my head from coming out of my mouth.

He looks down at his hands fidgeting with his phone. He obviously doesn't want to talk about this, but I can't let him off the hook. Not after how he ghosted me. And, okay, maybe I'm a teensy-weensy bit nosy.

"How did it go?"

"Okay, I guess. She doesn't blame me for Bill's death."

I squeeze his hand. "Of course not. She doesn't blame you because it's not your fault."

He flips his hand and laces his fingers through mine. My stomach clenches and warmth flows through my body. I am in deep doo-doo if holding hands with a man is causing stomach clenches.

"I saw my parents, too."

I guess the topic of Bill and his guilt over Bill's death is off the table. Does he not realize how tenacious I can be? But I let it go – for now.

"How are they?"

"Good. They helped me realize a few things."

I wait, but he doesn't fill me on what those few things are. He's silly if he thinks I won't come out and ask. "Like what things?"

"Stuff about Liz."

Could he be any more vague? Before I get the chance to ask him to be more specific, he moves on to another topic. "What do you want to tell the others?"

"Tell the others?"

"I won't be your dirty little secret, Munchkin."

"I don't know how you jumped from having sex to being a dirty little secret."

He raises our hands. "This is happening."

I try to snatch my hand away, but he holds tight. "I thought you didn't want a relationship."

"Maybe I've changed my mind."

Nothing can keep me from yanking my hand away from his now. "But I haven't. I told you I don't do relationships."

"Help me understand why."

I growl. I don't want to talk about my ex. It's embarrassing.

"I get it. You can't get over him," he goads.

"Get over him? I don't need to get over anyone."

"Really?" He raises an eyebrow. "Then you don't do relationships because …"

"Why is this any of your business?"

He snarls and grabs my chin to force me to look at him. "I spent the entire morning inside of you. It couldn't be more my business."

Shit. He's right. It's only fair I explain to him why I don't do relationships. It's freaking unfair, though. He said he didn't want a relationship either. If I had known his opinion had changed, I wouldn't have slept with him.

Adult Suzie laughs and laughs. She falls off her chair she's laughing so hard. *Yeah, right.* She manages to say between bouts of laughter. I guess Adult Suzie is not adulting today.

I jump to my feet. "I need a beer if we're having this conversation."

I stomp to the refrigerator and grab two bottles of beer. I take a gulp from one to give me some Dutch courage for this conversation. It doesn't help. I take another gulp before the bottle is taken from me.

"There's no need to be afraid. I won't tell anyone your deep, dark secrets," he says and then mutters, "unlike you."

"Hey! I didn't tell anyone your secrets." It's true. I didn't. Wally's the one who uncovered the secrets. I may have talked to Liz about Grayson's guilt, but I didn't tell anyone else about it. Except maybe I did tell the girls. Well, shit.

Grayson takes my hand and leads me back to the couch. He forces me to sit. "Come on. It can't be that bad."

I snort. Easy for him to say. I take a deep breath and dive in.

"I was dating this guy, Toby. We dated all through college. After we graduated, we talked about starting the micro-brewery together and getting married. I thought it was a done deal. I bought this house for us."

"For all the babies," Grayson growls. What is he growling about?

"Except it turned out Toby didn't want children. At least, that's what he told me after we'd been together for years. I was devastated, but I loved him, you know. I wasn't going to break up with him because he didn't want children."

Grayson chuckles. "And you thought you could break him down over time."

I don't bother denying it. He's right. I figured once Toby and I were married, he'd change his mind.

"Anyway, he asks me to marry him, and I am over the moon. Literally, over the moon. Of course, I say yes."

I fall silent. This time it's Grayson who doesn't have any patience.

"What happened?"

"Something felt off. Call it a hunch, call it women's intuition, call it what you will, but I knew something was wrong. I went to Hailey who was substitute teaching drama classes at the time and asked her to look into it. It took her less than a day to find out Toby had another woman. Another woman who was pregnant. Mr. I Will Never Want Children got another woman pregnant while engaged to me!"

Grayson gathers me into his arms.

"I'm sorry, Precious. But he's not worth your tears."

I push him away. "I'm not crying." It's true. I'm not. My eyes may have welled up, but no tears were shed this day by Suzie. "Now do you understand why I don't do relationships?"

"Are you going to hit me if I say no?"

I narrow my eyes on him, but I don't hit him. "Let me spell it out for you. Men betray you. I can't handle getting my heart broken again."

"I get it. You're protecting your heart."

"Yes." Finally, he gets it.

"But, Munchkin, the best way to protect your heart is to give it to me. I will guard and protect it with my life."

He is out of his danged mind if he thinks I'm giving my heart to him. Adult Suzie clears her throat and lifts one eyebrow, oh, so slowly. Shit. She's right. I may be lying to myself. My heart is already longing to be his. Nope. I can't allow it to happen. I shake my head at his crazy ass.

His grin is sly. "It's okay. I'm patient."

Chapter 25

Beer: It helps make things not suck.

GRAYSON

I know Suzie thinks we're back to being just friends, but she's dead wrong. And it's my job to show her how wrong she is. I need to wear her down is all. After this weekend, she can't deny how explosive our chemistry is. Besides, I've been thinking about what Mom said. She was right. Anyone willing to drive half a state to slay your demons for you is worth fighting for.

I may not be ready for the picket fence and the twenty children she wants to have, but I am ready to try for a relationship. I know I'll regret it if I don't, and I am done with having regrets.

With these thoughts whirling around in my mind, I open the door to McGraw's Pub. I haven't been here since two weeks ago when Liz showed up unexpectantly and I lost my mind. I know the uncles are ultra protective of Suzie. They probably weren't very impressed by how I acted. I need to man up and apologize to them for yelling at her. I will show them my head's screwed on straight now.

The uncles look up when I enter. Their eyes narrow and I know I'm right. I don't waste time heading their way.

I don't make them wait. "I'm sorry I yelled at Suzie the last time I was here."

Wally uses his foot to push a chair out from under the table. "Sit."

I bristle at the order, but I'm a soldier. I know how to take an order. I sit my ass down. I keep my mouth shut as I wait for them to begin.

"Is your head screwed on straight now?" Lenny demands.

"Yes, sir."

"Just like that?" Barney doesn't look like he believes me.

"I talked to Liz and my parents." When they continue to stare at me, I confess. "And I'm seeing a counselor."

"About damn time," Sid remarks.

"Sorry?" What does he mean?

"Son," Wally says and snags my attention. "Anyone with eyes can see you're struggling. We know a bunch of old farts like ourselves can't solve your problems, but a woman? A woman can soothe over those rough edges and make solving your problems worth your while."

He tilts his head toward Suzie who's sitting at a table with Phoebe and Hailey. She's giggling, but she doesn't fool me. I can see the strain around her eyes. She's worried I'm going to tell everyone we're in a relationship despite promising her I wouldn't tell anyone. I don't break my promises. Now, if people guess what's happening? An entirely different matter in my book.

"Ah, you finally hit that," Sid says when he notices me studying Suzie.

My nostrils flare as my anger blazes to life. "I didn't *hit* anything. Suzie is a woman, not some whore I took home."

Wally punches me in the arm. It isn't some play punch either. He's making it clear he can kick my ass if necessary. Message received. "He was testing you. Congratulations! You passed."

"Are you fucking kidding me? Do you think life is some fucking joke you can take bets on?"

Pops arrives with a tray of drinks and slaps me on the back. "No, this is not a joke. But Suzie is one of our own. We need to make sure she ends up with someone who won't hurt her."

"Like the asshat Toby did?"

"She told you about Toby?" When I nod, Pops' grins. "Good. She's opening up to you."

"Opening up? She slammed the door on any relationship between us besides friendship."

Pops squeezes my shoulder. "Give it time. You'll wear her down. Especially with us on your side."

He hands out our drinks and returns to behind the bar. I sip my beer while I try to come up with a plan to 'wear her down'. I've taken on insurgents, I won't let a little slip of a woman defeat me. Unfortunately, the only plan I've come up with thus far is to be around her as much as possible.

I watch as Barney's face turns red as he sucks on the straw in his coke. "You okay, man?"

He finally gives up and takes the straw out of the glass. He studies the bottom of the straw before throwing it on the table. I look closer. The end of the straw is sealed shut.

"Serves you right," Pops shouts from across the room.

"What did you do?" I ask.

Before he can answer, Wally's phone starts going haywire. Since he's obviously still involved with the government in some way, he doesn't hesitate to look at it. His jaw gets tight as he reads his message.

"Everything okay?" I ask, although I don't expect him to answer. If he's dealing with terrorist threats or something similar, he won't be able to tell me anything.

"I'm going to kill him," he says and throws his phone down.

I can't resist looking. There's a picture of a woman in a dominatrix outfit. A blindfold covers her eyes, but the rest of her body is on display since the only clothing she's wearing is a leather bustier with a matching pair of panties. I did not need to know Wally is into some BDSM shit.

"I am not a submissive," he growls before marching off.

I stand and follow him. This is going to be good.

"I'm going to kill him," Wally mutters as he rounds the bar.

Pops doesn't look concerned. He crosses his arms over his chest and narrows his eyes on Wally. "Maybe you'll think next time before you have some salesman call me at o-dark-thirty."

I obviously missed something when I was gone. This group of friends show their love for each other with practical jokes and gags. They're always trying to one up each other. It's a guy thing.

"Big deal. You lost a bit of sleep, you big baby. I'm going to be getting emails from dominatrixes for weeks."

"Who's got his phone?" Sid asks. "I want to see those pictures."

Lenny raises an eyebrow at him. "Since when do you let a woman take charge in the bedroom?"

"Never, but those women look hot in those leather outfits." Sid wiggles his eyebrows.

"What do you call a potato dominatrix?" Barney asks. "A mashochist." He chuckles and raises his fist. Suzie walks over to give him a fist bump.

She takes a step back, but I move to trap her in place. My nose fills with her herbal, spicy smell and my body instantly reacts. My pants are suddenly too small as my cock starts to fill. It hasn't had its fill of Suzie yet. I'm not sure it ever will.

"You haven't answered my texts," I whisper into her ear. I notice her shiver and I angle my head away to hide my smirk. She can fight it as much as she needs to, but she can't deny she wants me.

She takes a step away. "I've been busy. Some of us do have jobs you know."

Hailey chortles. "Poor Suzie is too busy eavesdropping on everyone else at the office to take thirty seconds to text you back."

"If only she could stick to eavesdropping," Phoebe mumbles.

My Suzie is a troublemaker down to her bones. There's never a dull moment when she's around. "What did she do now?"

"It's not bad enough Lola is overly affectionate with me."

"Is that what we're calling humping your leg now?" Suzie interrupts to ask.

Phoebe ignores her. "She squirted potty training spray on the legs of my desk to make Leroy pee there."

I cough to hide my laughter because Phoebe is not amused.

"And here I thought there was a problem with Leroy." Hailey frowns at Suzie. "I've taken him to the vet because he's way too old to be having 'accidents'."

Suzie shrugs. "I told you he didn't need to go to the vet."

"But you didn't tell me why."

"It was strictly need to know."

The uncles return to their table giving Suzie the space to move. She immediately backs up and starts to walk away. "Hey, Precious," I call before she can get too far. "You want to play pool?"

"I want you to stop calling me precious is what I want," she hisses.

Phoebe sighs and places a hand over her heart. "He calls her precious."

Hailey smirks before starting to sing, "Suzie and Grayson sitting in a tree." Suzie slaps a hand over her mouth before she can continue. She has to stand on a chair to reach Hailey's mouth since my munchkin is half a foot shorter than Hailey, but she's determined.

"Stop it. Nothing is happening between me and Grayson," she insists.

I don't contradict her. There's no need to when her friends are looking at her like she's the world's worst liar.

"This is going to be fun." Sid rubs his hands together. "I've got July."

"No." I'm putting an end to this shit before it can begin. "There will be no betting about our relationship."

"There is no relationship," Suzie continues to insist.

No one pays any attention to her. I'm not the only one who knows she's fighting a losing battle. Good to know I have her friends and family on my side. Together, we'll wear her down eventually. Hailey winks at me. Another ally in my fight. I think I'm going to enjoy this.

Chapter 26

Apparently 'beer' isn't a 'helpful reply' when asked how to improve team meetings.

HAILEY PARKS HERSELF ON my desk the next day. I push her off. "I don't want your butt cooties on my desk."

"I'm wearing jeans. Besides, cooties aren't real."

Phoebe enters with a tray of coffees and a box of donuts. Uh oh. Alert! Alert! An ambush is impending. It doesn't take a genius to know what this little ambush is about. They want to talk about Grayson. I am not discussing my non-existent relationship with the soldier with them.

I open the bottom drawer where I keep my purse, intent on making a run for it.

Hailey dangles my bag in front of me. "Looking for this?"

I make a grab for it, but she lifts her hand over her head – a place I can't reach. Stupid, obnoxiously tall woman. "You'll get it back as soon as we're finished."

I collapse in my chair. It goes flying backwards and hits the wall with a bang! Shit. I rub my lower back where it got jarred by the collision. My back is already annoyed with me after a night of tossing and turning. Sleep eluded me as my mind conjured up image after image of Saturday and all the delicious things Grayson did to my body.

Thinking of Grayson's magical tongue causes my body to heat and my cheeks to catch fire.

"Your look right now," Hailey's finger circles my face, "is why we're having this conversation."

Phoebe hands me a coffee. "It's only fair since you wouldn't leave me alone about giving Ryker a second chance."

"And I was right. You're now happily living together and engaged to be married." I pat myself on the back.

"What's to say you can't get your own happily ever after?" Phoebe asks.

Ryker walks in but comes to a halt when he notices the group of us drinking coffee at my desk. He shakes his head. "Call me whenever whatever this is, is done," he says and does an about-face.

"Don't you want a donut?" Phoebe yells after him.

"Babe," is his only response as he marches down the hallway toward the elevator.

Phoebe giggles. "He doesn't eat sugary stuff." She snags a chocolate glazed donut and takes a bite. She moans. "Yummy."

"You used to not eat sugary stuff either," I remind her.

"Nuh-uh." Hailey snaps her fingers in my face. "You are not changing the subject."

"Subject? I didn't realize this little meet and greet had an agenda. Do you want me to take notes?"

"Stop being a smartass," Hailey grumbles.

"I learned from the best."

She smirks. "I am the best, aren't I?"

"Neither one of you can keep to an agenda," Phoebe mumbles around another bite of donut.

"Excuse us for not being Ms. Richer Than God who grew up having board meetings at the breakfast table."

"No." Phoebe wiggles her finger at me. "I'm not letting you get away with getting off topic. Now, back to the matter at hand."

I don't want to. I really don't. But I ask anyway. "And what is the matter at hand?"

"You and Grayson," Hailey supplies.

I figured as much. "I told you. Nothing is going on between me and Grayson." But my body betrays me, and I feel my cheeks warm. Stupid cheeks need to stop betraying me!

Hailey snorts. "Liar."

"You know I don't do relationships," I remind them.

"Isn't a friendship a relationship?" Phoebe asks, and I snarl at her.

"I don't do romantic relationships then," I amend.

"Why not?"

"Yeah, Suzie, why not?" Hailey teases. I engage my eye lasers, but they have no effect on her. Damn it.

"Because."

"Not good enough. You insisted I give Ryker – who freaking kidnapped me in case you forgot – a second chance. You literally wouldn't shut up about it. You can be super annoying."

I grin. "I know. I kind of rock annoying."

Phoebe is not to be deterred. "If you don't want me bugging you day in and day out about giving Grayson a chance, then you're going to have to tell me your story."

"Do I have to?" I whine. I'm acting childish, but I can't help it. I already broke open my heart and told Grayson the whole ugly Toby story on Saturday. Do I have to do it again?

Adult Suzie rears her ugly self and reminds me, *You weren't heartbroken on Saturday. You were embarrassed.* You don't know everything, I tell her. *Sure, I do.*

"Fine," I grunt and tell her all about the lying, cheating scumbag also known as Toby, my ex-boyfriend.

"Let me get this straight." Phoebe holds up her finger. "He cheated on you and got another woman pregnant while his ring was on your finger."

"After he told me – someone who wants a whole gaggle of children – he didn't want children." Why does everyone keep forgetting this? It's the foundation of the betrayal!

"And, to be technical about it, she was pregnant before he proposed," Hailey points out.

"Thanks for the clarification. Glad we have all the facts perfectly clear now," I snarl.

"Did you miss what happened to me last year?" Phoebe asks.

Um, no. No one could have missed all the shit swirling around her. She was kidnapped not once, but twice. Although the first time wasn't technically a kidnapping. It's a long story. But the second time? Total kidnapping there.

"And yet, despite all of the shit he did and all the lies he told, you didn't hesitate to push me to get together with Ryker."

She must be serious. She's swearing.

"Of course not. It was obvious you were totally gone for the man."

Hailey pounces. "Let's imagine for a moment, if you will, someone else who is really into a man but said someone is being cautious because of her past. Would you as an innocent bystander push the woman toward the man? Or would you let her be?"

I seriously hate when she throws my actions back at me. "You've made your point."

"I don't think she has. I'm kind of pissed right now."

My eyes widen at Phoebe's declaration. The Phoebe I know doesn't use words like pissed, let alone actually get pissed.

"Why? What's wrong?"

I hope she's pissed at Toby on my behalf, but I'm worried she's angry at me.

"One of my best friends turns out to be a big hypocrite. No, not big. Huge hypocrite."

Hailey bobs her head in agreement. "I could have told you that."

I cross my arms over my chest. "I am not a hypocrite. I'm wounded. I need to protect my heart." I nearly cringe as I listen to myself. Convincing I am not!

"Seriously?" Phoebe bends over the desk and gets right up in my face. "He cheated on you. I agree it sucks. But get over it. My husband kidnapped me and was planning to rape me. He also set fire to Sid's house." She returns to her seat and crosses her arms over her chest. "If you want to compare exes with me, you're going to have to do better than he cheated."

"She's got you there," Hailey says before taking a bite of her cinnamon twist.

"I didn't know this was a competition."

"It's not. But surely you can see you're hanging on to what Toby did because you're scared."

I frown at Phoebe. "When did you get this smart?"

She shrugs. "Sometime after I was kidnapped and before I got engaged."

"Come on, Suzie," Hailey cajoles. "I've never pushed you about a man before. I've let you crawl into your shell and hide away. But I won't let you pull your tortoise act this time."

"Why not?" I pout. For good measure, I jut my bottom lip out.

"Because Grayson might be the one."

Pfff. This again? "I've given up on the one."

Hailey wags her finger at me. "No, you haven't. You might convince other people, but I know you. I know you kept the house you bought to live in with Toby because you still hope to fill it with children someday."

I shrug. "I can always get a sperm donor."

"Or you can woman up and give Grayson a chance."

I don't want to talk about this anymore. I stuff a donut in my face. There, now I can't talk about it.

Hailey goes for a compromise. "Promise me you'll think about it, and we'll leave you alone."

"What a minute. I didn't agree to leave her alone."

Hailey pats Phoebe on the arm. "It's okay. For now. We'll leave her alone for now. Not forever."

"Fine. I'll think about it," I mutter.

Phoebe shoves the box of donuts toward me. "Here. These will make you feel better."

I don't argue with her. I plan to polish off the entire box. It's my right after they ambushed me and forced me into considering giving Grayson a chance. As if my mind can think about anything else except Grayson and being together with him since Saturday when he announced he wanted to try for a relationship.

Try for a relationship? You don't try for a relationship. You're either in one or not. Men. They are such confusing creatures. They also smell good and taste good and make your body feel things your battery-operated-boyfriend can't. See? Confusing creatures.

Chapter 27

If you don't drink beer, then how will your friends
know you love them at 2 a.m.?

"I DON'T UNDERSTAND WHY we have to do a rehearsal. I'm pretty
sure all of us know how to walk down an aisle."

I might sound a teensy-weensy bit grumpy. I'm not exactly
grumpy. No, I'm scared. I'm seeing Grayson tonight for the first
time in nearly a week. And I still don't know what to do. My
walls are crumbling down, and it scares the absolute shit out of
me.

Phoebe smacks me. Or at least I think it's a smack. The
woman needs to learn to put a bit of oomph behind her smack-
ing. "Stop being a Debbie Downer. This is Hailey's big day."

"Isn't tomorrow the big day?" I ask to be contrary. Scared
Suzie is apparently no fun.

"Shush you or I'll laugh when you trip and fall walking down
the aisle."

My mouth drops open and I press my hands to my chest in
mock outrage. "How dare you assume I'll trip."

She giggles but before she has a chance to respond, Hailey comes rushing out of the dressing room. Her hair makes it abundantly clear exactly what she's been up to.

"Did you pet the magic dragon in a church?" I clasp my non-existent pearls and feign shock.

Aiden hears the word 'magic' as he walks by and smirks. He swaggers past to stand with the men who are gathering on the other side of the vestibule.

"I can't believe you … you know … in a church before your wedding rehearsal," Phoebe hisses.

"It was my last chance to have sex as a single lady. I wasn't passing it up."

In the tradition of not allowing the groom to see the bride on the wedding day before she walks down the aisle, Hailey is kicking Aiden out of the house for the night.

"I didn't peg you for a traditionalist." Ms. Breaks Into my Brew Shack Without a Second Thought wants to follow tradition?

"I read an article in Cosmopolitan—"

I gasp. "You read Cosmo?" Cosmo is way too girly girl for my Hailey.

Her cheeks darken and she points to Phoebe. "This one leaves them laying around everywhere."

Phoebe holds up her hands and takes a step back. "Oh no, you don't. I'm not getting in between you two and one of your 'arguments'."

The preacher arrives and claps his hands to get everyone's attention. Despite my teasing of Hailey, I snap to and pay attention. I'm not risking getting smote for misbehaving in a church. I do enough misbehaving as it is.

The rehearsal goes off without a hitch. Okay, there was a tiny hitch when I tripped walking down the aisle, but it wasn't my fault! I can't help it Hailey paired me with a mountain of a man. I had to run to keep up with his stride and running never was my strong suit. I didn't fall on my face, though, so there.

We walk from the church to the restaurant where the rehearsal dinner is happening. I don't open my mouth and complain about the rehearsal dinner and its lack of purpose although I really, really want to. I don't know why it's called a wedding 'day' when it's obviously a wedding weekend. There's even a brunch planned on Sunday. Told you scared Suzie is no fun.

I study the seating chart and grunt when I notice who's sitting next to me. Phoebe takes my hand and practically skips to our table.

"This is your fault, isn't it?" There's no possible reason he's sitting at our table unless Phoebe and Hailey decided to play matchmaker.

"It's called karma," she practically sings.

"You're enjoying this entirely too much."

"Enjoying watching you squirm while denying you're falling in love with Grayson you mean?" I narrow my eyes at her. I am not falling in love. I'm not! She giggles. "It's almost more fun than getting a fifty-percent off coupon for the fall sale at Chanel."

Grayson stands as we arrive at the table. He leans forward and kisses my cheek. Tingles erupt from where his lips touch my skin, and I can't help but remember other places his lips have touched. The memories cause fire to erupt across my cheeks. Great. Blushing and red hair do not go together. Not that I want to look good for Grayson. *Liar.*

"You look lovely," Grayson whispers as he pulls out my chair for me.

I narrow my eyes on him. "No jokes about me wearing a dress."

He chuckles as he pushes in my chair. "Feeling self-conscious, Munchkin?"

A little. I wear dresses for two occasions – weddings and funerals. I'm missing my jeans and boots. I feel naked without pants on.

A waitress appears and starts pouring wine into our glasses. Grayson holds a hand over my glass. "Can you get the lady a beer, please?"

"I can drink wine," I insist, although I can feel my lip curl at the idea.

"And I'm sure I'd enjoy watching you make faces the entire evening, but you enjoy beer, so you're getting a beer."

Who am I to argue? When the waitress returns with a draft beer, Grayson's eyes flicker with envy and I smirk. I take a sip and then smack my lips. "Aaahhh."

"You're mean, Munchkin."

The rest of the wedding party arrive and join us at the table. Hailey has two bridesmaids – me and Phoebe. Although she calls both of us her maids of honor, we all know I'm the maid of honor. Aiden's two groomsmen are Ryker and Sam. In addition to the wedding party, Sam's wife and Grayson are sitting at our table.

"I'm starving," Hailey announces.

Aiden laughs. "When aren't you starving?"

Hailey is the type of woman I normally hate. She can eat whatever she wants, and she never gains any weight. Of course, she constantly complains about not having any curves, but I'll take eating whatever I want over tits and ass any day of the week. Although, if I'm being perfectly honest, I usually eat what I want anyway. The proof is in my belly. My wobbly, pudgy belly.

The wait staff enter the room and start serving the first course. I nearly gag when the plate of oysters is set in front of me. Oysters? Knowing Hailey, I was expecting hot wings and potato skins. I raise my eyebrows in her direction, and she shrugs.

"Aiden's mom arranged the meal. She wanted to help since my mom…"

I hold up my hand in a *say no more* gesture. No one has seen hide nor hair of her mom for nearly two decades, although I sometimes get the feeling Pops knows more than he lets on. Wally may be a master in sneaky, but Pops is no slouch either.

I pick up my fork to force those slimy oysters down my throat, but when I look down, my plate has disappeared. It's a Valentine's Day miracle! Not exactly Valentine's Day. Hailey wanted to get married on the day, but it falls on a Sunday this year making her wedding an Almost Valentine's Day wedding.

"I got you," Grayson whispers as he places a basket of garlic bread in front of me. His hand moves to squeeze my thigh, and I nearly jump from the contact. My dress is silk and does nothing to prevent me from feeling the heat of his hand on my thigh. Little Susan wakes up and starts to tingle. I expect her to start a dance any second now.

Grayson leaves his hand on my thigh and his thumb presses circles into my skin. I shove a piece of garlic bread into my mouth before I moan out loud. Oh god. Why does his hand on me feel this good? Are his hands magic?

He smirks before petting my thigh one last time and lifting his hand so he can eat. He eats like he's a machine. Someone doesn't like oysters any more than I do.

"Why did you take my plate if you don't like them?"

"I'm not forcing you to eat food you don't like." My belly warms at his words. "Besides, I can eat anything. Trust me, when you're in the sandbox you get used to eating whatever's available."

He notices my basket is empty. "Do you need more garlic bread?" Before I can answer, he raises his hand and a waitress practically trips over herself running over to him. "More garlic bread for the lady, please. Oh, and another beer."

"I'm not helpless," I insist.

He grins and the two dimples on his right cheek come out to play. Dang those two dimples! I want to lick them while my hands pet his naked shoulders. My entire body heats up and the tingles spread from my belly and go south.

"I know you're not. But I want to take care of you." He leans close and whispers, "In every way imaginable, Precious."

In case I'm clueless about what he means, he comes closer and kisses my neck. His tongue swirls around my pulse point, which is beating out of control. His sneaky hand finds my thigh and his thumb starts those lazy circles in my skin again.

Is it hot in here? I'm burning up. A waitress clears her throat behind us, and I squeak.

"Your beer and garlic bread," she announces. Her voice full of mirth.

We separate. My eyes widen when I see Grayson reach down and adjust himself. He winks at me. "Later."

I clear my throat and grab hold of my lady balls. "We need to talk."

I expect him to snarl or frown or be generally annoyed with me, but no. What does the man do? He smiles and says, "Whatever you want, Precious."

Whatever I want? Too bad I have no idea what I want. Adult Suzie calls me a big fat liar. *You know exactly what you want and it's sitting next to you.* I want to ignore Adult Suzie. How the hell did she get out of the box I trapped her in anyway? *Stop being a pussy.*

Yeah, Little Susan gets in on the action. *Give us what we want.*

Is this what going crazy feels like? My mind, heart, and body are fighting for control and I'm terrified my mind is going to lose. Oh, who am I kidding, my mind has already lost.

Chapter 28

The difference between beer and your opinion is
that I asked for a beer.

I'M RUNNING DOWN THE stairs of my house the next day when someone knocks. "I'm almost ready," I shout.

I'm expecting Phoebe. She's picking me up on her way to Hailey's to get dressed for the wedding. Unfortunately, 'getting dressed' is a major understatement. In addition to getting into super uncomfortable dresses, we are also having our nails, make-up, and hair done.

Phoebe insisted. She went so far as to bribe Hailey by paying for the entire thing and making all the necessary appointments. I'm telling you – the more she comes out of her shell, the more sneaky the woman gets.

I open the door and rush out without bothering to look up. I slam into a body. A hard body. Not Phoebe then. I tilt my head back to find Grayson standing there looking edible. My palms begin to sweat.

"What are you doing here?" I ask when I manage to force myself to take a step back from his body.

"You said we needed to talk but then you snuck out of the party before we had the chance."

True story. I totally snuck out of the back door at the end of the party after putting off 'the talk' all night long.

"I don't have time for this now." For once, I'm not lying. Phoebe will be here any second.

Grayson smirks. "I'm your driver, and you have an hour before you have to be at Hailey's."

Shit. Phoebe and Hailey the matchmakers from hell strike again! Sneaky Phoebe is getting out of control, and Hailey is the worst influence on her.

"You might as well come in." I motion him inside with a frown on my face.

I shut the door and spin around to find him standing in my foyer. He lunges forward, hauls me into his arms, and slams his lips down on mine. The second his soft lips meet mine, I melt. He smiles against my lips when he feels my surrender and lifts me up. I respond by wrapping my legs around his waist. He moves until I'm pinned to the wall by his body. *Yes.*

He punches his hips forward and his hard cock hits me in exactly the right spot. I groan before grinding down on him. He moans before tearing his mouth away from mine.

"Shit. I didn't come here to do this."

I frown. "You don't want me?"

He presses his lower body forward so I can feel his hardness. "Don't ask silly questions." He pats my legs until I loosen them, and he sets me on my feet. "I'm sorry. I didn't mean to attack you."

"You didn't hear me complaining, did you?"

"No. Some moaning and groaning but no complaining."

I slap him. "No making fun."

"I wasn't making fun. Did you miss my groaning?"

"You need to stop talking about moaning and groaning." My body is already primed and ready to take him, but he wants to talk. The last thing I need is to have a serious talk with wet panties. And this talk of moaning and groaning is not helping the panty situation.

"You wanted to talk," I say once we're seated in the living room.

Grayson smirks. "I believe you're the one who said we needed to talk last night."

Oh right. My brain goes on the fritz whenever he's near. Darn. I thought I could put this talk off until after the wedding.

I stand. "Do you want a drink?"

He wraps his fingers around my wrist, thwarting my escape. "Stop running away."

I yank my hand from his and collapse on the sofa. I wring my hands together as I gather the courage to start this conversation. Ugh. I hate having 'the talk' with a man. Although, if I'm honest, I haven't had many 'talks' with men. Once Toby and I had our blow out, I was done with men. Hailey isn't kidding when she calls me a man-hater. Damn Grayson and his ability to break through all my walls.

"Why don't I start?"

My head whips up at his words. Start? What is he going to start with?

"In case I haven't made it perfectly obvious, I want you, Suzie. And not only to warm my bed at night. Although you and me in bed is fucking fantastic." He wiggles his eyebrows. "I want a relationship and I think you want one, too."

I open my mouth to respond but let's face it, I have no idea what I'm going to say.

"I can be patient. I know I can wear you down. But why waste the time? I think I proved my point last night." He winks.

"What do you mean? You proved your point last night? Was last night about proving a point?" My voice may sound slightly hysterical. I need a man who plays games like I need another fermentation bucket. Oh wait. I could use another fermentation bucket. Never mind.

He clears his throat. "No. I didn't set out to prove a point. I can't resist touching you when you're near. But how you melt when I touch you proves my point. We are explosive together."

"Sex a relationship does not make."

He takes my hand and threads his fingers through mine. "No, sex is not enough. But we're friends. Friends and smoking hot sex does equal a relationship."

Ugh! I hate when he's right. "I thought you didn't want a relationship."

"Like I explained before, I'm ready to try again."

This is all my fault. Why did I have to fix him? Damn me and my awesome ability to help people. I should have let him wallow in his guilt about his best friend's death. Oh boy. Bitchy Suzie has arrived. I tell her to get lost before looking over at him.

"I don't know."

He tugs on my hand until I'm close enough for him to grasp my hips. He maneuvers me until I'm forced to straddle him or fall off the sofa. Forced. Yeah, right.

"Much better."

I roll my eyes. Typical man.

He smooths his hands up and down my sides. "Talk it out."

"You can't seriously want me to talk about my ex-boyfriend with you."

He smirks. "Where are you sitting?"

Did he hit his head? "In my living room."

"No." He squeezes my hips. "Where are you sitting at this moment?"

"On your lap." Where is he going with this absurd line of questioning?

"Exactly." He leans forward and kisses the tip of my nose. "You are currently in my arms, not your asshat ex's. Now, lay it on me. What's your excuse this week for not wanting to be together?"

"This week?" I bristle. "You act like I'm making up excuses."

He raises an eyebrow. "Aren't you?"

I try to stand, but he holds me tight. I cross my arms over my chest and narrow my eyes on him. "I am not making up excuses! I don't want a relationship."

"Okay. Let me ask you this. How would you feel if I hooked up with one of the single women at the wedding tonight?"

I will kick her ass. How dare some woman move in on my man? My man? Well, shit. My head falls forward and hits his shoulder. "What if this all blows up in our faces?"

He grasps my chin and lifts my head. "What if it doesn't? No." He shushes me when I try to speak. "Don't start listing all of the reasons this won't work. Think about how glorious it will be when it does work."

"You sound awful sure of yourself."

"I'm not saying I'm ready to move in and get down on my knee to propose, but I am sure you are worth taking a risk for."

What can I say when his gorgeous face is grinning at me, sincerity is shining from his eyes, his dimples are out, and his mint and vanilla scent is surrounding me? Ugh. "Fine. We'll give it a try. But when it all burns to ashes, I get to say I told you so."

"Nothing is going to burn to ashes, except for your reservations about being in a relationship."

"I—"

"No. The time for talking is done. We have fifteen minutes before I need to drive you to Hailey's house."

"Fifteen minutes is not enough time for a quickie," I protest. I'm sure in a year or two I'll be okay with having a quickie with the man. For now, though, I need all the time possible to explore his body properly.

"Who said anything about a quickie? We're going to make out like teenagers on the sofa until it's time to go."

In the end, I'm ten minutes late arriving at Hailey's and it's a good thing a hairdresser is available because my hair is an absolute mess from Grayson running his hands through it. I'm also glad I packed an extra pair of panties in my bag because mine nearly went up in flames when Grayson yanked off my jeans and decided he just had to taste me before we left.

You won't hear me complaining.

The wedding preparation distracts my mind from the terrifying fact that I made a decision – a decision that may very well blow up in my face. I don't want to lose Grayson as a friend. But he's right. I'd be a fool – and a wimp – to not take a chance and see where our relationship takes us. I'm okay with being a fool. But a wimp? Suzie is not a wimp. Besides, I have a butcher knife perfect for cutting off his balls should he ever decide to cheat on me.

Chapter 29

Everybody believes in something. I believe I will
have another beer.

Pops gasps when Hailey steps out of the bride's room into the hallway where the wedding party is waiting for her in order to start the ceremony.

"Babycakes," he mutters as he envelopes her into his arms. "You are the most beautiful bride in the world."

He's not wrong. Hailey's ivory wedding gown is made of shiny satin and fits her to a T. It's also sleeveless, backless, and sexy as hell. Aiden is going to lose his mind when he sees her. When Hailey sniffs, I look away to give them some privacy for their father-daughter moment.

"At least she doesn't have to worry about who will walk her down the aisle," Phoebe complains.

"Pheebs, you have five men vying for the privilege of walking you down the aisle. Sure, your ex-husband is a total a-hole rotting in prison and your birth family sucks donkey balls, but your *real* family is way cooler than those asshats."

I hold up my hands and make devil's horns to illustrate to her exactly how cool her new family is.

"She's right." Ryker kisses her forehead. He holds out his elbow for her. "You ready?"

Ryker and Phoebe are first up to walk down the aisle. I make sure they are in place in front of the closed doors with Sam, Aiden's best man, lined up right behind them before approaching Hailey.

"Are you ready?"

She sniffs again. I wag a finger at her in warning. "Oh no, you don't. No crying. At least wait until Aiden sees you before you ruin your make-up. Probably best to wait to ruin your make-up until after the pictures are taken too. The photographer looks mean."

"Hey!" The photographer who is kneeling in the corner taking pictures doesn't think much of my comment. I wink at her to let her know I'm merely calming the bride down.

Hailey throws her arms around me. "I love you, Suzie Q."

"Okay, okay." I bat her arms away. "Stop with the emotional stuff before a rumor starts you're pregnant."

"After all the champagne I drank this morning?"

Good point. I squeeze her hands and get serious for a second. "I'm happy for you, Hailey. You done good."

I can't express how happy I am for her. My best friend has been pining for Aiden since she first set eyes on the boy in high school. It took more than a decade for them to get over themselves and find love with each other, but they made it. And today they're getting hitched.

I release her hands and pat her thigh. Hold up. Why am I feeling something hard? "Are you armed?" I hiss at her.

She giggles. "Of course, I am."

Is she kidding? She better be kidding. "You can't go into a church armed in a wedding dress. God will smite you!"

"Smite me? Look at you using big words." She leans close and whispers, "It's a garter belt."

Pops walks over. "Time to get you married, Babycakes."

I wave and make my way to my position in the line. The music starts and the doors open. Ryker winks at Phoebe, and they start up the aisle. Once they arrive at the altar, it's time for Sam and me to make the trek.

Don't trip. Don't trip. I concentrate on putting one foot in front of the other. When I manage the first steps without tripping over my own two feet, I exhale in relief. I got this. We make it to the front rows where the uncles and Grayson are sitting without a problem. Grayson turns toward me, and my mouth drops open when I see him wearing a suit and tie for the first time. Grayson in jeans and a t-shirt is hot. Grayson in a suit is sizzling. Oh my.

My heel catches on the carpet and I stumble. Sam lifts me by my arm to stop me from falling on my face. "Steady on, klutzy girl."

I roll my eyes but manage to reach the altar and take my place next to Phoebe without further incident.

"You lost me ten bucks," she hisses.

I am not dignifying her words with a reply. If she was stupid enough to bet on me not tripping while walking down the aisle, it's her own fault. Besides, I blame Grayson. If he didn't look good enough to eat, I wouldn't have tripped.

The wedding march begins, and everyone stands to watch Hailey walk down the aisle. I concentrate on Aiden instead. I can tell the exact moment he sees Hailey in her wedding dress for the first time. His eyes light up and heat flares in them. His hands ball into fists as he watches her walk toward him. I giggle when he takes his first step forward. He doesn't stop with one step. Not Aiden. He marches straight down the aisle and meets his intended halfway.

Hailey laughs, but Pops does not look happy. He refuses to let go of his daughter. A tug of war ensues, and the music stops. The guests are now all laughing. Finally, Hailey grasps Aiden's left hand in hers and tugs as she starts moving. The wedding march resumes, and the three of them walk down the rest of the aisle together.

"Who gives this woman to be married to this man?" the preacher asks when the gaggle of three finally reach the alter.

Pops looks down at Hailey and winks. "She gives herself but with her father's blessing."

"And her uncles' blessings!" The uncles can't help themselves from adding. I'm surprised they let Pops walk Hailey down the aisle by himself.

Pops kisses Hailey's forehead and gives Aiden one last scowl before moving to his seat in the front pew. Hailey hands her bouquet to me and the ceremony begins. The ceremony itself is short. Hailey wanted a big wedding but not a long and boring ceremony. In no time, the preacher is asking for the rings and the vows are being recited.

As soon as his ring is on Hailey's finger, Aiden bends forward to kiss her. The preacher clears his throat. When Aiden looks over, he shakes his head. "Not yet," he whispers.

"Then get to the part where you declare us man and wife," Aiden insists. Someone is more than ready for Hailey to be his wife.

I wish I could find a love like theirs. But love and marriage are not in the cards for me. My eyes drift to where Grayson is sitting. He meets my gaze and smiles, causing his dimples to pop out. My knees go weak. What is wrong with me? I don't do weak knees! The man is going to make me forget men are scum who are not to be trusted.

Why did I agree to give a relationship with him a try? I'm obviously losing my mind being surrounded by all these loving couples and their icky shows of personal affection.

"By the power of your love and commitment, and the power vested in me, I now pronounce you husband and wife! You may kiss each other!"

"Finally," Aiden grumbles before drawing Hailey into his arms and bending her backward to kiss her.

The uncles hoot and holler until Aiden releases Hailey. When Hailey looks my way, a smile stretches across her face from ear to ear. I barely manage to hand her the bouquet before Aiden rushes her down the aisle. I shake my head as I follow.

I'm surprised to find Grayson waiting for me when the photographer is finally done with taking pictures. I was kidding earlier about her looking mean, but now I know the truth — she is mean! She had to have been lying when she said my eyes were closed. There's no way my eyes were closed for ten straight pictures!

"Why are you here?"

Grayson doesn't bother responding to my question. "You have everything?"

At my nod, he places his hand on my lower back and escorts me to his truck. He has to help me into the truck since my bridesmaid dress was not made for movement. Seriously. I feel like someone rolled me into a swath of satin. Uncomfortable is entirely too mild a description for this dress.

"By the way," he says as his hands skim over the satiny material of the dress, "you look beautiful."

I roll my eyes. Me and beautiful don't belong in the same sentence. "No need to flatter me. You're getting laid later either way."

He snarls and leans forward to get all up in my face. "You are beautiful, and I'll compliment you as often as I want. I'm not saying the words to get laid. You hear me?"

"Yes," I agree because he's kind of freaking me out right now.

When we arrive at the reception, I'm not surprised to see Grayson is seated at the table for the bridal party. Hailey and Phoebe think they're being sneaky and pushing us together. They can think whatever they want. It doesn't mean they're right.

While we eat, Grayson and I laugh and joke. I'm relieved we can still act like friends despite the basis of our relationship changing. It's not exactly the same, though, with him causing a trail of fire to break out on my skin whenever he 'casually' touches me. The man is a great big tease I tell you!

When the dancing starts, I abandon him and rush out onto the dance floor. Hailey and Phoebe follow me, and we get our groove on to the eighties music the DJ is playing. I thought Phoebe would be too stiff to dance with us. She is a recovering spoiled rich girl after all, but she has no problems abandoning decorum to strut her stuff.

When the DJ announces he's taking a break, I make my way back to the table and collapse in my chair. Grayson hands me a glass of water. I make a face at him – where's my beer? – but dutifully drink the water.

I haven't had the chance to catch my breath before Phoebe arrives. "Come on." She takes my hand and tries to tug me out of my chair. I don't know what she's up to, but I'm not going anywhere. "It's the bouquet toss."

"Hard pass." I have no intention of trying to catch the bouquet, let alone actually catching it. No way. I may have agreed to attempt a romance with Grayson, but this girl is not willing to go any further. I am not getting married. Never ever.

Oh, grow up, Adult Suzie orders. Her voice is slurred – someone has been hitting the open bar hard – which means I'm free to ignore her.

Phoebe grunts and suddenly I'm flying out of my chair. "How the hell did you manage to pull me out of my chair?" I ask when I find myself in her arms.

She doesn't answer. Instead, she maneuvers us toward the dance floor where Hailey stands waiting. Phoebe doesn't stop until we're smackdab in the middle of the floor directly behind the bride. I, for one, am not liking the current situation.

The music starts and Hailey twirls around. The DJ starts counting down. "Three, two, one!"

The bouquet flies into the air. Shit. It's heading straight for me. I take a step to the side and it falls to the floor. I watch as it lays there. No one pounces on it. What the hell? I'm used to all the single ladies diving for the bouquet. What's going on?

I look around and notice I'm standing all alone on the dance floor. The uncles and Pops are guarding the edge of the area while holding the other women back.

"You promised no pranks!" I shout at them.

"It's for your own good," Pops claims. Easy for him to say. He's not in the line of fire.

Hailey marches to me, picks up the bouquet, and slaps it into my chest. I grab it before it can fall again. Cheers ring out.

I hold out the bouquet to Hailey. "Nope. I am not taking it back. Deal with it," she says and stomps away. It's kind of impressive watching her stomp in those obnoxiously high heels Phoebe insisted she buy.

I know when I've lost. I walk back to the table and slam the bouquet on the table. "This is ridiculous!"

Grayson doesn't have a chance to answer before the DJ announces it's the men's turn. My mouth drops open as he stands. He winks at me before sauntering off to the dance floor.

"What are you doing?" I scream at his back. Confession – I may be screeching at this point. What? Give me a break. I'm starting to panic here.

I stand and walk to the edge of the floor to watch. Maybe I can prevent whatever disaster is about to happen. Hailey is now sitting on a chair in the middle of the dance floor and Aiden is on his knees in front of her. She gathers the folds of her gown and starts to drag it up her legs, but he growls to stop her.

"These fuckers are not going to see your legs." He dives under her dress.

Someone grumbles, and I look up at Pops next to me. "I thought you liked Aiden."

"Doesn't mean I need to see him with his head under my baby girl's dress."

Before I have a chance to remind him Hailey is no longer a baby, Aiden emerges and lifts his hand holding the garter in victory. He doesn't bother turning around and counting off. He throws it straight to Grayson with a smirk.

"This is some bullshit right here."

I lift the hem of my dress intent on making a run for it. I don't make it one step before Pops blocks me. Then, Grayson is there taking my hand and leading me to the dance floor. How is this happening? The lights dim, the music starts up, and Ed Sheeran's voice begins to sing.

Hailey and Phoebe shout and clap. I flip them off behind Grayson's back. Their response? They laugh. They fricking laugh!

"This doesn't mean a thing," I tell Grayson as we sway to the music.

"I know, Precious. I know."

He draws me close and I lay my head on his shoulder. His arms wrap around me making me feel like the precious person he calls me. Well, shit. This is not good. Adult Suzie disagrees. *This is not good. This is fantastic!* I tell her to shut up and enjoy my moment with Grayson. Because there is no doubt in my mind, this can't last.

Chapter 30

If beer isn't the answer, your question sucks.

BACK AT WORK A few days later, I find myself slamming the phone down.

"What did the phone do to you?" Phoebe asks as she walks out of her office and sits on one of the chairs in front of my desk.

"Stupid clients and their stupid prejudices."

"You certainly cleared things up for me."

I snarl at her. "Since when are you snarky?"

She ignores my question. "Are you going to avoid the question all morning?"

"Don't you have work to do?"

"Not really. Things are slow. Apparently, February is not a popular month to cheat your insurance company."

"Why don't you go play hide the cannoli with Ryker then?" I must be desperate to avoid her questions if I'm suggesting a little love in the afternoon to distract her.

She giggles while her cheeks flame. "Ryker's leaving in ten minutes to go chase a skip."

Great. Phoebe and I will be all alone in the office then.

"You and Grayson looked snug as a bug at the wedding on Saturday."

And now you know why I'm not excited to be stuck alone with her in the office. I don't want to talk about my 'relationship' with Grayson with her. I'm not ready to dissect my relationship with anyone. Least of all myself.

I decide to misdirect her by answering her initial question. "A potential client canceled her appointment."

"Why? Did something happen?" She leans closer. "Did she find her husband in the act with his secretary?"

"Why is it always the secretary?" I shake my head. "But no. She does need PI services just not our services. When I told her Hailey was on her honeymoon, she became belligerent."

"Belligerent?"

"You know aggressive, confrontational—"

Phoebe holds up her hand. "I know what the word belligerent means. Why was she belligerent?"

"She doesn't want a PI who is recently married. She started ranting about happily married women being horrible people who could suck her dick."

"I thought it was a woman?"

I don't get a chance to answer before the door opens and a delivery man steps inside. "Phoebe Adams?"

Phoebe sighs before getting to her feet. "Let me guess. You have a package for me."

After she signs for the delivery, he leaves, and she sets the box on my desk. "Aren't you going to open it?"

She motions to my desk. "Knock yourself out."

She doesn't have to tell me twice. I rip off the wrapping paper to find a bottle of Stolichnaya vodka. Phoebe's brand of vodka. She's a bit of a vodka snob who's addicted to vodka martinis. Ryker tried to switch her onto American vodka, but he failed – big time.

"How much do they think I drink? At this rate, I'll have enough vodka to drink until I'm old and gray."

"Like you will ever go gray."

"Not on purpose anyway."

"And who's they?" I tap the card that came with the gift. The card I didn't touch because opening someone else's gift is totally normal but reading the card? That's an invasion of privacy. "You didn't even look at the card."

"I don't need to. It came from one of Hailey's uncles."

Ryker steps out of their office. "Princess, you need to make up your mind who is going to walk you down the aisle."

"And stop getting deliveries of vodka?"

Deliveries she was not two minutes ago complaining about. Someone's dragging her feet. Interesting.

Ryker grunts. "You need to set a date. I want you wearing my rings and my last name."

"You don't wear a last name," she sasses.

"Babe."

I giggle. Whenever Ryker says babe, the conversation is over. It annoys Phoebe to no end, which naturally amuses me.

"Leaving, big guy?"

He leans down and kisses her forehead. "Be good. I'll be back in a day or two."

I wait until I hear the ding of the elevator before confronting Phoebe.

"Why are you dragging your feet about the wedding? I thought you loved Ryker and want to marry him."

"I do." She slumps in her chair. "But another wedding?"

I'm surprised she doesn't want a wedding. The woman does love to dress up. "Then don't have a wedding. Elope."

"I can't. I promised … Hold up." She wags her finger at me. "How come it's okay for you to ask questions about my love life but I can't ask about yours?"

"Because I can obviously solve all your problems. Now, tell Suzie all about it."

To my surprise, my tactic works.

"Ryker wants a wedding. I want to elope."

"The man who just left this office would give you the world. I'm sure he'll agree to elope if you give him the right incentive." I wiggle my eyebrows.

"But I love him, and I want to give him everything he wants."

"And he wants a wedding?" I'm surprised. I wouldn't expect the big, bad bounty hunter to care one way or another as long as Phoebe is his in the end – his to protect, his to love.

"What's wrong with having a wedding? You looked like you had a good time at Hailey's wedding."

"She had a fruit and bubbly bar. What's not to love?"

I can't argue with her there. I don't drink champagne, but I couldn't help but be impressed with the setup. Of course, the fact she also had cases of my beer didn't hurt.

I refuse to be distracted. I drum my fingers on my desk and wait Phoebe out.

"Fine. I wasn't allowed to give any input into my first wedding, okay? I have no idea how to put together a wedding."

Is she serious? Ms. Always Perfectly Put Together is worried about planning a wedding? "Do you think Hailey knew how to plan a wedding before she started planning hers?"

"Please. Hailey has been dreaming of her wedding to Aiden since she first caught sight of the man. She knew exactly what she wanted."

Ah, now we're getting to the heart of the matter.

"You don't know what you want at a wedding, do you?"

Her arms flail. "How could I? I don't have any idea what my clothing style is, how am I supposed to figure out a wedding."

I frown. Now she's looking for excuses. The woman has a very distinct clothing style. I don't argue with her, though. Nope. I said I would solve her problems. And solve her problems I will.

"You don't figure it out."

"What? Is a wedding going to magically appear in one of those packages from the uncles?"

"Although that would be cool, it's not what I meant. Hire a wedding planner. It's not like you can't afford it."

Phoebe is rich with a capital R. I don't know precisely how much money she has, but she comes from a wealthy pharmaceutical family. Although they disowned her, she still has a ton of stocks and investments. Why she works is beyond me. I certainly wouldn't if a pot of gold landed on my lap.

"Isn't hiring a wedding planner cheating?"

"Cheating? Who are you cheating on? Is Ryker insisting you put the wedding together on your own?"

"No?"

"There you have it. Pick a date and hire a wedding planner." I tap the bottle of vodka. "Oh, and maybe you can stop tormenting the uncles."

She giggles. "But it's fun."

I knew it! She's already picked out who she wants to walk her down the aisle.

"Who did you pick?"

She mimics a zipper fastening her lips closed.

"Fine. But I'm stealing your vodka, and I refuse to attend another game show set up by the uncles."

"Oh, come on. It was hilarious."

It was a blast, but I'm not admitting to anything.

"Now, it's your turn. What's going on with you and Grayson?"

My phone rings and I practically dive on it. Phoebe tries to get there first but I'm seriously motivated.

"You Cheat, We Eat, Suzie speaking. I'm here to make your life better today."

She narrows her eyes on me, but she doesn't linger. Good thing since I don't know how long I can pretend to have a conversation with a man who admitted he dialed the wrong number and hung up on me.

Chapter 31

Every loaf of bread is a tragic story of a group of
grains that could have become beer but didn't.

PACK A BAG.

Pack a bag? Why does Grayson want me to pack a bag?
Confession – I've kind of sort of been avoiding Grayson since
we decided to start our relationship. Not at Hailey's wedding.
No, Hailey's wedding was awesome. Except for the bouquet toss
stunt. Grrr. But after? It's been the avoidance game all day, every
day.

I'm not trying to be a bitch. That shit happens all on its own.
No, I need time to wrap my head around the idea of being in a
romantic relationship with a man again. Apparently, my silence
is not deterring pushy man Grayson.

Why?

Do as your told.

Do as I'm told? Has he not met me?

I'll make it worth your while.

Little Susan wakes up from her weeklong slumber and cheers.

Make it worth our while! Make it worth our while! Good grief, she got the pompoms out. I tell her to put the damn pompoms away and go pack a bag.

Gee. I hope he cleaned his place. I am not staying there unless he's learned what a vacuum cleaner is since the last time I visited. Oh, stop your judging. I'm not a complete clean freak. Just in case, I pack an additional bag with some cleaning supplies and equipment. Huh. I really proved my point there, didn't I?

The doorbell rings thirty minutes later. I saunter to the door. Oh, who am I kidding? I skip to the door and fling it open.

"Hey, stud muffin."

Grayson shakes his head before leaning down to gently brush his lips with mine. I chase him when he pulls away all too quickly. "Sorry, Munchkin. We've got somewhere to be."

"We do?"

He doesn't respond and instead picks up my bags from the spot next to the door where I left them. He grunts when he lifts them. "What did you pack? The kitchen sink."

"Just some cleaning supplies. In case…"

He drops the heaviest bag. "You won't be needing them. Come on. You ready?"

I eye the bag with my cleaning supplies as I walk to the door. Is he saying he cleaned his apartment? I know military men are supposed to be disciplined with cleaning, but my experience at his place says otherwise.

Grayson takes my hand and leads me outside. "Stop dillydallying."

"Dillydallying? What are you? My grandpa? Who says the word dillydallying anymore?"

He doesn't respond as he escorts me to his truck. Once we're settled, he starts up the vehicle and we're off.

"Where are we going?" I ask when I notice he's headed for the highway.

"I'll tell you where we're going if you tell me why you've been ghosting me all week."

"I haven't been ghosting you all week." I am such a liar.

"I guess I won't tell you where we're going then."

I switch the radio on and fiddle with the station for a few minutes in the lamest attempt ever to stop myself from asking him where we're going. It doesn't take long before I'm begging. "Please, please, please. Tell me where we're going." I flutter my eyelashes and everything.

He snorts. "Are you trying to look innocent? Did you forget I know you're anything but innocent?"

I collapse back in my seat. "Why won't you tell me where we're going?"

"Maybe it's a surprise."

I rub my hands together. "Oh goodie. Let me guess. We're going on a safari."

"It's February in Wisconsin. What kind of safari could we be going on?"

"True. Plus, you didn't tell me to pack my passport."

I drum my fingers. Winter. Winter. Winter. "Are we going bobsledding?" I clap. I've always wanted to try bobsledding.

"You know those bobsleds go like 90 miles per hour."

"I know! I feel the need, the need for speed!" I lift my hand to high-five Grayson, but he shakes his head at me.

"You're harshing my buzz," I tell him when he remains silent.

"All you have to do is tell me why you ghosted me this week and I'll tell you where we're going."

"You're mean. Really mean. Like dirty snake mean." And snakes are horrible. The absolute worst!

He hums like me calling him mean is no big deal. Ugh! Fine! "I wasn't ghosting you. I needed time to think."

He takes my hand and places it on his thigh. "Now, was that very hard?"

"I don't want to talk about it." I try to pull my hand away, but he places his over mine to capture it. And damn it, I like how much he wants to touch me. I am in deep doo-doo here.

"We're going to the brewers' conference."

My mouth drops open as I momentarily forget how to speak. Naturally, it doesn't last long. "*The* brewers' conference. The conference with hops workshops, basic microbiology, quality workshops, and much much more!" I may be screaming by the time I finish.

Grayson hunches over. Yep. I was totally screaming.

"Oh my god. Oh my god." I clap. "I've always wanted to go, but it's not cheap and—" I narrow my eyes and look over at him. "Grayson, tell me you didn't spend all your money on this."

"I didn't spend all my money," he quips.

I slap his arm. "You know what I mean. This conference costs like over a thousand dollars. You shouldn't be spending that kind of money on me."

Grayson growls. "I will spend however much money I want on the woman I'm dating." He holds up his hand when I start to argue. "No. I don't want to hear it. You are my woman, Suzie, and I want to spoil you. It's the least I can do."

His woman? I am no one's woman but my own. "I am not your woman."

"You're not?" he challenges. "Then, I guess I'm not your man."

"Your…" I trail off. Damn it. I hate it when he makes sense!

"Fine. Tell me all about the conference."

He smirks, and I narrow my eyes on him. If he starts to gloat, I'm jumping out of the truck. I don't care if we're currently driving 90 mph down the interstate. I'll do it!

"The registration details are in the glove compartment. I didn't know what add-on workshops you would want to go to, so I signed up for all of them."

I bite my tongue before I yell at him – again! – for spending too much dang money on me. Does he not understand the whole easing into a relationship thing? I open the glove compartment and find the folder with all the details. My eyes grow wider and wider as I scan the papers.

"You seriously signed us up for everything. Beer styles workshop, draft beer workshop, sensory training."

"Not everything. I didn't figure we needed to know about human resources or pairing beer with food."

Good call. "Hey wait. You said we. Are you doing all of the workshops with me?"

I watch as his cheeks darken to a dusty shade of pink. He looks adorable! "Um, I thought if I'm going to help you with the marketing, it would be helpful to know more about the brewing itself."

My heart speeds up until it's racing. Thumpity thump thump. I place my hands over my ribcage to stop the thing from beating its way clear out of my chest.

"I'm sorry. I shouldn't have presumed."

"No, no, no. You misunderstand me." I swallow and dive in. "You know how my ex Toby and I were going to start a brewery together?"

"I know. I don't mean to take his place."

"Silly man. You could never take his place." He looks over at me, and I see the flash of pain in his eyes before he blinks, and it disappears. I slap his thigh. "Don't be stupid. You could never take his place because you are twenty gazillion million times better than him."

"Twenty gazillion million? Is that the technical term?"

"Don't make fun of me when I'm trying to be honest."

He makes a motion with his hand as if to tell me to continue.

"Um…" I take a deep breath and try to sort through my thoughts. Why is this so danged hard?

"One of the reasons I felt betrayed when Toby … you know…" He nods in understanding and I force myself to continue. "He not only proposed after I found out about his pregnant girlfriend, which was after he told me he never wanted children." Growl. "He also wanted to continue our brewery business together. He didn't understand why I was upset. He said the business and our relationship were two different things.

Total and utter bullshit since the whole brewery thing was his idea. I only learned brewing for him."

Grayson wraps his hand around my thigh. "I want to say it's not a big deal I'm learning all of this for you because I know you are freaking out right now."

I am totally freaking out. We started a relationship a week ago. Seven measly days! I thought we would ease into this. But no, the Army man is jumping in combat boots first.

"But I'm not going to lie to you. I like my balls where they are, thank you very much."

"The knife I have picked out wouldn't be too painful."

"How did I know you already had the knife picked out?" He chuckles as if he's not afraid of my knife-wielding ways. "Precious, the truth is I am learning all of this for you. I know how busy you are between the PI business and your brewing. If learning about brewing allows me to spend more time with you, then that's what I'll do."

Damn him. He knows exactly what to say to melt my reservations away. Toby never wanted to learn anything for me. Everything was about him, him, him.

Did I say I was in deep doo-doo? I was wrong. I am knee-deep in doo-doo and sinking fast.

Chapter 32

Today I was a hero. I rescued some beer trapped
in a bottle.

"Today was the Best. Day. Ever," I say as I collapse onto the bed in our hotel room.

I am exhausted with a capital E, and my feet are killing me. Shitkicker boots is not the way to go if you're walking around a conference center all day. And I think my brain is about to burst from all of the information I learned at today's workshop. I thought I knew all there is to know about the different beer styles. I was wrong.

But do I care? Not even a tiny bit. I had way too much fun to care about silly things like my feet no longer being able to support my body and my brain exploding.

Grayson plops down on the bed next to me. "There is a lot more to brewing than I thought. And I am not looking forward to the microbiology workshop tomorrow. I am not into science. Give me a weapon, tell me the current wind speed and direction, and I can calculate the change in trajectory to hit my target, but biology and chemistry?" He shivers.

I pat his leg. "Don't worry. I'll let you cheat off me."

His stomach growls, and I groan. "I guess we have to move because someone needs to be fed."

"I can order a pizza. I saw a take-out menu on the desk."

"Oh, thank goodness. I don't think I can move." My eyes are already closing. Just a small nap and I'll be ready to go.

"Not even for a meat lover's double cheese pizza?"

My eyes snap open and now it's my stomach's turn to growl. I guess I'm hungry, too. "Sounds perfect."

Grayson stands and slaps my thigh. "Why don't you get showered while I order the pizza?"

Get showered? Is he out of his mind? I am not moving. I'm perfectly happy to sleep in my own filth tonight.

I startle awake when a weight lands on my chest. My eyes snap open to find Grayson smirking from above me. "What?"

He doesn't answer. Instead, his lips trace my neck as he nibbles and bites his way to my ear. "Too tired?"

Tired? Who's tired? "For some reason, I'm not feeling tired anymore."

"Are you sure?" He bites my earlobe and I moan. "I can get up and take my shower."

I wrap my legs around his hips. "Don't you dare move."

He presses his pelvis into mine and I can feel how hard he is. My stomach dips and tingles erupt in all the right places.

"Don't move at all?" His hand squeezes my breast and even through several layers of clothing, it feels incredible. "I shouldn't do this, then?" He pinches my nipple and my back arches of its own accord.

His hand drops and I open my eyes to glare at him. "Why did you stop?"

He crawls backward before standing. "I think you're wearing too many clothes."

I agree. Way too many clothes. "Race you," I say as I jump to my feet.

I whip my sweatshirt over my head and rid myself of my bra. Then, I unsnap and unzip my jeans and push them down my legs together with my panties. Shit. My boots. I forgot all about them. Stupid boots. I try to kick them off without unlacing them to no avail. They are laced up tight. I move to sit on the bed, but I miss my mark and end up sliding down the side of the bed to end up flat on the floor on my naked ass.

"Shit."

Grayson chuckles. "Need some help, Munchkin?"

I raise my head, ready to give him a piece of my mind for laughing at me, but when I notice he's stark naked with his cock hard and pointed in my direction, any response I had is completely forgotten.

I rise to my knees, the jeans wrapped around my ankles and the boots I was desperately trying to rid myself of mere moments before completely forgotten, and inch closer to his mouth-watering cock. I lick my lips.

Grayson groans. "Don't look at me like that if you want me to last until I'm inside you."

I wink up at him. "Maybe I want you to be inside another part of me."

In case there's any confusion as to what I'm referring to, I grab hold of his length and dart my tongue out to lick him from base to tip. He growls and his hands land on my head.

"You don't have to," he pants.

I smirk up at him. "What if I want to?"

Before he can respond, I take his cock into my mouth as far as I can. Not all the way. I may have a big mouth but apparently, it's not big enough for his cock. While my mouth moves up and down his length, I use one hand to cup his balls and the other to squeeze the base of his cock where my mouth can't reach.

Grayson's hands tighten on my head until I can feel his fingernails digging into my scalp. Being able to drive this man to the brink of his control makes me feel powerful and sexy. I squirm as I feel myself getting wet.

Pre-cum leaks from his tip and I swipe my tongue to gather it. Mmm… salty. I run my tongue around his tip until he's pushing on my head. I grin and take him in deep. When he hits the back of my throat, I swallow.

Suddenly, I'm flying through the air. "I wasn't finished."

"Yes, you are, you little tease."

Like he doesn't ever tease me.

I land with my back on the bed and Grayson tugs on my right boot until it comes free. He throws it behind him before doing the same with the other boot. Once my boots are gone, he yanks my pants off. Now I'm completely naked like the man standing above me. Hurray!

Grayson presses his palms against my inner thighs until I widen my legs. He runs his fingers up and down my legs. With each pass, his fingers come closer and closer to where I need him most before dropping back down again.

"Stop teasing me," I growl.

He smirks. "Like you didn't tease me."

I totally did. I guess I can take a bit of teasing. I drop my head and close my eyes to concentrate on the feel of Grayson's roughened hands against my thighs.

"Are you wet for me?"

Of course, I am. "Why don't you find out for yourself?"

His hands stop roving and his fingers dig into my thighs as he wrenches my lower body off the bed. I open my eyes to watch the show. His fingers separate my folds before his tongue swipes my seam. When his mouth latches onto my clit, I nearly come off of the bed.

"I love how you taste."

Those words from him are the sexiest thing I've ever heard. "Grayson," I sigh.

"Right here, Precious. Right here," he says against my skin and the sound reverberates through my body. My nerve endings catch fire and I forget how to form words. The only thing I can do is moan as his tongue swirls around my clit before dipping low and entering me.

The tingling in my stomach rushes through my body and I explode with a shout. "Yes!"

Grayson continues to lick and suck as I ride my orgasm. When the aftershocks finish, he releases me and places my lower body back on the bed before crawling forward.

"My turn," he growls before slamming into me.

My legs wrap around his waist and I arch my back. He leans forward and captures my right breast in his mouth. His teeth come out to play and it's like there's a direct line from my breast to my pussy. It flutters and I can feel another orgasm building. The things this man can do to my body.

"Feels. Good," he grunts as his strokes increase in pace. "Not gonna last."

Suddenly, he stops. What the hell? I pummel his back. "Why are you stopping?"

"Forgot the condom."

"I'm not on birth control," I squeak as I push on his shoulders in a complete panic.

"We could see what happens."

My eyes widen. "See what happens? Are you insane?"

"You do make me crazy."

"I don't think now is the time to discuss whether we want to bring a hellion into the world."

I swear I see disappointment in Grayson's eyes but when I look closer there's nothing there. I'm seeing things. Grayson doesn't want to have a child with me. We've been dating a week. A week, I remind myself.

He starts to glide in and out again and I nearly forget what we were talking about. "I'll pull out."

I want to remind him pulling out is not an effective means of birth control, but he pinches my nipple and swirls his hips and I forget my name.

His strokes speed up once again until I'm squeezing his length and screaming out his name.

Before my orgasm has waned, he pulls out. His hand jacks his length up and down until he explodes all over my stomach. He grins as he stares at his seed on my stomach before reaching forward and rubbing it into my skin.

Seriously? "Do you have to mark your territory?"

"Yep." He doesn't bother to look at me and continues to stare at his seed.

"Men." I slap his shoulder and push him to get off of me. "Now, I have to take a shower."

Grayson jumps to his feet and pulls my hand to help me up. "Excellent idea."

He slaps my ass as I walk past him to the bathroom. "And, if you're a good girl, I'll let you get me all dirty again."

"Wherever did you get the idea I'm a good girl?" I wink before racing to the bathroom.

Grayson catches me and throws me over his shoulder. "I guess I'll have to punish you then."

Who can say no to the sexy man? Not me.

Chapter 33

"Do you want another beer?" is the most ridiculous question I've ever been asked.

I walk into McGraw's Pub with my hand in Grayson's the following weekend but come to a complete and total stop when I see Wally's hair. Or what's left of Wally's hair I guess I should say. Although he usually has a short military-type haircut, his hair is nearly shaven now and there's a blue tint to it.

Wally points at me. "Not a word, kid. Not a word."

I cough to hide my giggle. "I can't wait to hear the story," I murmur to Grayson who shakes his head at me.

"You are a menace."

"Me? I didn't dye his hair blue."

"That was me," Pops announces to the entire bar. His attention focuses on Wally. "You deserved it and you damn well know it."

My eyes widen. What did Wally do? And why isn't Pops telling everyone? Oh, is it a secret? I rub my hands together as the excitement to find out what happened builds.

"No."

I blink up at Grayson. I kind of forgot he was there for a second. "What? No?"

He places his hands on my cheeks and leans in close. "No snooping around to find out what Wally did."

I flutter my lashes. "Me? Snoop?"

He smirks. "Try your little miss innocent act with someone else. I ain't buying."

"Hey, Suzie," Barney shouts. "What do you call a blonde who dyed her hair?"

"I don't know, what?" Watch out! Lame joke approaching.

"Artificial intelligence."

I giggle as I watch Sid's face darken. He smacks Barney across the head. "Hey, fucker, I have blond hair."

Barney bobs his head. "Exactly." Sid smacks him upside the head again. He kind of deserved it.

The door behind us opens. "Hey! What's the holdup?" Hailey says as she stands in the doorway right behind us. Her skin sports a dark tan, which stands out all the more since everyone else in Wisconsin is pasty white at this time of year.

I tackle her. "Welcome back!"

She cringes. "Can you not shout in my ear?"

I release her and step back. "Probably, but it doesn't sound like much fun."

I snatch her hand and skip to a booth while dragging her behind me. "Tell me all about your honeymoon. I want all the deets." I wiggle my eyebrows. "All the dirty, sexy deets."

Behind her, Grayson grumbles, "If this is going to be a girl talk evening, Aiden and I will be at a pool table."

Aiden chuckles and slides into the booth next to his wife. "Don't worry. Hailey knows better than to share our sex life with Suzie. Otherwise, I'll tan her ass."

"Maybe I like it when you tan my ass," she sasses.

Pops grunts as he arrives at our table. "I don't need to hear that shit."

Hailey pushes Aiden until he's forced to stand, and she rushes to her dad. "Pops!" He lifts her in his arms and twirls her around.

"Hey, Babycakes, how was your honeymoon?" He sets Hailey down and narrows his eyes on Aiden. "Did the kid treat you right?"

Hailey slaps his shoulder. "I thought you approved of Aiden."

"I do. Doesn't mean I have to like the fucker, though," he says and stomps off.

Hailey watches him walk off. "Was that weird? It was weird, right?"

Aiden takes her hand and drags her back into the booth. "He needs time to adjust is all. It's one thing to know your baby girl is getting married. It's another thing to know she's married and now has a man warming her bed every night."

Her brow wrinkles. "How do you know what he's thinking?"

"Because I plan to be the same way with our daughters."

Her eyes widen and she shakes her head. "Our daughters?" She gulps.

"What are we talking about?" Phoebe asks as she and Ryker join us.

I grin. "Hailey's panicking because Aiden brought up children."

Phoebe sits in the chair Ryker dragged over with a frown on her face. "Darn. I thought we were going to spend the evening teasing you for hooking up with Grayson."

Well, shit. This evening took a major nosedive. I push Grayson's shoulder. "Come on. Let's go play some pool." The man does not move. Not an inch!

"I thought you were hungry."

"I'm fine." My stomach growls and makes a liar out of me. Stupid stomach. Why does it insist on being fed?

"A little birdie told me Grayson took Suzie to a brewing festival last week," Phoebe tells Hailey.

"It wasn't a little birdie. I told you. I wasn't trying to hide anything. And it wasn't a beer festival, it was a craft brewers conference."

Hailey stares at me with her mouth hanging open. "Grayson took you to a brewers' conference?" I don't bother responding. I literally told her he did five seconds ago.

"Yep," Phoebe answers. "But she won't tell me anything about what happened. She's been holding out on me."

"What are you talking about? I told you all about the micro-biology class and the beer styles class and—"

Phoebe holds up her hand. "Let me stop you there. You did bore me with all those details no one in the world except you cares about. What we want to hear about is what you and Grayson got up to."

"Come on, Suzie, why don't you give us all the deets?" Hailey mimics my earlier remark.

I growl. She is not amusing.

"Yeah, what's good for the goose is good for the gander."

My brow wrinkles. "I don't understand your analogy. Aren't we both ganders? Wait. Which one is the female, and which is the male?"

Hailey slams her hand on the table. "We will not be distracted."

"I'm out." Aiden stands.

Ryker grunts, which I interpret as *me too*. He kisses Phoebe's temple. "Don't give her too hard of a time, Princess."

But when Grayson stands, I clutch his hand in a panic. "Where are you going?"

He leans down and kisses my forehead. "Don't worry. I'll be back when the food arrives. You can survive fifteen minutes with your best friends, can't you?"

He pries his hand free and follows Aiden and Ryker to the pool table.

"Oh good, now the men are gone, you can tell us how you're doing," Hailey says.

I'm confused. "How I'm doing?"

"You didn't believe I want all the deets of your lovemaking, did you?" Her lip curls. "No, thanks."

Phoebe raises her hand. "I'm okay with details." I raise an eyebrow at her. "What? I'll have you know I'm not a complete prude."

She sure had me fooled. "Whatever."

Hailey reaches across the table to grasp my hand. "Are you okay? Are you and Grayson okay?"

I look away and my gaze falls upon Grayson who is looking my way. He raises an eyebrow in question. He may have left but he didn't abandon me. Knowing he has my back warms my insides. "I'm okay."

Hailey releases my hand and uses her finger to circle my face. "Judging by the look on your face, you are doing more than okay."

I shrug. I can't deny it. I'm sure my face went all soft and smooshy when I looked at Grayson. I can't help it. The man makes me melt.

The door to the pub crashes open and a teenage boy steps in. "Where is he?"

Hailey stands and walks over to the boy. I rush after her. This is going to be good. Phoebe is hot on my heels.

"Can I help you?" Hailey asks.

The boy glares at her. "Are you the owner who hurt my mom?"

"Your mom? Who is your mom?"

"Faith."

My eyes widen. Faith as in the new cleaner, Faith?

Pops walks over. "Can I help you, son?"

"Son?" He spits out. "I am not your son."

Clearly. No child of Pops would be this rude.

Faith rushes in and grips her son's shoulder. "Oliver Benjamin Bakker, what are you doing here?"

"Oh, someone got the middle name treatment. Someone's in trouble," I sing.

Oliver turns his glare on me. "Who the fuck are you?"

Before I can blink, Grayson is looming over the boy. "Is that how you talk to a lady?"

"N-n-n-no, sir?"

"You do not speak to a lady in that way," he schools him. Huh. Would you look at that? I'm a lady now.

"And," Faith pushes her way in between Grayson and her son, "we do not use such language in our household."

The teenager rolls his eyes. "Whatever, ma."

"What's going on, darling?" Pops asks Faith.

"That!" Oliver points at Pops. "That right there is going on. You do not call an employee darling."

"Maybe we should take this conversation somewhere private," Hailey suggests. She gestures toward the back hall where the office is located.

Faith looks around as if she only now realizes she's standing in the entryway of a popular bar on a Saturday night. Her eyes widen before she seizes her son's hand and marches him to the hallway. When Hailey goes to follow, Pops stops her.

"I got this."

Hailey's eyebrows nearly fly off her forehead. "You sure?"

He doesn't bother replying before rushing off after Faith and her son. As soon as he's out of earshot, she starts clapping and jumping up and down.

"Um, why are you acting like me right now?" I ask as I watch her dance in circles.

"Because Pops is in love."

"Pops is in love?" I turn to Phoebe. "And I thought I was the one who leaps to conclusions."

"No, no, no, you don't get it." Hailey drags me back to our booth.

Once we're seated and the men have gone back to the pool tables, she leans forward to whisper. "I saw Faith coming out of his apartment this morning."

"This morning? Are you sure? And why were you here this morning? Didn't you return from your honeymoon this morning?"

She waves my questions away. "I'm sure. Do you want to hear this or not?"

I don't believe there's anything going on in Pops' love life, but I am not stupid. A change of topic away from love life? Yes, please!

"Tell us everything."

Chapter 34

I realize there are better things in life than beer, but beer makes up for me not having any of those things.

I ENTER MY WALK-IN closet on a mission to find my jeans with the pink back pockets and multi-colored patches on the knees. It's Easter and I'm dressing up for the occasion. I open the drawer containing my special occasion clothes, but there are no special occasion clothes here. What the hell?

I open the drawer beneath it and it's the same. Full of Grayson's clothes. I stand and place my hands on my hips. I am not going to panic. I'm not! I will calmly assess the situation. I can be calm.

Two minutes later any thoughts of calm have flown south for the winter with no plans of returning. It's not a big deal I tell myself. Take deep breaths. Inhale through your nose. Good. Now, exhale through your mouth. You can handle this. It's not a big deal I tell myself again.

You love Grayson. What difference does it make if he appears to have moved into your house without your knowledge? Wait!

What. The. Actual. Hell? I love Grayson? What? When? How did this happen?

We've only been dating – I count the weeks with my fingers – for eight weeks. Two months if you want to be technical about it. Not near enough time to fall in love with a man. *But you've been friends much longer*, Adult Suzie reminds me.

Screw her and her little voice in my head. I was sure I had banished her. Where does she get off telling me the truth? Does it look like I want to hear the truth now? In case there's any confusion, the answer is no. No, I do not want to hear the truth right now.

What am I going to do? I eye the suitcase on the floor in the corner. I can run. Not run away. I'm not a complete coward. But I can take a little vacation until my head figures out what the heck to do. My heart has no problems with the situation. She knows exactly what she wants to do. She wants to run downstairs and jump Grayson before telling him we love him.

My heart is the most stupid organ in my entire body. I was with Toby for over a year before I told him I loved him. I snap my fingers. Aha! I simply won't tell Grayson I love him. I'll keep this nugget of information to myself.

What about the clothes in your closet? Adult Suzie asks. I wag my finger at her. She will not goad me into hyperventilating again. Grayson spends nearly every night in my bed anyway. Now that I'm thinking about it, I can't remember the last night the man didn't sleep in my bed. I slap my forehead. The man has committed a sneak attack and I'm the idiot who didn't notice. I promise I'm not always completely oblivious.

"How bad are you freaking out right now?" I startle and jump at the sound of Grayson's voice. "A lot then?"

I am freaking right the eff out, but not for the reason he thinks. But he can't read my mind. He may think he knows me and what I'm thinking most of the time, but he can't literally read my mind. He doesn't need to know about the big revelation I just had. Nope. I am not telling him.

I clear my throat. "I'm not freaking out." Lie. Total lie.

He chuckles. "Sure, you aren't, Munchkin." He gently pushes me down until I'm sitting on the chaise lounge in the middle of my closet. Yes, my walk-in closet is big enough for a chaise lounge. Eat your hearts out, bitches.

Grayson kneels in front of me and takes my hands. "Now, how are you actually doing?"

Umm, I bite my lip before I can shout, *I Love You!!* at the top of my voice. No, I remind Adult Suzie. We are not telling him we love him yet. She pouts and goes off to consult with Little Susan. Great. We all know whose side Little Susan is on.

"I'm okay. But when did this happen? Did you move in and forget to tell me?" I go for sass. My tried and true method of hiding how badly I'm freaking out.

"I didn't exactly move in."

Yeah, right. I motion with my hand to the closet full of his clothes. "How is this not moved in?"

"I still have my apartment."

I raise an eyebrow. "And when was the last time you went there?"

He takes a moment to think. "I picked up my mail there two weeks ago."

"Really? Because I'm pretty sure I found some mail from your college addressed to this address." It may be painfully obvious what's happening here, but I am determined to get him to confess.

I try a different tactic. "I thought your counselor said you shouldn't be making any big decisions now?" He's been seeing a counselor since our big blowout over my visiting Liz.

He shrugs. He hates talking about his counselor. Annoying.

"You promised you would always be honest with me," I remind him.

"I thought if I moved in nice and slow you would accept it better than me showing up with boxes and boxes of stuff."

He's not wrong. "Is there any stuff left at your apartment?"

He shrugs. "The furniture. But it's shit compared to yours."

Am I doing this? Am I letting him move in? Pfff. What am I thinking? The man has already moved in and I didn't notice. I am such an idiot.

"Fine. We live together now. Whatever. I expect you to start taking out the trash and helping do the dishes."

"Precious, who do you think's been taking out the trash and shoveling the snow for the past two months?"

He's got me there. A-freaking-gain.

"Since we're finally discussing this, we need to talk about the mortgage and bills."

I stand. "Nuh-uh. I've had enough of the adult stuff for one morning. We'll discuss financial stuff tomorrow." Or never, I think but don't say. "I have an Easter egg hunt to get to."

Grayson studies me for a long minute and I worry he's going to push it. I check to make sure I have my big girl panties on in preparation for a fight. But, lucky for me, because we all know I'm bound to lose any fight this man starts, he drops it.

"Why are we going to an Easter egg hunt anyway?"

"Because it's fun." I don't say duh, but I definitely think it.

"You do realize they won't let an adult participate, don't you?"

Oh, thee of little faith. Oh, thee of little faith.

When we arrive at the Easter egg hunt an hour later, Grayson shakes his head at me when he figures out what's going on.

"You realize this is cheating, right?"

"Cheating?" What is the man talking about? "I'm not cheating. I'm helping."

And I am helping. I may have a ball while helping, but that's not the point. The point is I'm helping young mentally challenged children have an awesome Easter.

"Ms. Langley," a woman shouts as she rushes to me. "Thank goodness, you're here. We have some last-minute details to discuss."

I roll my eyes. "It's Suzie, Emily. You call me Suzie. What last minute details? We do this every year; we should have it down by now."

"Wait." Grayson snatches my hand to stop me before I can follow Emily. "You organized this?"

I blush. He wasn't supposed to find out! I don't need to brag about what I do. I don't do this for me after all. I do it for the kids. In case there's any doubt, I love kids. And not because I'm a big kid myself. Or at least, my disregard for anything resembling adulting isn't the only reason.

Grayson yanks on my hand until I'm in his arms where he squeezes me tight. "I always knew you were hiding a big heart under your sassy mouth but this? You humble me, Precious." My face goes from a slight blush to code red on fire. "God how I love you."

My ears must be deceiving me. He did not just tell me he loves me, did he? I lean away and search his face. His smiling face greets me as if he has nothing to hide.

"Suzie!" Emily yells to get my attention. The chant is picked up from the group of children waiting for the Easter egg hunt to begin. "Suzie! Suzie! Suzie!"

"I need to go," I say and try to conceal the relief on my face. I am not ready to talk about whether he loves me or not. No way, Jose. That particular discussion can wait a while. Like maybe a year or two.

Grayson isn't fooled for one minute. He chuckles and pats my ass. "Go. Go find those Easter eggs."

Two hours later I'm exhausted as I walk toward Grayson. My knees ache and I think I have a bump on my head. I'm also rethinking giving out prizes for the most Easter eggs found next year. One thing is for sure. I'm wearing protective gear next time.

"Why are there grass stains on your jeans and leaves in your hair?" Grayson asks as he plucks a leaf from my hair.

"It was an accident."

Accident my ass. I know Denny pushed me on purpose, but when I spun around to confront him, he looked too dang cute with his bottom lip in a pout and batting his eyelashes at me. I couldn't force myself to yell at him. I am such a pushover.

"What's next?" he asks.

"You can find a chair and relax. Lunch will be ready soon."

"What are you going to do?"

"I need to help prepare the food."

He takes my hand. "Come on then. Let's go help get lunch ready for the kids."

Damn it. He needs to stop being so darn sweet and helpful. How am I going to manage to stop myself from telling him I love him when he is helping out the kids? How?

Chapter 35

Ashes to ashes, dust to dust, life's a bitch and beer's a must.

I'M TRYING REALLY, REALLY hard not to get excited, although it's difficult. Incredibly difficult. But I refuse to bounce in my seat all excited when we're driving to Grayson's hometown to commemorate his best friend's death. And yes, I realize how fucked up I sound.

Before you bring out the rocks to stone me, let me explain. I'm not excited we are commemorating Bill's death. What happened to Bill and how Grayson handled his death is nothing short of tragic. Then, why am I literally sitting on my hands to stop myself from dancing in my seat?

Because Grayson asked me to accompany him to meet Liz today. Eek! I know he told me he loved me at Easter, but we haven't talked about it in the two months since then. Not due to lack of trying on Grayson's part, mind you. He has brought up his love declaration more times than I can count. And I have had an onset of stomach cramps forcing me to rush off to the bathroom every single danged time.

I expect Grayson to recommend I see an internist any day now. Who am I kidding? The man knows exactly why I rush off each and every time he starts talking about his feelings. Because I'm a big fat chicken. Bwak! Bwak!

I'm working on it, promise. I've been practicing telling him I love him in the mirror for weeks. I have no problem telling the mirror I love it, but whenever I can sense the words coming out of my mouth in the presence of Grayson, I freeze, and panic ensues.

Hailey would laugh her ass off if she knew how tongue-tied I am around the man. Me? Tongue-tied? I can hardly believe it myself. Good thing my best friend has no idea I forget how to speak when Grayson is around.

The man himself pulls my hand out from underneath my thigh and places it on his thigh where he laces his fingers with mine. "Don't be nervous."

I'm not nervous. Oh shit, should I be nervous? Now, I am nervous.

He squeezes my hand. "Thank you for coming with me."

"Of course. There's nowhere else I'd rather be."

I'm not blowing smoke up the guy's ass. I'm serious. I don't care where I am as long as Grayson is next to me. I could be hiking through the jungle surrounded by snakes and other creepy crawlers and I'd be fine as long as the man is next to me. And if I had any doubts as to whether I loved the man, those thoughts would have cleared it up.

I cannot allow my thoughts to go down this path. I am not going to blurt 'I love you' out to him while we're on the way to a cemetery.

"What's on the agenda for today?" I ask to get my mind off emotions and feelings and all the icky stuff.

"First, we'll meet Liz and little Grayson at the diner. After lunch, we'll head to the cemetery to see Bill."

"Is Bill buried in Merrill?" He nods. "Is there a veteran's cemetery in Merrill?"

Unlike Hailey, I didn't grow up with a father and a bunch of uncles who served in the military. I don't know much about how these things work.

"No. Bill wanted to be buried near his family."

"His family? Will there be other people there today besides Liz and her son?"

Now, I am starting to get nervous. Don't get me wrong. I usually charm the daylights out of families. I'm the fun sidekick after all. But this is a serious occasion. I can hardly laugh and joke and be klutzy when we're remembering the death of Grayson's best friend.

Grayson squeezes my hand. "His family as in his wife and son."

I let out the breath I didn't realize I was holding. Good. No family to impress.

"We're here," he announces as he parks his truck in front of an old-fashioned diner. "Don't worry. I'm sure Liz forgives you for ambushing her."

My jaw tenses and I snarl at him. How dare he say those words right before we walk inside to meet her? Oh, he is mean.

"I'm teasing," he says as he helps me out of the vehicle.

I slap his shoulder. "You are not funny."

"I'm a little funny."

I purse my lips. "Whatever."

He chuckles as he takes my hand, and we walk into the diner holding hands. As soon as the door opens, little Grayson shouts and runs to us. "Uncle Grayson!"

Grayson picks him up and twirls him around. "What's happening, little man?" he asks when he sets him down.

"It's Daddy's birthday," he announces with a loud voice causing everyone in the place to look our way. When their eyes catch on the little boy, sympathy blooms in their faces.

Geez. Does everyone in the town know Liz's story? I'm not sure I could live in a small town. Oh no. Does Grayson want to move back here since he's finally dealt with his guilt over Bill's death? Grayson takes my hand and drags me back into the present. I guess I can worry about stupid stuff like where I'm going to live for the rest of my life later.

"Liz." Grayson drops my hand and hugs her.

While the hug lingers, I kneel down to face her son. "Hi, Grayson. Do you remember me?"

He nods but moves to hide behind his mom's leg. I tug on my ear lobes and my tongue pokes out. He giggles, which of course encourages me to make more faces because I'm an adult like that.

Grayson pulls me to my feet. "You remember Suzie?"

I smile and wave at Liz and then I ruin everything by opening my mouth. "I'm sorry. I shouldn't have ambushed you. It was unfair to you and—"

She cuts me off when she hugs me. "Thank you. I can never thank you enough," she whispers.

Tears gather in my eyes at her sincere words. "Why are you thanking me?"

"You got him here, didn't you?"

I bite my lip to stop the tears from falling. "I'd do anything for him," I confess in a soft voice.

She ends the hug but keeps her hands on my shoulders. Her smile is blinding. "You would, wouldn't you? I'm glad. Make him happy." She shakes her head as her hands drop. "What am I saying? Keep him happy."

A man behind Grayson clears his throat. "Sweetheart?"

Liz's eyes light up. "Jerry," she murmurs before walking around Grayson to greet him. "I thought you couldn't make it." Jerry? Who's Jerry? Is this Liz's boyfriend? Oh shit, I'm not sure how Grayson will handle his best friend being replaced.

Jerry's cheeks darken. "I, um, switched shifts."

Liz draws him closer. "Grayson, I'd like you to meet Jerry."

Grayson swallows before offering Jerry his hand. "Nice to met you, man."

"I'm sorry for your loss," Jerry says as he engulfs Grayson's hand with both of his. "And thank you for your service."

Grayson coughs and tugs his hand away. "Thanks."

"Should we sit?" I ask to try and draw Jerry's attention away from Grayson who – judging by his inability to look Jerry in the eye – is feeling uncomfortable.

"And this is Suzie," Liz introduces.

I wave and move to take my seat, but Jerry doesn't let me escape. He enfolds me in his arms. "Thank you." Geez. What is it with people thanking me today? "Liz missed Grayson. Thank you for bringing him back into her life."

I can feel the heat emanating from my cheeks. "I didn't do anything."

Grayson hauls me away from Jerry and helps me into a seat. "You did everything," he whispers into my ear before taking a seat next to me.

"Now," he says in a louder voice, "who's hungry?"

"Me!" Little Grayson raises his hand.

I giggle. "Your mini-me is hungry."

Grayson messes with Liz's son's hair. "Then, we shall feed him. What do you feel like? Waffles and ice cream?"

His eyes widen. "You can have ice cream on waffles?"

I laugh. "Little one, much to teach you we have."

To Liz's credit, he looks at his mom. "Can I, Mom?"

"Whatever you want, baby."

He grins. "It's Daddy's birthday. Mom said I can have whatever I want."

I tilt my head and tap my cheek as I pretend to study him. "In that case, I think we're going to need some cake too."

Grayson throws his arm around my shoulders. "You are going to be a great mom."

I snort. "I'm corrupting the child."

He kisses my temple. "No, you are comforting a child who has lost his father on the toughest day of his year."

My stupid eyes well with tears again. What is wrong with them? Do I have extra tears or what? "I'm happy to help," I quip in an effort to tone down this stupid emotional reaction I'm having.

"You're a miracle worker is what you are. I can't wait until you shine your light on our children."

"Grayson Eliot Neill, you will not bring up having children with me today!"

And at least not for a year. Maybe longer. Definitely longer. Much longer. I am not ready to discuss having children with him. Adult Suzie laughs. *Wrong. You want those children bad.* Shut up, I tell her. *This is going to be fun to watch,* she says in a voice full of glee.

Grayson the boy giggles. "You got the middle name treatment. You're in trouble."

I laugh with him. For the rest of the meal, I keep my attention centered on Liz's son. I'm not ignoring Grayson the man. Seriously, I'm not. And I'm not a liar. Well, maybe a little.

Chapter 36

You can't find happiness at the bottom of a beer. Obviously. Who's happy when their beer's gone?

I SIGH AS I collapse on the bed in our hotel room that night. Today was exhausting. Not exhausting as in I walked five miles – although we did walk around the cemetery a lot – but mentally exhausting. To my surprise, it was also a fun day.

Liz and Grayson told a ton of hilarious stories about Bill and how much trouble they got into growing up. Grayson's mom is a saint to have put up with his shenanigans. How many times can a kid get suspended from high school? Isn't there a limit? I should probably feel sorry for all the kids who ended up with frogs and other icky stuff in their lockers, but Grayson says they only targeted kids who were bullies. Bullies suck.

When Grayson and Jerry stalked off to have a man to man talk, I panicked and rushed after them. Liz held me back. I had nearly bit off all my fingernails by the time they returned. I grabbed Grayson's hands and checked his knuckles for bruising and blood. To my relief, there was no sign of a fight. Although I'm sure Grayson could cause a man a ton of damage without getting a mark on himself.

After the cemetery, Liz invited us to her house where we had dinner and cake. Jerry appears comfortable in the house. It's obvious he's spent a lot of time there. I kept my eye on Grayson, but he seemed to handle the replacement of his best friend in stride.

We finally left when it was time for little Grayson to go to bed. But first, he insisted Uncle Grayson read him a story. I may have snuck to the door of the bedroom to watch. My heart about melted when I saw the two of them cuddled up on the bed.

Grayson lays on the bed next to me and wraps his arms around me.

"Now, it's time to talk."

I groan. "We've been talking all day. Can't you just rip my clothes off and ravish me?"

He smirks. "While your idea has merit, we do need to talk."

"About what?" I ask all innocent like.

Grayson chuckles. He doesn't buy my innocent act. Of course not. It is an act after all. He tucks a strand of hair behind my ear. "I told you something important on Easter and you never responded."

I close my eyes and bury my face in his chest. Ugh. His declaration of love is the last thing I want to talk about. "Why can't we avoid talking about this for a bit longer?"

He threads his fingers through my hair and tugs my head away from his chest forcing me to look up at him. "I think two months is enough avoidance."

"You do?" I wrinkle my brow. "Two months is nothing."

His hands tighten on my hair. "Don't be glib."

"But I'm so good at it."

"Enough," he growls. "I know you're scared." I bristle. "No. Don't try to deny it. I know Toby messed your head up to the point you are now afraid I'm going to betray you or some shit."

"I'm not afraid you're going to betray me. I trust you."

I'm not just spouting words. I do trust him. I trust him more than I ever trusted Toby. And therein lies the rub. How can I possibly trust someone I've known for less than a year more than the man I loved for years?

Adult Suzie tuts at me. *You didn't love Toby. You thought you loved Toby. You were wrong.*

Have I mentioned how much I hate Adult Suzie? She's a total pain in my ass. She's also right, and she doesn't hesitate to rub it in. Bitch.

"Then what are you afraid of?" Grayson asks and my attention returns to the man staring down at me with love clearly reflected in his eyes.

"It's all happening too quick. I've known you less time than the time it took me to fall in love with Toby."

Grayson grunts. "Are you seriously going to keep lying to me about loving Toby? You and I both know you never loved the man."

"What? I did love him!" Can you go to hell for lying? Because I am a big fat lying mess.

Grayson doesn't argue or get mad. No, he grins at me and releases my hair to cradle my face with his hands. "Let's forget about Toby. Let's stick to the people in this room on this bed right now. They're the only people who matter. You with me?"

I swallow the lump forming in my throat and nod.

"I love you, Suzie Langley." My heart flutters as my entire body heats and goosebumps erupt across my skin. "And I know you love me."

I roll my eyes. "You had to ruin it, didn't you?"

He ignores my disruption. "I've given you two months to hem and haw and overthink things. Are you about done now?"

Um, no. Hello! Have you met me? I have tons of more problems and obstacles to throw at him. "What about when you move back to Merrill?"

His thumbs rubbing circles into my skin pause. "When I move back to Merrill? When am I moving back to Merrill? Why am I moving back to Merrill?"

"Since you and Liz made up and all, I thought you'd want to move back to your hometown. Wally said you didn't move back here after you got out of the Army because of the situation with Liz and Bill's death."

"Ah, I see." His eyes move to a spot behind me as he formulates his answer. Shit. I was right. He does want to move back here. I panic and verbal diarrhea spews forth from my mouth.

"I can't move here. My whole life is in Milwaukee. My friends, my business, my brewery. I mean, I guess I could move the brewery, but all my contacts are there. And I don't think I could manage living in a small town. Everyone in the diner knew Liz and her story. I couldn't handle walking into a room and knowing everyone knew everything about me. I like my privacy."

"Are you done ranting now?" I wasn't ranting. But I don't bother with an explanation. He's a man. He wouldn't understand.

"Whatever."

"I never planned to move back to Merrill. There aren't a whole lot of job opportunities here. And moving here after ..." He pauses to clear his throat. "... everything I've seen and done seems like moving backwards."

"Oh." I fiddle with a button on his shirt. "Are you planning to stay in Milwaukee then?"

He grasps my chin and forces me to look at him. "I'm not leaving Milwaukee unless you are. I love you, Precious. I'm not going anywhere."

I close my eyes and let the feeling of belonging wash over me. I didn't realize how much I was worried about him moving back to Merrill until we visited today. But he's not moving back. He wants to stay with me.

"Now, is there something you want to say to me? Something about love maybe?"

I slap his chest. "Don't push me."

"Munchkin, if I don't push you, you won't tell me you love me until we're old and gray sitting on our rocking chairs on *your* porch at *your* house."

"Please. Like I'm ever going to go gray."

Grayson wraps his arms around me and hauls me close until my body is flush with his. "I need to hear the words, Precious."

"Fine! I love you. Are you happy now?"

"Ecstatic," he whispers before he molds his lips to mine. I immediately open my mouth and his tongue invades to duel with mine.

I end the kiss before I completely lose my mind in a Grayson fog. We have other things we need to clear up before I forget my name.

"You're not going to propose, are you?" I tilt my head back so I can look him in the eyes. "I'm not ready for an engagement." I'm not sure I ever will be if I'm being perfectly honest with myself. Adult Suzie laughs and laughs and laughs. *Liar. You want to be married to this man more than you want your next breath.*

"No." Grayson chuckles. "I'm not going to propose this minute."

"You need to know I may never be ready to get married." It's important to be honest about these things.

"Not a problem. Wisconsin is a common law state."

I narrow my eyes on him. "What do you know about common law?"

"You're the one who's always bringing it up every time Sid claims he's only been married four times."

"He has been married five times," I insist. "Common law marriage is still marriage."

Grayson rolls us and I find myself on my back with him hovering over me. Sparks erupt when I feel his hardness pressing into my belly. *Yes.*

"Finally, we get to the ravishing portion of our evening. Time to rip my clothes off, bad boy."

"I am not going to fuck you."

My bottom lip juts out in the biggest pout ever.

"No, silly girl, I'm going to make sweet love to the woman I love who finally admitted she loves me, too."

I am totally down with his plan. Totally!

Chapter 37

The past, present, and future walk into a bar. It was tense.

"Where are you going?" I ask Grayson when he misses the exit for the highway the next morning.

"To my parent's house."

"To your parent's house?" I screech and my hands go flailing about. "You want me to meet your parents?"

I am not prepared for this! I need time with my girls to discuss strategy, maybe even a shopping trip with Phoebe to pick out the perfect outfit. And now you know how serious meeting the parents is. I would brave a shopping trip with Phoebe to prepare.

Grayson catches my hand and kisses my knuckles. "They're going to love you."

I am not touching his comment with a ten-foot pool. "I can't believe you want me to meet your parents."

"Do you love me?"

I roll my eyes. The guy needs to stop asking me that question. Last night he made me say *I love you* before he'd let me come. I'm pretty sure his actions constitute cruel and unusual punishment.

"Yes," I grit out.

"Is this relationship serious?"

Oh great. Are we going to have another one of our talks? I could do without. "Yes."

"Then, you're meeting my parents."

I release the breath I was holding thinking this is the end of the conversation. What am I thinking? Of course, it's not.

"And I want to meet your parents when they visit at the end of July."

"We're living together. My parents will be staying with us. I wasn't planning on hiding you in the closet." Don't get me wrong. I'm tempted, but my mom would ferret out Grayson living in the house in a minute flat. The woman is part bloodhound I tell you.

"They're staying with us? Can't we get them a hotel?"

I throw my hands in the air. "Can we talk about this later? Right now, I need to spend my time panicking about meeting your parents."

"Too late," he says and parks the truck on the side of the road. "We're here."

My heart starts to beat at a frantic pace and my hands tremble. Oh shit. Oh shit. Oh shit. Grayson jumps out of the truck and comes to my side to open my door. I debate taking off in his truck, but the uncles never taught me how to hotwire a car. Gross oversight on their part.

"All you have to do is be yourself. They'll love you. They'll probably spend the entire time telling embarrassing stories about me."

My ears perk up. Embarrassing stories? Maybe meeting the parents won't be too bad after all.

Grayson helps me out of the truck, and we walk hand in hand to the front door. Before we reach the porch, the door flies open and an elderly man who looks a whole lot like an older Grayson steps out.

"Grayson? We weren't expecting you."

A woman pushes the man out of the way. "What a way to greet your son, you cretin. Grayson!" Her eyes widen when she notices me. "And a girl!" She claps. "Grayson brought a girl home!"

Grayson chuckles as he steps forward. "Mom, Dad, this is Suzie. Suzie, this is Norman and Armela, my parents."

I reach out my hand. "Mr. and Mrs. Neill, it's lovely to meet you."

His mom swats my hand away. "None of this Mr. and Mrs. Stuff. You'll call me Armela," she says before wrapping her arms around me.

Grayson separates us. "Mom, don't scare her away."

His dad chortles. "Scare her away! This is the woman who slays demons for my son. She isn't scared of a little old hug." He yanks me away from Grayson and pulls me into a bear hug, which lifts me off my feet. To my relief, he lets me down and motions us into the house before he can squash me.

I start to walk inside, but my foot catches on the door sill and I go flying. Grayson wraps an arm around my waist to stop me from falling flat on my face. In my defense, the door sill is elevated way higher than normal.

"Would you look at that? The demon slayer is a klutz." Norman chuckles.

"Dad."

"It's fine." I smooth my hand down Grayson's arm. "He's not wrong."

"And we both know you're not as klutzy as you pretend to be." I ignore him. Now is not the time to discuss my inability to walk with two left feet.

"Come in. Come in." Armela ushers us into the kitchen where we take seats around the table. Before I can blink, there's a coffee cake in front of me and I can smell the coffee brewing.

"When did you get into town?" Armela asks as she serves us cake.

"Yesterday."

"Of course, Bill's birthday." She sniffles but blinks away her tears before they have a chance to fall. Of course, Grayson's parents practically raised Bill. They must be feeling his loss too.

"Where did you stay last night?" Norman asks.

"At a hotel."

"Why didn't you stay here last night?" I blush as memories of all the things Grayson and I did last night flitter through my mind. I wasn't exactly quiet.

Norman looks at my face and winks. "We wouldn't have minded. I'm half deaf anyway."

Armela slaps him. "Stop embarrassing them." Lucky for me, she deliberately changes the subject. "I'll bring out Grayson's baby album as soon as you finish your cake."

I bite my tongue to stop myself from cheering in excitement. Grayson groans.

Armela points at him. "Don't you dare say a word, young man. I have waited a long time for you to bring a woman home."

My eyes widen as I glance over at Grayson. "Have you never brought a girl home before?"

He shrugs. A shrug is not an answer.

Armela pats my hand. "He was waiting for the right woman."

"Mom, stop scaring her."

"What? I'm not scaring her."

She totally is, but I'm not admitting my fear to his parents on the first meeting. What I am going to do is kill Grayson as soon as we leave. How dare he ambush me like this! And could he have warned me his parents are crazy? Yes, yes, he could have.

I shovel my cake in my maw. I want those embarrassing Grayson stories. The shoveling is not due to my desperate need for an excuse to not talk. Nope. This coffee cake rocks.

An hour later I find myself sitting in Grayson's childhood living room laughing my ass off. "He didn't!" I exclaim.

"Oh, he did." Norman frowns at his son. "Nearly got expelled for it too."

"What were they thinking bringing a live animal into a school full of teenagers?" Grayson grumps as I continue to giggle. "It was entirely too much temptation."

"Then it wasn't your fault you set the donkey free?"

"How was I supposed to know the donkey was going to find its way into the cafeteria and steal all the bananas off students' trays?" Notice he didn't deny freeing the animal.

While I wipe tears of mirth from my eyes, Grayson stands. "We need to get going. Suzie has work in the morning, and I have a class."

"You don't get a break for summer?" his mom asks.

He shakes his head. "Summer school."

Armela envelopes me in a hug. "Thank you for bringing Grayson home."

"I didn't—"

She places a finger over my mouth. "Shush. I don't want to hear it."

Her arms have scarcely left me before Norman's grabbing me and giving me another one of his bear hugs. I barely stop myself from squealing as I'm lifted from the ground and twirled around. "You're all right, demon slayer. You're all right."

"Dad," Grayson grumps before freeing me from his dad's hold.

"You'll come up for our July 4th picnic." Armela more or less orders as we walk toward Grayson's truck.

Grayson raises his eyebrow at me. Smart man. He's leaving the answer up to me.

I grin. "Sounds like fun." And I'm not lying. After I got over my nerves, the day ended up being fun. And meeting his parents wasn't too bad. They speak my language – crazy. Looking at Grayson's diaper-clad bottom didn't hurt either.

Besides, wherever Grayson goes I go. I will put up with crazy parents and fireworks for the man. Hell, I'll put up with nearly anything for the man. I'm not quite sure how it happened but I love him more than I could have ever imagined. I can't wait to spend the rest of my life with him. Maybe we'll even get married.

Adult Suzie gives me a thumbs-up. Uh oh. I must be talking crazy if she's agreeing with me.

Chapter 38

Beer! Because no great story ever started with someone eating a salad.

I OPEN THE DOOR to my house – *our* house, Adult Suzie reminds me – and nearly run smack dab into Grayson.

"Hey, what are you doing here?"

"Is that any way to greet your man?"

I roll my eyes before lifting up on my tiptoes to kiss his cheek. "There. Happy now?"

"Yes." He smiles and his dimples come out to play.

What was I thinking? Why did I only kiss his cheek? I lift up on my tiptoes again, but Grayson places a finger over my mouth before I can reach him. I drop down with a big pout on my face.

"What's going on? I thought you were working."

Since there's a the month-long break between the end of summer school and the start of the fall semester, Grayson took a job with a protective services company. Apparently, there are private companies that provide patrol services to towns. Who knew?

Anyway, it turns out Grayson has some super-duper mega top-secret clearance from his time in the Army. The company couldn't hire him quick enough. Unfortunately, he works all hours – nights, weekends, you name it. It's Labor Day weekend and he's scheduled to work the entire three days. I planned to spend the entire weekend in my brew shack.

"No. I have the weekend off."

"What? Since when?"

Grayson looks at his watch. "No time to explain. Come on," he says and picks up two bags. He places his free hand on my back and steers me out the door and toward his truck. "I'll explain on the way."

Except he doesn't explain on his way. He's being all mysterious. Gosh. I hope he's not taking lessons from super-spy, Wally. I'm not sure I can live with a mysterious man. I don't like surprises and I'm nosy as hell.

Maybe he's taking us on a romantic getaway. Little Susan fans herself with both hands. Shut it, I tell her.

He pulls into the parking lot of the airport. *We are going on a romantic getaway!* Little Susan is jumping up and down now. There's no controlling her when she gets like this.

Grayson shuts the car off and turns to me. "Is there any chance I can get you to wear a blindfold and earplugs?"

A blindfold? Earplugs? Little Susan is practically melting. *Tell him yes and ask if he brought handcuffs!*

I look around. "We're at an airport. If you bring me in there blindfolded, Homeland Security will have you arrested so fast it will make your head spin."

Trust me on this. I once made a teensy-weensy, minuscule really, joke about Osama Bin Laden while I was checking in for a flight to Florida for spring break during college. I won't go into details, but someone did not make it to Florida for spring break that year. That no-fly list stuff is no joke.

"Will you at least agree to the earbuds?" He holds out a pair of brand-spanking-new Beats headphones in bright red.

"Dude, those are not earbuds."

I don't mention the price. Grayson loses his mind whenever we talk about money. Maybe because I refuse to let him help pay the mortgage or other bills for the house. Adult Suzie shakes her head. *When are you going to stop being stubborn and grow up?* I don't answer her, but the answer is never.

"Please. For me?" He gives me puppy dogs eyes. And with those whiskey-colored eyes of his, I'm helpless to say no. Don't judge. You couldn't tell the man no either.

And thus begins the weirdest adventure at an airport ever. I wear the headphones and listen to my brewers' podcast the entire time. The only time I'm allowed to take them off is when the security personnel insist. Then, we're off speed walking to a gate. Grayson wasn't kidding when he said we need to rush. The plane is nearly done boarding when we rush on.

"Can I take my headphones off now?" I ask when we take our seats. Grayson cringes. "Am I talking really loud?"

Confession: I totally know I'm talking too loud. What? He's the one who made me wear headphones through the entire airport like an anti-social bitch.

Instead of yelling at me to keep it down, Grayson uses a tactic of which I wholeheartedly approve. He kisses the daylights out of me. The headphones fall off and the talk of long term yeast storage completely leaves my mind as his tongue explores my mouth and his hands fist into my hair.

He pulls away with a smack and leans his forehead against mine to catch his breath. "Vegas," he whispers. "We're going to Vegas."

My arms shoot into the air. "Yee-Haw! Vegas baby!"

The other passengers who, let's face it, should probably be annoyed with me by now, clap and laugh.

"Why didn't you tell me where we're going?" I ask as I rescue my headphones from the floor. Ew. It's icky down there. I wonder what— Nope. I am not going to think about what could have possibly made the yucky mess. Note to self: Never, ever drop anything on the floor of an airplane again.

Grayson shrugs. "I wanted to surprise you."

I normally hate surprises. Seriously, they freak me out. But I'll have to forgive him this one time and one time only since this is the best surprise ever. A weekend away in the city of entertainment. Yipee!

"Mission accomplished!" I grab my phone to start researching all the fun stuff we can do but then realize I don't have any connection.

"Here." Grayson hands me a guidebook for Las Vegas.

I snatch the book from him. "How did you know?"

"It's a four-hour flight. I knew you'd need something to keep your mind busy."

I frown. What does he think? I can't sit still for four hours? I look down and notice my knees are bouncing up and down. Unfair! It's not because I can't sit still. I'm excited is all.

By the time, the captain does his little prepare-for-landing speech, the guidebook is practically bleeding blue from all the notes and underlining I've done. Too bad I didn't have a highlighter. I store the book in my bag and take Grayson's hand.

"I can't wait! I've never been to Vegas before. Have you been to Vegas before? Did you book a hotel? Should we book a hotel? There were tons of recommendations in the book."

Grayson leans over and kisses me. I can feel him laughing through the kiss. I slap his shoulder and push him away. "No laughing. I'm excited. Isn't it good I'm excited? Would you rather I didn't like your surprise?"

He kisses my forehead. "I'm glad you like your surprise. And yes, the hotel is booked."

It doesn't take long before our taxi is pulling up to a hotel on the strip. My mouth drops open when I see which hotel it is. The freaking Venetian! Holy moly!

"Are you out of your mind? How much is this costing?"

"Since someone won't let me pay my share of the mortgage, I thought I'd splurge." Notice he didn't answer my question.

When we walk into the lobby, I start to worry I'm going to get lockjaw from my mouth gaping open like the village idiot. The Venetian seriously looks like an Italian palace with marble everywhere. There are even murals on the ceiling. On. The. Ceiling. This is so cool!

While I look around like a fish out of water, Grayson checks us in. He hands me the hotel brochure as we walk to the elevator.

"Did you see this? There are forty restaurants onsite, ten outdoor pools, and a fitness center, which has a forty-foot rock-climbing wall. Forty feet!"

Grayson shakes his head as the doors open and we walk onto our floor.

"This is our room." He waves the key card in front of the electronic pad and pushes the door open. "After you."

My feet immediately carry me to the window where the city is displayed. "Wowza. This place is the bomb." I turn around and notice a garment bag draped over the sofa. Yes, there's a sofa in the room because it's a freaking suite.

"I think we're in the wrong room."

"We're not."

"Um, dude, do you not see the bag that is clearly not one of ours? It's right there." I point to the bag.

"Look at me."

"Look at you? Why? Are you making funny faces?"

I turn back to the window where Grayson is now down on one knee. I start backing up. No, no, no. I don't want this. *Shut up,* Adult Suzie says, *and act like an adult for one minute.* Little Susan nearly swoons. She places the back of her hand on her forehead and everything. *Isn't this romantic?*

"I know you're scared."

I narrow my eyes at him. How dare he? "I am not scared."

He smirks. "Sure, you aren't, Precious. Just like you aren't backing away from me now."

I force my feet to stop moving. "We agreed to not get married."

"I never agreed to not getting married." I open my mouth to tell him he's wrong, even though it would be a lie, but he speaks before I get a chance to spew my lies.

"Suzie, Precious, I love you and I want to spend the rest of my life with you. I want to wake up every morning to your grumpy face. And fall asleep with you every night. I'll let you hog the covers every night of the week."

I cross my arms over my chest. "I am not grumpy in the morning and I don't hog the covers." And I never, ever lie. Not me.

Grayson ignores my comment. "I want to spend my days working on the marketing side of Shorty's Brewing Sensation while you sweat away making new and exciting beers in your obnoxiously clean brew shack."

"Hey!" Clean? Yes. Obnoxiously clean? No.

"But mostly I want to put my babies in you and watch your belly round with our children. I vote for starting our family immediately." He waggles his eyebrows.

My eyes well and my hands shake. "Are you sure?"

"Am I sure?" He chuckles. "Look around you. Everything is arranged."

He nods to the garment bag. "Your wedding dress is in there. The chapel is booked."

He digs in his pocket and pulls out a jewelry box. "And the ring is bought." He flips the box open and I gasp.

"I want you to always wear your ring and a solitaire would get in the way when you're brewing." When I don't say anything, he starts to sweat. "We can get a solitaire if you prefer. There's a jewelry store in the hotel."

I snort. "There are probably several."

"Okay." He starts to stand. "We'll go get you a solitaire then."

I put my hand on his shoulder and push him down. "No."

His face crumbles. "No? You won't marry me?"

"No, I don't want you to exchange my ring. I want that one."

His face lights up. "Then, you'll marry me?"

I bite my lip as I stare at the ring. *Come on,* Adult Suzie pushes. *You know you want to say yes.* Ugh. She's right, the bitch. *And we want to make babies!* Little Susan shouts and starts to strip. Geez. Can I get married first?

"Yes." Deep breath. "I will marry you."

Grayson whoops before springing to his feet and pulling me into his arms. He twirls me around until I bat him on the shoulder. "My ring. I want to see my ring."

"Such a girl," he mutters.

The ring is gorgeous. It looks like two rings intertwined. On the front, there's a gap between the intertwining two rings where three diamonds sit. It's different and perfectly perfect.

The bell rings. "Your entourage has arrived."

"What?"

I'm still sputtering when an entire crew of women arrive.

"When exactly are we getting married?" I ask Grayson who is trying to sneak out of the room.

"In one hour."

"In one hour!" I screech.

"I'm not giving you a chance to change your mind."

"I haven't even seen my gown yet."

"It's lovely!" he shouts from the hallway. "Phoebe picked it out."

Fifty-five minutes later, I've been transformed into an honest to goodness bride. I'm never going to hear the end of it from Phoebe, but the gown she picked out is perfect. How did she know? It's a strapless hi-low gown in white silk. And by the way, hi-low means knee-high length in the front and floor-length in the back. Yeah, I didn't know that either.

The suite door opens and Grayson walks in wearing a dark gray tuxedo. My mouth waters and I feel flush. I didn't think the man could get any better looking. I was wrong.

"You're beautiful." While I've been staring at the – gulp – groom. He's been staring at me. Actually not me. My breasts that are straining against the front of the gown. He leans forward to kiss me, and I scream.

"No. Lipstick!" For good measure, I hold my hand up in front of my mouth. "The crew took ten minutes to do my lips alone. I want to look perfect in the pictures. You did hire a photographer, didn't you?"

Grayson holds his elbow out to me. "Yes. I promise everything is arranged and you're going to love it."

I don't bother denying it. So far, the man is hitting it out of the ballpark. "You are so getting laid tonight."

He chuckles as we walk to the elevator.

"How far do we have to walk? I'm not sure I can wear these heels for more than five minutes." When did Phoebe ever get the impression I can wear five-inch heels? Oh shit, Phoebe. And Hailey. They're going to kill me.

Grayson squeezes my hand. "No one is going to kill you. As long as you go ahead with the wedding reception planned for next weekend everything is fine."

"Wedding reception next weekend? Is there anyone who didn't know about our elopement before me?"

He cringes and looks away. "Um."

"You are not to be believed." The elevator doors open and I stomp out. This doesn't go well for me when the little itty bitty heels hit the slippery marble floor. My right leg flies up and I'm pretty sure I flash everyone in the hotel.

Grayson wraps his arm around my waist and steadies me. "It wouldn't be a wedding without klutzy Suzie in attendance."

"Oh, hush you. Where are we going?"

"Come on." He takes my hand and leads me toward an exit. The exit opens to the large body of water surrounding the hotel also known as the Grand Canal. A white gondola awaits us.

"Get out of here! We're getting married in a gondola!" I clap but manage to stop myself from jumping up and down. We all know how well moving in these high heels works for me. As in it doesn't.

A man in a blue and white striped shirt and red sash smiles. "Good afternoon. Mr. Neill and soon-to-be Mrs. Neill."

"Hold up. I never agreed to take your name."

Grayson rolls his eyes. "You are seriously the most stubborn person I know. I don't care if you take my name. Now, get your gorgeous ass in the gondola so we can get married and start making babies."

"Um…" The gondolier's eyes widen. "You can't …er…"

I slap the man. "He doesn't mean right here, right now. We'll save the naked festivities for our suite. Don't you worry."

He sighs as he helps me into the gondola. Grayson sits next to me.

"Who's going to marry us? Elvis?" I giggle. Elvis has to marry you if you're in Vegas, doesn't he?

"I am not getting married by Elvis," Grayson growls. "A celebrant will perform the ceremony. Ah, here he is now."

A man smiles down at us as he takes the seat across from us. The gondolier pushes off from the side and we're off. I can't help giggling.

"Stop giggling. This is important." Grayson isn't annoyed though. I can see the humor in his eyes.

"Good afternoon, Mr. Neill. I'm Mr. —"

I hold up my hand to stop him. "First names only."

"Of course. I'm Braydon."

"I'm Suzie and this is Grayson. Now, Braydon, get us married as quickly as possible. Then, I think you'll want to disembark from our white gondola as I plan to make out with my new husband as soon as you pronounce us husband and wife."

He laughs. "I can do that."

I wink. "I know you can."

"What if I had elaborate vows planned?"

I raise a brow at Grayson. "What more is there to say besides you love me and promise to cherish me and love me even when I'm old and gray and fat."

"I think it's supposed to be in sickness and health."

Braydon clears his throat. "Shall we get started?" Grayson and I nod in unison. "Do you have the rings?"

Grayson produces a man's ring. "We can get you another ring, but I thought your ring could be both an engagement and wedding ring."

He actually looks like he's sweating as he waits for my answer. I don't make him sweat. Now that I've decided I am going to get married, I want to get it over with and move on to the good stuff. *Yeah! The good stuff!* Little Susan says. I don't think anyone will be surprised to hear she's got the pompoms out again.

I wiggle my hand at him. "This ring is perfect. I don't need another one."

He blows out a breath and turns his attention to Braydon. "We're ready."

"Do you have vows prepared?"

Before Grayson can answer, I do, "I love him, he loves me. I promise to put up with him. He promises to love me when I get fat. We're good."

"Do you, Grayson, take Suzie to be your lawfully wedded wife?"

Grayson smiles at me. "I do."

"Do you, Suzie, take Grayson to be your lawfully wedded husband?"

I wink at Grayson. "Yep. I sure do." I look around. "Where's the ring? I want you to wear it."

Grayson takes the ring out of the box and hands it to me.

I slide it onto his finger. "I know there's all this stuff about with this ring, but I'm not much for traditions."

"You don't say?"

"Shush, you. I have something to say. I give you this ring as a symbol of my love and as a reminder that I am by your side always, even if I'm physically elsewhere."

Grayson stares at his hand for a moment before raising his head to smile at me. "Thank you."

"Now, by the power invested in me by the state of Nevada, I declare you guys married. You may kiss the bride."

"I love you," Grayson whispers before his lips meet mine.

"I love you more than beer," I say when the kiss ends. And I do. The man snuck past the ten-foot fence around my heart and made a home for himself. Good luck trying to escape. Not on my watch!

D. E. Haggerty
Love and Laughter in Every Chapter

About the Author

D.E. Haggerty is an American who has spent the majority of her adult life abroad. She has lived in Istanbul, various places throughout Germany, and currently finds herself in The Hague. She has been a military policewoman, a lawyer, a B&B owner/operator and now a writer.